ONE SINGLE THING

HUNTER GRANT SERIES

TINA CLOUGH

ONE SINGLE THING

Copyright © Tina Clough 2019

PAPERBACK ISBN 9780473469139

Disclaimer

Most locations in this book are real places, but details have been changed to avoid comparisons with real businesses and individuals. The characters are the author's invention and are not based on any particular persons.

Lightpool Publishing

www.lightpoolpublishing.com

Cover design by Tara Cooney Design

A catalogue record for this 5x8" edition is available from the National Library of New Zealand

To order copies of this book please contact Publishers Distribution Limited orders@pubdist.co.nz

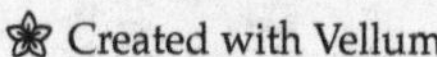 Created with Vellum

PROLOGUE

Four weeks into our South Island exile, Benson calls. We are standing on a sunny mountain-top in a bone-chilling wind straight off the Antarctic ice. Dao is taking photos of panoramic scenery with serious calendar potential: mountains all around, Queenstown on the far side of the lake and a white boat carving a wake through the dark water.

'We got that guy called Mint,' says Benson. 'He got dobbed in by an informer in exchange for a small favour. I'm afraid we're going to need Dao when his case comes up in court. She's the only person who can testify that he picked up the drug parcels from the island.'

'What about the other one – John?'

'I don't know yet. He's gone AWOL and he lives on his boat, so he could be anywhere. I'll let you know when it's safe to come back.'

Now that Bramville and the Boss are dead, there are two men left for whom Dao poses a threat. John worries me the most, the man who retrieved the drug deliveries from where the ships dropped them into the sea off the Northland coast and brought them to the place we call 'the island', though it is in fact a remote bay on the north-east coast. Bramville had threatened to give Dao to John, if she didn't behave and she was terrified of him. She said, 'He would use me first and then throw me in the sea to drown.' The other one was Mint, who delivered consignments to the Boss's customers. A middleman, and less dangerous, who has now been caught.

'That was Benson,' I say and hunch my shoulders against the biting wind. 'They've got Mint. John has taken off on his boat or gone into hiding.'

The tip of Dao's nose is red, and her fingers are white. She puts the phone in her pocket. 'Can we go back to Auckland now?'

'Not yet, but he'll let us know. Have you got enough photos? Please put your gloves on before your fingers drop off.'

When I whistle Scruff appears from behind a rocky outcrop and takes up his customary position beside Dao. We climb back into the helicopter's bubble of warmth and discuss where to go in the three hours that remain of our charter.

Four weeks ago, we drove off the ferry in Picton and set out to explore the South Island. We had no idea when it would be safe to return to Auckland and no specific plans.

'Isn't it lucky that you can work from anywhere,' said Dao cheerfully as I drove very slowly towards Nelson.

'My arms aren't feeling lucky', I said. 'Nobody's told them that having knife and bullet wounds is good luck.'

'Yes, but we're both alive.'

'True.'

Not long ago she saved my life in a deadly situation when I was seconds away from disaster in an abandoned factory. I will never ask her if she intended to kill the man they called the Boss. She managed to throw a large and very heavy circular-saw disc like a frisbee. To divert his attention, she said, but it was hard to aim, and it hit the Boss and nearly took his head off; I lived and he died. And there we were, exiled for our own safety and driving slowly towards Nelson on a very scenic road that wound in a thousand bends through native bush. My stitches had come out two days earlier, but I had little faith in my ability to control things at speed.

I pulled over to let backed-up traffic pass us and Dao wound her window down. 'Listen to the birds! And that smell, I love that damp smell.'

I checked the side mirror and pulled out on the road again, thinking how surprising that statement was. An unexpected sentiment from someone who, not long ago, had trekked barefoot through the forest for days to escape enslavement. A girl who had lain down in a damp hollow to die rather than be caught by her tormentor.

Instead of commenting I said, 'Did I ever say thank you for saving my life?'

'Yes, twice. You can stop now, Hunter. I just did what I had to do.'

Benson wanted us to go into witness protection. Dao is the only living witness who can connect those still alive to the drug distribution from the place we still call 'the island'. She spent a decade there at the mercy of an abusive man and thought she was on an island. But she refused the witness protection offer in that way she has that leaves no room for negotiation.

Benson's second approach was to threaten to arrest me for illegal use of a firearm unless we left town for a while.

He doesn't know that I still have one of Charlie's Glock pistols, loaded, under the front seat of the car, but I'm sure he suspects it. Neither does he know for certain that I had our armed intruder at gunpoint before the cops came, but he's pretty certain.

He issued a strong and unofficial threat, hoping to change my habits. He pointed out that he can have me stopped and searched at any time, repeatedly, and make my life very uncomfortable. He made it clear that he thinks I am dangerous and prepared to do whatever I think needs doing, even if it is illegal. He also pointed out that he doesn't give a shit about me, but he doesn't want anything to happen to Dao. To keep him happy we left Auckland for an extended tour of the south the day after the funeral for Paul, the innocent victim of the factory drama. At one stage it looked as if we would have to tour in a campervan because Dao refused to go without Scruff, then she found a website that lists pet-friendly motels.

Four hours after leaving our perch on top of the Remarkables mountain range we are back in our dog-friendly motel. The helicopter tour has shown us things neither of us have ever seen before. We landed on a glacier, where Dao made me hold on to the back of her jacket, so she could lean right out over the edge of a deep crevasse. We saw a frozen waterfall, where she would have liked to climb in under the frozen cascade, but thankfully the pilot said it wasn't allowed. We got a quick overview of Milford Sound thrown in as a bonus and I finally understand why people rave about Mitre Peak. Since the first time my mate Charlie took us flying in her helicopter, Dao has considered it the ultimate form of transport. The South Island is the perfect place for it: choppers available everywhere, and every flight a scenic wonder.

A week or so later we are in the Woolstore Café in Oamaru, having a late lunch. Dao is drinking an apple and carrot smoothie and watching a blurry CCTV image on a little monitor beside our table: a penguin sitting on a nest under the floor of the café.

'Right under your feet,' says the waitress, when she brings our lunch. 'It's the same pair as last year. They marry for life.'

My phone buzzes. 'Benson again. He can wait.'

'No, no, please take it,' says Dao. 'He might say we can go home.'

'Two things, Hunter.' Benson sounds serious. I see him in my mind's eye, medium height and a bit chubby, shirt coming untucked. But his appearance is very misleading, when he drills into you with those piercing grey eyes you know he is not as harmless as he looks.

'You can come back now if you're done with the touring. Word on the street is that John sailed to Tonga a couple of weeks ago. With that size boat he could roam the islands for years without being noticed or checked. So, it's safe to return, I think.'

'Great. We'll book a ferry crossing and drive up in easy stages. What's the second thing?'

'Check in with me as soon as you're back, would you?'

It sounds more like an order than a request; there is more to this than meets the eye.

'Why? Haven't you got all the information you need from us?'

'Not quite. Some additional stuff has come up.'

We continue slowly up the east coast of the South Island. The vagabond life has become

addictive. We go for walks and watch seals sunbathing on rocks. A whale-watching cruise at Kaikoura leaves us with dozens of photos of whales' tails disappearing into the water and not a single shot of a whole whale. I do a lot of work in the evenings, while Dao studies and Scruff sleeps beside her.

Thanks to the Internet, my London partner and I manage to run a very efficient business without meeting more often than once a year at most. When people ask me what I do, I usually say that I run an employment agency. What we actually do is provide highly trained ex-military personnel for those who can afford it. Those who need a private army, a butler who won't hesitate to shoot an intruder or a driver who knows how to handle three tonnes of armoured Mercedes-Benz at high speeds.

The ferry crossing to Wellington is a hair-raising test of fortitude for both of us; we picked the roughest day this year, and a few days later, on a rainy Wednesday we drive straight through Auckland and across the Harbour Bridge to the North Shore.

'Let's go to the supermarket on the way home,' says Dao. 'If we do the shopping on the way we don't need to go out again. I can't wait to get home. Do you know that it's eight weeks since you were shot?'

So that's how we are going to define it, I think: that night in the abandoned factory with a man who was going to kill me, if I didn't tell him where Dao was and neither of us suspecting she was right there in the shadows, looking for a way to save my life. From now it will be 'the night I was shot' – which is fine with me.

By early evening we are back to normal. The fridge is full of food, the washing machine is doing a second load and Scruff is in the courtyard garden sniffing around and re-marking his territory. I stand in the bedroom, vaguely wondering why I have three odd socks, when Dao comes running upstairs with my phone. 'It's Nigel. He wants to talk to you.'

Nigel lives in the townhouse next door, a retired fusspot who likes to keep an eye on things, sometimes excessively so.

'Welcome home, Hunter,' he says. 'It's nice to have someone living next door again. I worried while you were gone. But I kept an eye on things in case there was any more trouble.'

'Everything's fine, Nigel. I don't think there is any reason for you to worry now. It's all over.'

The poor old chap hasn't been the same since the guy with the sawn-off shotgun invaded my house. He is not really that old – he just acts like he's ninety.

'I hope so! I get a bit nervous these days when I see people near your house or in the lane at the back. I saw a guy a couple of weeks ago who looked a bit suspicious. I think he was looking in through that narrow window beside your garage door. I'll bring your mail over tomorrow morning. It's just junk mail.'

A text to Benson, to say we were back, generates an instant reply: *Please come and see me tomorrow at 1 pm.*

1

Benson smiles at Dao. 'How was the South Island? Did you see lots of lovely scenery?'

'Amazing – it's very beautiful. We flew in helicopters quite a lot. But it's nice to be home again. Is this talk about my mother?'

Sooner or later the body of Dao's murdered mother will be released for burial after being found buried on the island. It is very important to Dao, who has no family left and spent years of her childhood believing her mother had abandoned her with Bramville.

'No, I'm sorry Dao. I'll chase it up and let you know, but it shouldn't be long now.'

For a brief moment he seems uncomfortable. He looks down at the papers in front of him, then at me. 'How many times did you and Charlie go to the place we call the island?'

'We flew over it twice. Once when we took the photos and got the GPS location. And then again on our way back from my cabin – that time Charlie flew us up to find the black book Dao had hidden when she ran away from the island. Dao wanted to see how far she had walked.'

'Did you land there?'

'At the island? No, I've never set foot on the ground there, I've only seen it from the air.'

'And you haven't gone there by car?'

'No.'

I can sense Dao's tension building with every question he asks. 'What's this about, Benson?' I ask keeping my eyes on his. 'Has something new come up? Why are you asking me about the island?'

He looks at me, straight-faced and unreadable. 'We want to know where that barrel full of drugs went. The one that was in the shed when Dao escaped.' His eyes lock on mine, watching for reactions.

'I have no idea. All I know is what you told me when your guys raided the island – that Bramville had gone and there was no barrel in the shed. I presumed he had taken it with him when he fled, maybe delivered it to the Boss. Or perhaps he hid it somewhere.'

Does he really think I took it? Or does he suspect that Charlie went back and grabbed it? Has he already talked to her, or did he start with me?

'It wasn't at the Boss's house in town or his holiday place at Raglan. We're starting a separate investigation – someone has that barrel. It's worth a fortune and there are plenty of people who'd like to buy it. Whoever has it could make a great start on their retirement fund.'

His gaze shifts to Dao and he smiles again. 'You must have seen many barrels come and go over the years. What happened to the empty ones?'

'Mint used to take them. Sometimes when he came to pick up a parcel Bram would say there was an empty barrel and ask Mint if he wanted it. He always took it. We kept a couple in the generator shed, smaller ones from earlier, when they used little fat ones.'

'Yeah, we found those. But we know from Bram's black book that the last barrel hadn't been there for long. Mint had only made three pick-ups, one or two packets each time. What we need now is a description of the barrel – size, color and anything else you can remember. And the size of the drug parcels.'

Dao is silent for a moment, thinking back. Then she holds out her hand level with the desk. 'The barrel is about this tall, dark blue plastic. The lid is black – it screws on. On top of the lid is a sort of handle – like a bar across a dip in the lid. The barrel is about this wide and it's cylindrical.' She holds out her hands, about sixty centimetres apart.

'Great,' says Benson. 'I thought you'd be able to tell us.'

'Of course, I can.' Her voice is neutral; her calm face betrays nothing, but I feel her unease. 'I was chained up in that shed every night for years and there was nearly always a barrel there. The parcels were about the size of a half-kilo butter packet. Each one was wrapped in grey paper and then – what's it called, Hunter?'

'When you told me about them, I thought they must have been shrink-wrapped from the way you described them.'

She turns back to Benson. 'They kind of looked hard, very tightly wrapped in plastic. You could see the grey paper inside, kind of creased.'

'In the daytime, once he released you, were you allowed to go back into the shed?'

'I went back most days. There was stuff I needed in there – the spades and the wheelbarrow and some of the bigger tools. But I only ever saw the barrel without its lid on once. I would never have dared open it. What if he had come back and seen me? I would have got beaten again . . . or worse. At night, or when he went away for the day, he chained me up and then I couldn't reach the barrel.'

I get up, make no pretense of friendliness. 'Is that all, Benson? If it is, we're leaving now.'

Outside Dao stops and grabs my arm, alarmed and upset. 'He thinks perhaps you took the barrel! Why? Bram would have taken it when he left, after I ran away. Why is he asking you?'

'I don't know. Something must have come up. Let's take Scruff for a run on the beach.'

The main objective now is to restore some sense of normality. At the beach Scruff and Dao chase each other along the water's edge, splashing and noisy. I follow further up on the dry sand, my mind busy with conjecture and then I call Charlie and leave a message asking her to call back.

My phone buzzes before we get to the end of the beach, it's Charlie getting back to me.

'Great to have you back! I just turned my phone back on – I've been flying clients to Kauri Cliffs. How are your arms? We must get together soon.'

'Listen, Charlie, Benson's sure to call you any minute. We've just been talking to him at the station.'

She interrupts before I get any further. 'He called me last week and we've made two appointments that I had to cancel because of new flight bookings. I'm due to see him tomorrow morning. What's it about? He seemed a bit curt, I thought.'

'It's about that barrel of drug parcels from the island. They can't find it and they think you or I might have taken it. He asked if we had landed there.'

'For fuck's sake! After all we've done for him. What sort of things did he ask?'

'Just basic stuff – did we land at the island, or did we go there by car and boat at any stage. Can you prove we didn't land when we flew over?'

'No, I can't. I filed a flight plan, of course, and I keep a flight record as well as the automatic recording of what we call time-in-service. But that means nothing. Even the transponder isn't totally tamper-proof. All those things mean nothing if you're determined to keep something secret.'

'Let me know how it goes with Benson.'

Later on, when Dao is watching a TED talk on her laptop, I open the CCTV surveillance program on mine and go back over the time we were in the South Island. We had the cameras set to motion activation while we were away, so only someone who came onto our strip of grass between the sidewalk and the front of the house would set it off. There are a few shots of the postman, who rarely stops at our letterbox because I get most things by email, and one morning two ducks land on the grass. But a few days later, nine days before we returned, a man walks right up to our garage and peers into the narrow window beside the door. He stands there for a moment, shading his eyes with his hands before he walks away, but he never faces the camera squarely. I snip the side view of his face and save it. I have never seen him before.

Next, I scrutinize the recorded views of the courtyard behind the house. A cat activates the camera a couple of times each week. It belongs to the couple next door and climbs their lemon tree, leaps onto the two-metre wall between us and drops down on our side. It gets back by taking a flying leap from our table to the top of the wall. Very impressive.

Eight days before we returned, at 3.18 in the morning, a man comes over the wall from the lane behind us. He sets off the outside light and ignores it, walks right up to the house and looks in the windows. He shakes his head, looks up at the higher windows, spots the camera and turns back. He is too short to make it back over the wall. He grabs one of the chairs by the table and clambers up and over; I presume he had something on the other side to stand on as well. The shot of his face when he looks up at the camera only shows his mouth and chin clearly. His cap casts a deep shadow over the top half of his face, but I snip and save it. After the armed invasion I had mesh-reinforced glass installed downstairs on the courtyard side of the house. I wonder if he would have smashed the glass otherwise, despite the clear warnings about an active alarm system. Is this guy looking for the barrel?

Three weeks later I get a call from Benson.

'We haven't found the barrel,' he says, 'but I thought you'd like to know we no longer think you or Charlie took it.' He sounds pleased.

'So, you found out something new? Or can't you tell me?'

'Yeah, I think it's OK to tell you. We've spent a lot of time searching for shots of Bramville's vehicle on CCTV cameras, tracking him after he left the island. We have a good one from a camera mounted high up on a lamp post at a supermarket in Whangarei. We think it was the day he left. We missed it the first time we checked that site – the barrel was on the back of his pick-up truck. The following day he was caught on camera on the harbour bridge, but he had a cover over the back. Then four hours later he was filmed at a BP station in Manurewa – the cover was off and there was no barrel on the back. So, either he sold it already or he's stored it somewhere. We know one of the gangs is trying to find it, so we presume he hid it before the Boss killed him. Maybe that's what the Boss was trying to find out and he died too soon? Perhaps cutting

Bramville's foot off with that machine was only meant to make him talk.'

'Or maybe he did tell the Boss where it was, and he killed him anyway,' I say. 'After my own encounter with him, nothing would surprise me.'

Benson sighs. 'Tell me about it! Endless possibilities and nobody alive who can tell us.'

'Thanks for telling me I'm not a suspect any longer,' I say. 'I'll tell Dao – she was a bit pissed off that you thought it might have been me.'

2

E ighteen months later life has settled down and we have established a routine that suits us both.

'Do you want to go out for dinner?' I ask. No answer. 'Dao, can you hear me? Dinner out somewhere?'

Dao looks up from her laptop with the dislocated expression of someone woken from a deep sleep. 'You mean go out – to eat? Tonight?'

It's astounding, this ability to concentrate for hours. It's usually when she is immersed in something mathematical. First it was something called fractals, then it was linear algebra. Currently she is learning algebraic number theory, which I freely admit I know absolutely nothing about.

'Don't you want to go out?'

'I'd rather stay home and have soup or whatever. Or toasted sandwiches and ice cream if we have no real food?'

'There's plenty of real food in the freezer, don't worry. I'll start making dinner if you go down and get Scruff in from the courtyard before he gets really wet.'

Dao runs down the stairs. I am hesitating between frozen meatballs and smoked salmon when she comes back up the stairs very fast. She has snatched the tablet from the dining table on the way and she is opening the security system screen as she comes.

'There's a guy outside – I went into the garage to pick up the towel to dry Scruff off and I saw him through the narrow window. He's acting strange.'

Even now, when her life is no longer in imminent danger and nearly everyone concerned is either dead or in jail, we have the system active all the time. Sometimes the ground-floor alarm is on, even when we are at home. I've got used to always checking before I go downstairs, so I don't set it off. Scruff has learnt to pause on the top step and look for reassurance. The loaded Remington shotgun is always beside the stairs on the living-room level. The Glock pistol I borrowed from Charlie is still under the front seat of the car, loaded. While Dao was the only living witness who could testify against a major drug king, we got into the habit of leaving nothing to chance. The man they called the Boss was determined to eliminate her; we both bear the scars to remind us of his efforts. There is one man still out there, John, who would love to see her dead. From what Benson told us last year it seems likely that he is no longer in the country, but I'm not taking any chances.

Now and then Dao asks, 'Is that gun still loaded?' and I say, 'Of course it's loaded. Not much use otherwise.'

My brother-in-law Matt says the alarm system is Dao's comfort blanket. She is hooked, and either cannot or will not give it up. Have patience, he says. I have unlimited amounts of patience.

Now she holds the tablet up for me to see. 'Look! Quick!'

A man is walking away from our front door. He gets to the footpath, turns and approaches the door again.

'He was doing that when I first saw him, then he just stood there for ages.'

After the trial of Mint last year people got very interested in Dao, too interested. Everyone was fascinated with her; a few turned into temporary stalkers and hung around outside the house. Two families offered to 'adopt' her, which annoyed the hell out of her. Being twenty-two and looking like fourteen can be a pain.

The doorbell rings. 'Stay here,' I say and go down.

He is a skinny guy, forty-ish. Medium height, untidy dark hair, sweatshirt and jeans; could be anyone or anything.

'Sorry,' he says. He's moving from one foot to the other, nervous. 'You don't know me. I read about you last year . . . when that boat chap was in court . . . the drug-smuggling guy. My sister has disappeared.'

'I'm very sorry to hear that,' I say. 'You should go to the police.'

I start closing the door, but he grabs hold of the edge.

'Please! Just let me tell you. The cops aren't interested. It's really ...' His voice is rising, his face creased with worry. 'And my parents are going crazy. Something has happened to her and nobody will do anything!'

Dao appears beside me.

'Hunter is not a detective,' she says kindly. 'It's not his job. You should get a real private detective.'

'I don't know anything about them.' His voice drops back to normal. He is focusing on Dao now, calmer. 'How would I know if they are any good? It's not as if it's, you know, a case of adultery or whatever. And there are some things I found. Some weird things.'

I can see his brain doing a fast search for something that will convince us to let him in.

'I found her flat unlocked, her things were still there. Nobody knows where she is.'

'You have to go back to the police,' I say. 'I really can't

help you. Tell them what you found and insist on talking to someone a bit more senior than the front-desk constable.' I close the door.

The doorbell goes late in the evening a couple of days later; we have just come back from dinner at Willow and Matt's place in Castor Bay. I grab the tablet, which is always on the dining table, and see a man looking up at the camera.

'It's that guy again, the one who came the other day.'

He starts talking very fast as soon as I open the door. 'Please let me tell you about it. I know something is terribly wrong. I did go back to the cops, but they just won't listen. Please!'

Once again Dao appears silently beside me. She moves around the house like a shadow on bare feet; unnoticeable unless Scruff is following her, and I hear his claws click on the floor.

'Come in.' She reaches out as if to take his hand. 'You can tell us about it, but you have to understand that Hunter might not be able to do anything.'

Upstairs in the living area he comes to a halt beside the dining table, looks around the room and at the stairs to the next level. He is jiggling a bunch of keys, a continuous clicking sound. I go to make coffee and Dao stands where she can watch him and see me at the same time.

We sit at the dining table and I push a mug in his direction. 'What's your name? You know that I'm Hunter and this is Dao.'

He picks up the mug and puts it down without drinking, his hand is trembling. 'My name is Noah Barber. My sister Hope is a photojournalist. She's brilliant. She writes long articles about humanitarian issues. Her agent gets them published in magazines and newspapers – often abroad. She takes wonderful photos. She has been to Pakistan and Afghanistan many times, knows everything about the culture. She came back not long ago. She'd been there for a few weeks researching those so-called honour killings. You know, when families kill their daughters because they've brought dishonour on the family.'

He stops and looks as if he has forgotten what he was going to say.

'And? Go on.'

'It's hard to know where to start.'

He is turning over information in his mind. Some part of him is always moving, fingers, hands, feet tapping against the chair leg. It is distracting and irritating. I need to speed this process up or we will be here all night. I look hard at him, make eye contact, make sure he is listening. 'Take it from the start and in order. Only what is relevant – like verbal bullet points.'

A long pause. 'Well, she got back. I suppose she started working on her material. I saw her twice, maybe three times. We visited my parents and one evening we had a meal together. We're always in touch by text, several times a week. Then I went to Australia for a holiday. I called her once and she said she thought she had a stalker, but she kind of made fun of it, said he was too young for her. The last two days I was away I heard nothing from her. I got back and called my parents and asked if they knew where Hope was. They said they had called her a couple of times and left a message, but she hadn't called back. They live in Hamilton.'

He stops again and stares into the distance. Dao nudges me under the table, frowns and shakes her head; I keep my mouth shut.

'Right,' he says after a while. 'That's what started this

bloody nightmare. After I talked to my parents I went straight over to her place – she lives on the top floor of an old building in Shaddock Street. It's an attic that someone converted into a big open studio. One huge space plus a little bedroom.'

He fiddles with the keys, pushes the coffee mug to one side. Just as I am about to tell him to continue, he starts up again. 'I came up the stairs, turned the corner to the top flight of stairs and her door was open, just ajar. The flat was empty. Her laptop was there, still on, in sleep mode. It looked as if she had rushed off in a hurry and not locked the door – like an emergency. Only she would never do that. Never!'

'And that's what you told the cops?'

'Yeah. I locked the place and went straight to the police station and reported her missing. I told them nobody had heard from her and she hadn't responded to calls for at least two days.'

He rubs a hand roughly over his face, probably reliving the scene in his mind. Dao never takes her eyes off him. My sister Willow is a lawyer with a law firm specializing in trust and tax matters. She says she would like to have Dao with her sometimes, when she meets with difficult clients. She reckons Dao has a finely tuned instinct for body language, or perhaps she notices something in people's voices that we miss; possibly because she spent a decade with an abusive man and had to be always alert.

We wait again and neither Dao nor I say anything.

'I told them something must have happened to her. They got me to describe exactly what I had found and wrote it all down – and the details of how long it had been since she had answered her phone. All sorts of questions about her age, any male friends, what she does for a job. Get in touch with her friends, they said they'd make some enquiries in the neighbourhood. Make sure to tell us if she turns up, they said. She might have gone off with a friend or a boyfriend. They said they'd be in touch.' His voice tapers off.

'And then? Did they get in touch?'

He shakes his head. 'I went back the next day. I knew a bit more then and I was sure they would take it more seriously. But no – they listened to what I said, told me adults often take off for short periods of time and it's everyone's right to do so, said people don't always tell family what they are up to. They said it didn't sound like a crime had been committed, and for me to come back if we hadn't heard from her in a week.'

He does his looking into the distance trick again, lost in thought for a moment. 'I've stayed in her flat since. I wanted to see what I could find. I've set up all her electronic gear – I know her laptop password and how to unlock her phone, her PINs.'

Dao bends down to pat Scruff who is beside her chair and Noah stops talking, his eyes follow her movements. He is very easily distracted. 'And another thing.' He rubs his hand hard over his face again, stretching the skin under his eyes; it's painful to watch.

'It was really strange. It must sound mad. The second time I went back to the cops I got this weird feeling, like they were stalling. When I told the woman at the desk what I had come about, she looked something up on her screen and then she went and got a guy from the back somewhere. A more senior guy, not in uniform. And he just kind of blocked me, deflected everything I said. Like a politician avoiding straight answers, lots of stock phrases.' He shakes his head and sighs.

'But you have a theory about it,' says Dao, and I wonder what she noticed that I didn't.

'Kind of, yeah. Not very specific. Would you give me your email address? I'd like to send you a couple of things to read. It might explain some things. Hope writes about things that happen to her, not as a diary – more sporadic. Little stories. She's been doing it for years, hundreds of them.'

On the doorstep he turns and says, as if to reassure us, 'I have her laptop and I've put an extra lock on her door.'

He walks across the street towards his car, shoulders hunched, hands in his pockets. I stand in the open doorway and look after him for a moment. I am wary and intrigued in equal parts.

3

efore breakfast the next morning I go back to the CCTV recording from Noah's first visit. I have a vague impression there was another person in the picture, when Dao held up the tablet for me to see. I find the place and slow the recording down. Noah is nearly at the front door and a man comes into view on the other side of the street, on the extreme left. He stops and takes a couple of steps sideways into the shadow of the big tree nearly straight across from my house. Noah stands indecisively at the door for a while, before he reaches out as if to press the bell. He pulls his hand back and turns, walks down the short path to the street. The man on the other side stands immobile in the deep shadow of the tree. Noah changes his mind and approaches the door again, hesitates for a minute and finally presses the doorbell. I never noticed the man when I was standing in the doorway talking to Noah, but he was there all the time. When Noah leaves the man is still there, but the recording stops after a minute, when nothing new close to the house triggers the motion sensor. I can't tell if he followed Noah. I mark the place and decide not to mention it to Dao yet.

We are at the breakfast table doing what we do in the mornings: I am reading news online and Dao is probably reading about some esoteric form of mathematics. There is an email from Noah, with two attachments.

'Check the email from Noah I've just forwarded. He's sent us those stories of his sister's. Let's read them now.'

'Hunter and Dao, thanks for letting me talk to you last night. Please read the two attached stories from Hope's "journal". If you want to talk to me again you can reach me on my cell phone, number below. I would prefer not to discuss this via email. Noah.'

THIS TIME IN PAKISTAN

I concentrate on north-western Pakistan, visiting the shelters I have managed to find out about. I want to talk face-to-face with the women who live in these sanctuaries for so-called shamed women. The 'dishonour' women, the ones who have escaped being killed by their families. Before I left, I tapped into my networks of friends, NZ refugee centres and immigrants I have known for years. Many of them used their connections to find out where the shelters are. Mostly they are just a house like any other; anonymous and without any external sign of what they are – a refuge.

In Pakistan I always wear shalwar kameez, the traditional long tunic and wide pants. And a dupatta, to cover my head and shoulders like a big loose cowl, so I look like a Pakistani woman – black hair, local dress and sandals. I look down as I move around or wear sunglasses – or my blue eyes attract attention. I don't use taxis unless I have to, just local buses. I try to avoid being noticed as an outsider when I visit the houses.

In the first town I walk from a bus stop; I have memorized the route by studying it on Google Earth. A street of narrow houses with shuttered or barred windows on the front and small courtyards at the back. There is a little market along one side of the street. I walk along stalls selling melons and vegetables, pass for a local in the crowd. I count front doors without being obvious about it, move slowly along, occasionally stop to look at something on a stall.

The woman who owns the house is called Aghala. She has been told to expect me. I take my sunglasses off and greet her by name when she opens the door. The house is one room and a passage wide – three rooms and a lean-to at the back for cooking. The first room has worn rugs and a scatter of cushions on the floor, a couple of low tables and six women sewing and embroidering. Aghala sells what they make in the markets; it is their only income. They hardly ever go out: a couple of them are hideously disfigured and all of them are terrified of being recognized.

I progress from that house to other towns and other safe houses. I sit for hours with damaged women, listening to their stories and asking questions, very carefully and slowly. Some let me video or take photos of faces and bodies damaged by fire or acid. I ask all of them to choose an assumed name for the articles they know I will write. I have planned exactly how I will get the photos and my notes through airport security. The material I am collecting would be regarded as critical of the culture and the regime; if it is found I will get arrested.

I meet eighteen-year old Samika, in hiding since she was thirteen. She allows some photos of the petrol burns that scar her upper body, her neck and face. She has no hair on one side of her head and practically no ear. Samika brought dishonour on her family, as they say, by secretly meeting a boy from her village. She was promised to a much older man from another village – but she got pregnant. The pictures of Samika's damaged body are hard to look at. Her father and oldest brother took her some distance outside the village and near a cluster of scrub and trees they set fire to her – they thought they had strangled her first, *but she was alive. They left her lying on the ground — they thought she was dead. She knew her mother and her aunts would come to get her body later. She rolled to put out her smoldering clothes and hair as soon as the men had gone. She was in agony and shock and just managed to crawl away among the bushes. Two women with a donkey cart collecting firewood heard her crying. They took her on the cart to their village, covered with sacks — not the village where she came from. They knew of a woman who was part of the shelter network and Samika was smuggled away. She nearly died from the burns and she lost the baby. The shelter is her life now, forever. Nobody will ever want her, but she is alive, and she is safe.*

Those women were born into a culture where girls and women are possessions and the so-called family honour is paramount. Women's lives can be disposed of at will by their men, if religion and custom deem it right. Sometimes their mothers kill them. It is illegal, but it goes on all the same. All those lives that end in pain and terror at the hands of the very people who should protect them — it seems deeply primitive to me.

I wanted the personal stories, so I could make the issue come alive for the readers, to create greater awareness. Their stories will be part of me forever. I cannot file them away, I cannot un-remember them. I might never be able to go back there once the articles are published. This sixth trip to Pakistan might have been my last. I thought I had perfected my ability to distance myself from the things I investigate, to maintain a professional separation, but this time it feels too personal and too real to tuck away in some recess in the back of my mind.

'Have you finished reading the first one?' Dao looks up from her laptop, sad and serious. 'It's awful, cruel. At least it wasn't my own family who abused me.'

She rarely refers to what she endured during her decade of captivity. She knows I will not let anything happen to her, if I can possibly prevent it, but Hope's story has brought back the past.

'It's a brutal culture in some ways, very different from ours,' I say slowly, feeling my way. I want to establish a point of difference between her situation and the girl in Hope's story. 'We were briefed on this sort of thing before the army sent us to Afghanistan. They regard daughters and wives as possessions, just as Hope says. The man who enslaved you had no cultural or religious so-called excuses – he was a criminal and a sadist, unacceptable in our society.'

She nods, and we read the next story.

ABDUL AND AFIA

Occasionally I get valuable information and introductions from someone who has heard third or fourth hand that I am interested in something. They pass my email along and I get another piece of the puzzle from a person I will never meet. But today was different. I was sitting at my desk, eating lunch, and reading something I had just written when an email notice popped up in the corner of the screen. For a moment my mind was blank, but then I remembered. I had talked to Abdul Malik and his sister Afia on the phone, a few weeks before I left on my trip; they came here from Pakistan several years ago. I got a message from someone in my extensive network saying that a young couple would possibly get in touch. And then Abdul and Afia called one evening and said that they had contacts who might be helpful. I never met them, but they provided some useful information over the phone.

The email message was very brief: 'Afia and I would like to hear about your trip. Can we meet somewhere? Abdul.'

I replied, 'Come and see me. I work from home, so you can come nearly any time, but I am out all day tomorrow (Sat). The contacts you gave me were very useful. Let me know when it would suit you to come.'

We made a date for Sunday morning. They called from the street and I gave them the door code and waited on the landing as they climbed the stairs. They were very alike, slim and good-looking, both wearing jeans and sweatshirts.

'Khush aamdeed, good morning,' I said. 'It's lovely to meet you finally. Come in and sit down. Would you like a cup of tea or coffee?'

Afia handed me a little bag with a strong scent of cardamom. 'This is for you. We hope you like them.'

'Gulab jamun, my favourite! Thank you. I always buy them when I'm in Pakistan. Did you make them?'

Abdul laughed. 'No, I made them – Afia is too impatient to wait for the milk to reduce, she only makes things that are really quick. She'll have to marry someone who is a good cook like I am.'

I talked about where I had been and showed them some of the pictures I had taken on my trip, without mentioning anything specific about which shelters I had visited or the stories I had heard.

'The contacts you gave me were really useful, so thank you for that. Most people were helpful, and I have a lot of material for my articles. I have just started working on them, but it's a bit slow at the moment. I can only type for an hour or so and then I have to rest my arm, but at least I can work. I shouldn't moan about it.'

'I noticed your arm. What happened?' asked Abdul. 'Did you have an accident while you were away?'

'Yes, but it was right at the end, luckily. I fell on some broken concrete. But it's not serious, just a bad sprain and some cuts.'

I had no idea what the Maliks did for a living, or whether

they were refugees or immigrants. 'How did you end up in New Zealand? Did you emigrate or did you feel you had to leave – were you refugees?'

'No, we came from choice,' said Abdul. 'We both found the social expectations hard to live with and at the time we left, the general political situation was changing – things were getting even more restrictive.'

'Abdul is a baker,' said Afia, 'and he's gay, so living here is better for him. And I teach French, so I can get a job nearly anywhere. We have residency status now and will get citizenship in another couple of years.'

Dao looks at me over the screen of her laptop, puzzled. 'Why did he send us these? Is he hoping to make us realize how special Hope is, to make us feel more like helping him find her?'

'Maybe. Or perhaps he's worried that she got into trouble over there, upset someone in Pakistan or someone from Pakistan, who lives here in New Zealand.'

'It must be connected somehow – or at least Noah thinks it is. Will you help him?'

I know she wants me to. My only reservation is how it might affect her. She made incredible progress right up to the trial of Bramville's accomplice Mint, the drug delivery man. During the trial details of Dao's enslavement and some of the subsequent events became public knowledge. Not all of it through the court proceedings, possibly by police or others talking about her. The rumors and the media attention caused a setback and I want nothing to drag her down now.

'I think we should, Hunter. Someone must try to find her.'

'OK. Not that I know what we can do, but let's see if we can think of something.'

I know why she wants to help Noah. Because nobody searched for her; she just dropped out of sight and lost ten years of her life.

In the evening I call my sister, Willow. She went back to her law firm last year when the twins were a year old, and they promptly made her a partner. I imagine they wanted to make sure she was back to stay.

'Missing persons,' I say. 'Say an adult disappears? The family knows nothing. Some of the circumstances are odd – a computer was left on and the front door was open. Wouldn't you expect the cops to take it seriously?'

'I imagine it depends on who it is and what else is going on in their lives. And also on who reports it. Do you know someone who's disappeared?'

'It's the sister of a guy I know. He got fobbed off by the cops for some reason. They told him adults are free to take off whenever they want to – it doesn't mean they are missing. When he went back a second time with some new information it got a bit weird and they still wouldn't help him.'

'For God's sake, Hunter!' says Willow impatiently. 'What does that mean, "it got a bit weird"? Tell me exactly what happened.'

'As soon as he said what it was about, they got someone from higher up the food chain to come out to the front desk and this person did a snow job, fobbed him off. He has no idea why.'

'It does sound odd. But I can't make enquiries just out of the blue. Has your friend got a lawyer? Someone making an official call might get more answers.'

'I haven't asked him. Can I give him your number if he needs help?'

I call Noah as soon as I've finished talking to Willow. 'You should ask your lawyer to talk to the cops. I presume you have one.'

'Yeah, kind of, but he's a patent specialist that I've used – I invented a couple of things. I don't think he'd be interested. But I can find someone.'

I hear a tapping noise in the background, little clicks at regular intervals. Even at home in the evening he is fiddling with things and making noise; the most restless person I have ever met.

'You can call my sister Willow if you like. She's a lawyer and she's extremely good at her job. I've told her about your problems with the cops, didn't mention any names. I can text her number to you.'

'Thank you, that would be great.' His voice is muted and tired.

When I come down the next morning Dao is already at the table with her laptop.

'I'm searching for stuff about Noah. I want to know what he invented. We don't even know what he does.'

By the time I have made porridge she is done. 'Noah has registered patents for two inventions, both electronic things.' She looks at her screen. 'He has a business called Barber Innovation and quite a nice website. One invention is a kind of switch that reacts to various things like barometric pressure and wind speed and some other things. It's a safety thing that you can attach to machinery with something called a controller. I haven't read all the details. The other patent is for – this is a quote – an embedded software control unit for robotic processing of very small components. He's on LinkedIn and he studied electronic engineering at Auckland University. He is not on Facebook or Twitter. He also works for a company that makes electronic stuff. His own business must be a background job.'

We are still sitting there reading and discussing the news when Willow calls. Suspecting it might be about Noah, I turn the speaker function on so Dao can hear what she says.

'Your mate Noah called. I didn't realize you've only just met him. Not very coherent, is he? I got his permission to keep you informed, not that I have anything much to tell you, but I have called the cops and asked for a progress report on Hope's case. The response was slightly unusual, so I'll try to find out why. I've got several appointments this morning, but I'll get on to this after lunch.'

'What was it that seemed unusual?'

'Same thing that seemed odd to Noah – evasive answers, platitudes. I think he's right about the police stalling, but I fail to see why. I would have thought the open door and her bag left behind should be enough to make them take it seriously. Even if they think she might have committed suicide somewhere, they should have investigated her flat first. Noah says not to email him or you about this, so I'll call tonight. Talk later, bye.'

Dao is intrigued. 'Why doesn't he want us to use email?'

'I was thinking about it earlier when I read his message. Perhaps he's one of those people who don't trust anything and constantly think they are being spied on. Paranoid.'

She frowns. 'I wonder if he's just unusual or if he is scared of something. I got a feeling that he hasn't told us everything yet, that there's something else that he knows or suspects.'

Over the last year and a half of police interviews, a

court case and various discussions about what happened at the place we refer to as 'the island' I have learnt that Dao is very precise about how she words things. If she says, 'There's something else that he knows about,' then it's best to pay attention. She is right more often than not. If she is uncertain or guessing, she will say so. And if something she says carries an implication of more to come, then it is useless to try to extract it from her until she has worked it out.

When I found her nearly dead in the forest and brought her to my house in town, she knew nothing about the world as it is today. She had been isolated and deprived for a decade. One night when she could not sleep, she said, 'There is so much I don't know. You must teach me everything or I might never catch up.'

I promised I would. Since then, she has also taught me more than I would have thought possible. The fact that she is eighteen years younger than I am, and still catching up, means nothing.

4

We are doing the Takapuna to Milford loop walk with Scruff when Noah calls again.

'Thanks for putting me in touch with Willow. She's good. I've just talked to her. She got the same treatment from the cops that I did ... kind of evasive. She's going to try some other ... avenues.'

Dao and Scruff are playing a noisy game of catch-me around my legs. I put a finger in my free ear, so I can concentrate on Noah.

'It's pretty strange, all right. Any new developments?'

'Not really. Willow is coming to see Hope's flat tonight after dinner. Just to see it, you know ... to sort of understand how strange this is. I mean, that she should have just left or run away. Could you come too? I'd like you to see what I found – how unlikely it is, this idea that she left voluntarily.'

'Yes, we'll come. Where is it?'

'I'll text the address to you. I'm meeting Willow there at eight – I'm going to my flat after work to pick up some clothes and stuff first. I think I told you I've been staying at Hope's place.'

I text Willow and say that we'll pick her up after dinner.

We arrive as dusk is deepening into night. The weather is changing; the air feels damp, like a too early foretaste of autumn. The street looks deserted. It is in the eastern part of Eden Terrace, a mixture of light industries and small businesses. There is little to indicate that Hope's building is residential. An upholstery business has the main part of the ground floor and a smaller space on the corner seems to be a dressmaker's studio. Close to the other corner is a solid-looking wooden door with a keypad. Noah enters a code and leads the way up the stairs.

'There are a couple of small flats on the next floor,' he says over his shoulder. 'And then Hope's flat in the attic.'

The top landing is like a long mezzanine gallery with bare concrete walls, a cast-iron railing and ancient-looking patterned tiles on the floor.

'Don't trip on those broken tiles,' says Noah. He swipes a card over a sensor on the door frame. 'I put this in the other day for some extra security.'

Why extra security? Does he think someone is going to break in – and in that case, who? Maybe Dao is right, and he knows something he has not told us yet; or did he decide to do this because it makes him feel better? His motivations are not easy to get a grip on.

He goes in first, waits until we follow and flicks a switch. At the end of the long room a single spotlight comes on, lighting a carved sculpture and casting a long shadow on the white wall. We take a few steps in and an up-lighter throws an oval of light over a painting on the wall beside us, then more lights in a choreographed sequence until the long room is lit like an art gallery.

'Beautiful!' says Dao. 'Can you do it again please?'

Noah reaches for the switch and the lights go off, one

by one in the reverse order they came on. He presses it again and the lightshow starts anew.

'My God!' says Willow. 'I've never seen anything like it. It's mesmerizing.'

Noah smiles, possibly the first smile I have seen on his face. 'Yeah, it worked out OK. I set it up as a birthday present for Hope. We spent hours discussing which objects should be lit first and how the room would come to life. This non-linear sequence is important to her – she calls it a non-verbal narrative. The lights show you things in a specific order. Not just first this wall and then the next – you have to turn your eyes to look at each thing in isolation, as they are illuminated. She's collected these things on her trips for years.'

'Did you invent it? It's very clever.' Dao is remembering what she found out this morning, wants to know more.

'It's just an electronic control unit and a bit of software to control the sequence. I had to adjust it over a period of days to get the timing right. Endless tweaks, but we cracked it in the end. There are a couple of single light switches here and there, so you can turn on one light or another, for convenience.'

'It's a work of art,' I say, impressed by how absorbing it is; impossible to look away until the last light has come on. 'Perfect for this big space. You've done a great job.'

Noah points at the desk at the far end of the room. 'That's where she sits and works. The laptop was turned on, plugged in and in sleep mode. Hope is very organised. She would never leave without checking the door was locked. Her bag was on the little table over there by the door and her keys too. Only her phone is missing. She is the kind of person who tries the door handle every time she leaves, to check she really locked it. But the door was open.'

We walk slowly around the room and study the art works. Hope bought these things when she travelled, so they mean something to her. They are exotic and interesting in themselves, but they also reflect a deliberate choice, there is a theme: women and children. Dao disappears into Hope's bedroom at the kitchen end of the studio and I go to look out of one of the three long windows in the wall opposite the door. Dao comes out of the bedroom and starts to say something to Noah, but I interrupt her.

'Hey, listen, let's go out on the landing and have a look at the outside of the door again.'

They stare at me, as I walk towards the door. 'Right now, please. I've just thought of something.'

They think I've lost my mind, but they come. I push the door nearly shut and go to the far end of the landing and beckon them to follow; keep my voice low. 'Noah, did you install a camera in there?'

'No, why?'

'I think there's one in the window frame.'

'What the fuck! Are you sure?' His voice is rising. 'Show me!'

'Not so loud. I might be wrong, but if it is a camera, it might have audio as well. I think we should go somewhere else and discuss it before you do anything.'

'Yes, let's,' says Willow. 'If you're right we need to decide how to deal with this. And I have some questions I want answers to, Noah. Where could we go?'

'I suppose we could go to Verona in Karangahape Road, it's not far,' says Noah. 'They'll serve anything at any time of the day or night.'

'Now then,' says Willow crisply, when we have found a

table in an alcove, 'what makes you think it's a camera, Hunter?'

'There's a hole in the top right-hand corner of the window frame and I think there's a lens in it, recessed a tiny bit. I noticed because I'm tall enough to look straight at it. I caught a glint of reflected light. To someone shorter it might look like a counter-sunk screw. If it is a lens, I suppose it could be wired to something and send images, video.'

Noah nods, his face grim. 'I need to have a look. If you're right, it means someone was watching her.'

Willow says mildly, 'You don't seem totally surprised. Why?'

He hesitates before he replies, nearly as if he would rather not tell us. 'You're probably going to think I'm crazy, but I've been worried she got involved in something in Pakistan, either this trip or the one last year.'

'What do you mean by "involved"?' Dao asks, not prepared to accept a vague 'something'.

'I don't know, anything. That area is full of stuff that seem far-fetched to us but are everyday events there. What if someone blackmailed her to do something, or if they tricked her to carry something or to forward messages? She'd never do anything illegal on purpose, but you read about people who get trapped like that . . .'

He stops talking and runs his hand roughly down his face. It reminds me of that film with the alien who'd been pretending to be human and then he peeled his face off.

'But that camera – shit! It means something bad. Someone's watching her. Maybe it's that stalker, or is it the authorities? Or criminals?'

'Oh, sorry,' says Dao. 'I didn't tell you.' She pats her pockets and pulls out a phone. 'I found this in the bedroom. Is it hers?'

Noah turns it over in his hands. 'Yeah, it is. This crack in the screen, it happened when she was in Pakistan. She showed me when she came back. Where was it? I looked everywhere in case it was still there somewhere and I called the number, but I couldn't hear it ringing. Maybe the sound is turned off.'

'It was inside the magazine on top of that low bookshelf beside the door. I saw there was a bulge in it, like there was something inside, so I had a look. Maybe she was sitting on the bed reading and her phone rang. And then she got up and left the phone folded in the magazine.'

Noah looks up from the phone. 'The battery's flat. I'll charge it and have a look. Maybe there'll be something helpful on it.'

On the way home Dao says, 'He's scared that he'll find out something bad about Hope. Maybe that's why he seems so nervous. I bet he's been thinking of all the worst things, like drugs or helping terrorists.'

5

It is the day after the visit to Hope's flat. I am working on a proposal that my London partner wants by the weekend, so he can start drafting the personnel contracts. Dao is sitting cross-legged on the sofa with Scruff beside her with a textbook open beside her, untouched since lunch. She just sits there absent-mindedly patting Scruff.

'What's wrong, Dao?'

'Nothing,' she says and then she remembers that we have agreed this is not a great answer, unless it is true.

'I just keep thinking about Hope and where she is now – what might be happening to her. Did Noah tell us how old she is?'

'No, but I think he said she is older than he is. There must be stuff about her on the Internet. Bound to be, if she's a well-known journalist.'

I've hardly finished speaking when Willow calls. 'Hunter, this business of Noah's sister is getting complicated. I called Benson after I had no luck with the guys at Central. He said he would check it out as a favour. He owes me. I sorted out the complications when he was winding up his parents' trust fund last year – he knows he got the job done for very little. He came back to me just now with some stock phrases about how adults can leave when they like, and they don't have to tell anyone where they are going, it doesn't mean they are missing. The same stuff they keep trotting out at Central. But I had the strongest feeling that he was embarrassed – that he knows something he can't tell me, and he hated lying about it, even by omission. The only reason I can think of is that Hope's file is flagged with a notice that the cops are to leave it alone.'

'And what do you think that means?'

'Probably that some other authority is involved – our intelligence services or those from another country or Interpol. Or possibly one of those private surveillance firms the government agencies use. It couldn't really be anything else.'

'Have you told Noah?'

'Yes, just now on the phone. He's asked me to make an official information request to the GCSB, the SIS and the Police. He's more frazzled than ever – unfinished sentences all over the place. Remember that conversation we had in the car? He's definitely worried that she got involved in something very dangerous. I don't think he actually knows anything specific, but he might. If he does, I must find out what it is. I can't represent him if he withholds information.'

I end the call and turn to tell Dao about it, but she beats me to it. 'There's lots of stuff here about Hope.'

She holds up her laptop for me to look at something. I sit down beside her to have a closer look.

'Which one is Hope?'

'She's the one in the red dress. She got an award for investigative journalism – that photo is from a hotel in Sydney. Doesn't she look great? Not a bit like Noah.'

Hope is in a line-up of four men and two women on a stage. She is probably somewhere north of forty, quite short with black wavy hair worn long. She is in a bright red dress and very high heels and she has a great smile. Not pretty in the conventional sense, but very striking.

'There's lots of stuff about her in all sorts of places. She's really well known, and she got another award – in New Zealand – a couple of years before this one.'

Dao points at all the tabs she has open. 'She's been interviewed on radio a couple of times. I've bookmarked a few of her articles to read later.'

I go back to work on my proposal; I am deep in a database of ex-military personnel for hire when the doorbell goes. Dao checks her phone. 'It's Noah.'

We have the app for the CCTV system on every device in the house. Turning a three-level townhouse into Fort Knox got complicated. I used to have a simple alarm system that I never used. Now we have a sophisticated system with all the bells and whistles. We also have twice the number of devices in the house. Aside from the inherent complications that arise when Dao sets the alarm on the ground floor without telling me, the system has been useful. Without it Dao might well have been killed by the clumsy armed intruder a couple of years ago.

Noah starts talking as soon as he is inside the door, so intent on what he wants to tell us he has no time for greetings.

'I've just talked to Willow. I said I'd show you all the stuff I found – I'll get it to her later. I've been working through files on Hope's laptop. I had to come over here for a client.'

This guy is so disorganised, I think, he even interrupts himself. What the hell is wrong with him?

'I was just about to make coffee. Sit down, Noah. It won't take a moment.'

When I bring the coffee mugs, he is sitting at the dining table sorting sheets of paper into little piles. Dao stands behind him, watching over his shoulder.

'I found quite a lot of things. Some of it makes no sense. And some photos from her phone but . . ."

He leaves the sentence hanging and puts two sheets of paper face-up in the middle of the table. One is a picture of a bearded man with unruly grey hair standing in a doorway with a hen to one side of his feet and two cats on the other. The other is of a young man, taken on a street at night. He stands in a wide recessed doorway with bright lighting.

'I have no idea who these people are. I've had a closer look at the one of the young guy and played around with some software to sharpen it. I know where it was taken. He's standing across the street from Verona in K Road, where we went last night. Hope and I often go there. It's one of her favourite places.'

'Do you have the dates?' says Dao. 'Were they taken before or after Hope went on her trip?'

'After.'

He puts a third print on the table: a thin woman with very short grey hair, possibly in her late fifties. She is smiling and has a glass of wine in her hand.

'This is Hope's agent, Samantha. It was taken forty-three minutes before the one of the young guy ... maybe forty-four. My guess is she and Hope were having a drink in Verona ... but probably a meal actually, seeing what time of night it was ... and when they came out Hope took this photo of him. I think he's the one she told me about, the one she called her stalker ... said he was too young for her.' Suddenly he seems to be losing focus, his thoughts drifting.

I pick up the print and look closely at the young guy. He is looking straight across towards Hope and even in this less-than-sharp picture I can see that he is very good-looking.

Noah has a quick sip of his coffee. 'I also went through her text messages – there are loads of them. I have copied out some that puzzle me, in case they have a bearing on what's happened. Nothing definite, but . . . interesting.'

He pauses with a startled look on his face, as if he can hardly believe he is talking about something relating to his sister's disappearance as 'interesting'.

'This is an exchange of text messages that I typed up for you. They start in Pakistan and continue after Hope returned – the other person was still in Pakistan. I can't make head or tail of them. Nothing she told me about her trip explains anything about this. She always tells me things. Well, not this time obviously.'

He hands me a page and Dao and I read it together:

1. Sent from a Pakistani cell phone number a couple of days before Hope returned to NZ:

My son is concussed, four stitches in his head. They say he will be OK. I am in your debt.

2. Sent from the same number in Pakistan the day after Hope returned:

Are you ok? Are you back in your country?

3. Hope's reply eight minutes later:

I'm back home, bruises and cuts, nothing serious. Thank you very much for what you did!

4. The person in Pakistan replies 45 minutes later:

You saved my son. I saved you. Now we owe each other nothing.

'So, she *was* involved in something,' says Dao slowly. 'She did something for a boy, and his father helped her in return. And both of them got hurt? I wonder what it was.'

'She had sprained and bruised her arm, quite badly,' says Noah. 'She fell over some broken concrete – that's when she cracked the screen on her phone. She never said anything about someone helping her or saving her. This is so strange, some dramatic event and–'

'Two events, I think.' Dao picks up the text message sheet again. 'First something that involved a boy and then another thing where Hope was saved or helped. How can we find out? Did she write one of her journal stories about it perhaps, one you haven't found yet?'

Noah shakes his head. 'Both those "saves" could have been one event. I was thinking about it on the way here. What if something like a riot or an accident happened? Say Hope jumped in to save a boy from some danger, but she in turn got into trouble doing that. And then the boy's father rescues her – so, now they're quits. He's told her his son is going to be OK, she's told him she got home and there's nothing much wrong with her.'

'I suppose it could be,' said Dao doubtfully. 'But he did say first he was in her debt, and then a couple of days later that they were quits. It seems like two events to me.'

Noah thinks for a moment. 'Yeah, you're right.' He sounds slightly reluctant.

He is not flexible, I think, he finds it hard to let go of a theory once he has formed it. Which is a disadvantage in a situation like this: it precludes him from looking at things from several points of view.

'What about that camera in the flat? Or was I wrong?'

'No, it was a camera all right. Well, it's only a lens in that little hole in the window frame, the rest is inside a unit mounted on the outside wall. The encrypted video would have been streamed to another location using a P2P – sorry, point to point wireless link. So somewhere within line of sight there is a receiver. From there they could have sent it further afield, anywhere at all.'

His eyes move from Dao to me and back again, making sure we understand what he is saying. 'But I couldn't reach to remove the unit by myself, so I called in a friend to help – well, not just to help, I wanted a witness too. We removed it and he took it away to look at – he's a bit of a specialist.'

'You didn't think of telling the police to come and see it while it was in place?'

'No – I'd rather check it out first, just in case…'

Of course, you would, I think, because you think they might take the equipment away and you won't be able to prove it was ever there.

He pulls a pile of papers closer and flicks through a bunch of photos. 'These are all the parts and the serial numbers. I asked my mate to take them, for evidence, if we need it. Here is the unit that was on the outside wall.'

Next he holds up a picture. 'It's small and the housing is grey, so nobody would have noticed from the street. You can see it here … I took this photo from the other side of the street. There was no way for us to work out where the video was streamed to, not now.'

When he is talking about his own specialist field of knowledge there are no half-finished sentences, no hesitations. He speaks fluently and coherently; it makes him a different person.

'Who knows how to do this and how hard is it?' says Dao. 'And how did they mount stuff on the outside of the building that high up? And where does the electricity come from?'

'They must have put it up the same way we took it down. One person in the window at the kitchen end and one by the middle window. Both reaching out and across, drilling anchors into the wall, getting things fastened, inserting the camera in the wooden window frame and so on. A bit laborious, but not difficult. Those long windows have small opening panes at either end, otherwise it would have been impossible. There was a power cable running from the box, in at the lower edge of the kitchen window, down behind the full height cupboard unit that butts up against the window frame and then into the power point for the dishwasher in the cupboard under the sink. Very cleverly done and most people wouldn't notice.'

'Why not batteries?' I ask. 'Wouldn't that be simpler?'

'Well, yes – but if they thought it would be there a long time?'

He stops talking and drinks some coffee, his eyes constantly moving around the room over the rim of the mug. I am impressed by how complex the whole set-up was, and the time it must have taken.

'Quite a risky thing to do, breaking into her flat and doing something that took so long. What if she had come back? And the way it was done, obviously very tidy. So, we know two people are involved, or more. Not a lonely stalker, unless he brought someone with him. If it's official surveillance, who would it be?'

He doesn't answer, just gets up and scoops up the

papers. 'I have to go and see that client. Samantha says I can see her tomorrow morning. Do you want to come?'

We say we will, and he leaves at a run.

When he has left the house feels calmer. His behaviour adds stress to every situation; I find him intensely irritating. His mannerisms are disruptive, his half-finished sentences mean you never know if he has finished talking or if there is more to come. He is easily distracted and goes off on a tangent. But maybe he was different with Hope; he seems to have been a supportive brother, someone she felt she could rely on. Or was she the strong older sister and involved him closely in her life, perhaps to give him something he could not provide for himself?

While we are making dinner Dao asks, 'Do the police spy on people? I mean, in their homes?'

'The police can use listening devices, but only if they think someone's involved in serious crime. Willow will be able to tell us. And then there's the intelligence services – I think they can do just about anything they like. Or it might be a private surveillance firm. God knows if Willow's request for information will produce anything.'

6

S amantha's office is a surprise. We take the lift to the fourth floor in a relatively modern office building in Hobson Street and find ourselves in a replica of a 1960s living room. The only sign of the present era is a laptop open on a desk to one side. She herself looks exactly like the photo from Hope's phone. Tall and thin, short grey hair and a beak of a nose.

As soon as we introduce ourselves, she asks, 'Any news yet?'

Noah shakes his head. 'No, nothing. But I've got a few things to ask you.'

She is clearly very worried, but there are no questions or exclamations of dismay. A low-key, self-controlled woman, I like her.

We sit in armchairs with wooden armrests around a kidney-shaped coffee table with splayed legs. It is an oddly comforting room. Not a single mass-produced decorator item in sight; no glass-topped desk making a power statement, just a quaintly old-fashioned, comfortable space.

Noah brings out his folder of papers and hands

Samantha the photos. She flicks through them and goes back to the first ones.

'These were taken when Hope and I went out for a meal about ten days after she got back. That young chap was on the other side of the street when we came out. She said he was her stalker, but that he had never approached her, just kept turning up.'

'Did she say how often she had seen him?'

'I got the impression it was only the last week or two – since she got back, anyway. She said he was never outside her flat. He would just turn up where she went in the evening. He would be somewhere close by, when she came out from a restaurant or a bar. She'd been out quite a few times since she got back, catching up with friends. She said she noticed him because he was so good-looking and such a smart dresser. She didn't seem particularly worried, more amused than anything else. She said he never tried to talk to her.'

Dao and I exchange a look. We have done some research on stalker behaviour and what motivates them. Dao had commented on how common it seems to be that stalkers keep sending things to the person they are fascinated with like notes, emails, flowers.

'They want a response from you,' she said. 'If someone is being generous you might feel you should say thank you, even if you don't know them – and then they can reply to that and so on. Start a conversation.'

Samantha looks down at the photo again. 'He *is* handsome. I noticed that even from across the street. Hope attracts a lot of attention herself. Men often look at her in the street in that particular male way – turn around for another look. She always laughs it off, but I have seen it many times. She has something that really makes men pay attention. I said she should take a photo of him, let him see she was doing it. Maybe that would discourage him from following her around.'

'He turned up when she was leaving places,' says Dao. 'But he didn't follow her there. So how did he know in advance where she was going to be? He could only know that if he's—'

I know she is thinking of the camera in Hope's flat and overall surveillance; so does Noah. He interrupts quickly, as if to stop her mentioning it in front of Samantha. I have no idea why.

'Yes, very strange,' he says hurriedly, his voice a bit too loud. 'Now, the next photo is that guy with the hen and the cats. Since I talked to Dao and Hunter, I've identified him. He's Spencer, the documentary maker. I've heard Hope talk about him.'

'That's right. He's a very good friend of Hope's and also a client and friend of mine.' Samantha looks at the picture and smiles. 'Quite eccentric and very charming. How did you work out who he was?'

'He is in one of Hope's journal stories. Last night I trawled through more files on her laptop and I discovered that she occasionally saved things in random places, not with her other stories. By mistake, I imagine. I'll have to go through everything, but it takes time. The Spencer story was where she saves articles she is working on. I printed a couple of copies for you guys to read.'

VISITING SPENCER

Spencer opened the door, with two cats and a hen crowding around his feet. I had to laugh. 'Two cats, OK — but a hen inside? Let me take a picture of you and your family.'

'Oh, she's very good.' He shooed his pets out of the way. 'She

comes in the back door and just potters around and picks up crumbs from the kitchen floor and she gets on fine with the cats.'

'House-trained?'

'No, sadly not.' He looked fondly at his hen. "I think I could have done it, if I had started when she was a chicken. I close the door to my bedroom which is the only room with carpet. Yesterday she laid an egg behind the sofa.'

The discussion about the documentary went in a different direction from what I had imagined.

'I'm thinking more of a sort of kaleidoscope format,' said Spencer. "You know, having bits of your filmed interviews and the voice clips interwoven with other material, still photos, library footage of towns, markets, interviews with refugees and asylum seekers. Painting the big picture from a mosaic of snippets – images and words.

'Like a general impression of the overall culture?'

The two cats were sitting on the windowsill, basking in the sun. Spencer reached out a hand and absently stroked the nearest one. I thought what a great photo it would be, geraniums in pots, cats and his bearded face.

'Yes, the overall ambience of the country, which you know so well – but showing good and bad without prejudice. Wonderful food, markets, fabrics, metal work, but also the cruelty and cold-blooded abuse of those who break the rules. And all under the shadow of the Taliban and endless strife and uncertainty.'

Ever since he rang, I had wondered what had started this. As far as I knew he had not been there since he did a gap-year trip through Asia thirty years ago; now he appeared to be infused with an almost missionary zeal to present it to the world in all its glory and horror.

'Why do you want to do it? What started this idea?'

'A woman,' said Spencer and cast a glance of shy glee across the table.

'A woman! I thought you had sworn off women years ago.'

'I know. Funny, isn't it? But I met this woman and she's inspired me. She is an immigrant and she has told me so much – and then Samantha told me about your trip and it just seemed as if it was meant to be.'

We spent an hour looking at the material I had on my USB drive. Even as we talked the thing started coming alive. When I left, we had a basic plan for working on it together. Spencer promised to write an outline and email it in the next couple of weeks.

'If we can get some funding, or even a small advance, I'll be OK. It's not an expensive thing in itself, nobody needs to go off for another trip and there aren't any film crews involved apart from someone to do the voice-over – and, of course, lots of editing.'

I promised to show him the draft for the articles as soon as they had taken shape. My head is full of half-formed ideas.

'Yep, that's Spencer all right,' says Samantha and shakes her head. 'Very interesting guy. Not business-orientated and not commercial enough to earn big money, but he has produced some very good work.'

Noah picks up the pages and returns them to his folder. 'I'm going to call him later. I want to know if she told him anything useful. I have Hope's phone with me – there are some contacts on it that I'm not familiar with. Can I run them past you?'

'Of course.' Samantha casts a quick glance at her watch. 'Fire away.'

'Jane H is the first one.'

'Probably my hairdresser. I recommended her to Hope a couple of years ago. We can cross-check the number.'

'Louise.'

'Don't know.'

'Mirrie.'

'Miranda Hanson, friend of ours, editor.'

And so it goes on, until Noah says, 'And last of all, Willard.'

'No idea. I've never heard the name.'

We get up to leave and I look around the room again. Samantha smiles. 'I did it like this when I took the lease here nearly twenty years ago – not that I knew then that it would turn into a precursor to the current craze for mid-century style. I just liked this kind of stuff, bought it from second-hand shops and it cost practically nothing.'

'I presume you're going to call all these people and see if they know something?' I say to Noah as we go down in the lift.

'Yeah, I've got to try everything.'

'Noah,' says Dao seriously. 'You have access to her emails on her laptop and her texts and the call log on her phone. Have you checked everything by date to see who she was in touch with after she came back? Someone she might have told about some drama that happened on her trip? Perhaps someone who's not in her Contacts list – just a number.'

'No,' he says slowly. 'There might be somebody I've missed. Very good idea. Thanks, Dao.'

He is learning to pay attention when Dao suggests something.

7

E arly the next morning Noah calls. 'This Willard guy – he only met Hope recently, on the flight back from Pakistan. They seem to have gone out together a couple of times since. I didn't have long on the phone with him – he was pretty frantic about some kind of transport issue, something to do with a turbine. I'm seeing him tonight after work at his place. He said you can come too.'

Today he seems quite coherent, no half-finished sentences. I have a few questions about Noah that I would like answers to. There was a guy in my unit in Afghanistan who was a bit like him; he got pulled out halfway through a deployment.

'OK, text me the address,' I say, a bit taken aback by how involved we have become in this.

I turn off the heat under the porridge pot and go upstairs. Dao is getting dressed after her shower and I sit on the bed and talk to her. In her usual methodical way, she has laid out what she is going to wear in a line on the end of the bed. Today it's dark grey jeans, a bright red T-shirt and her striped, white-and-grey hooded zip-top. The hoodie is exactly like the one I bought her after I found her in the forest. She was devastated when it wore out from constant washing, but we managed to find another just the same. All her things look like doll's clothes; she can pack for a week in a carry-on bag.

'We've been invited to meet the mysterious Willard tonight at his place. Are you OK continuing with this or would you rather we get out of it somehow? We don't actually have to be involved from day to day.'

Dao slides the T-shirt over her head and reaches back with both hands to lift her long hair out from under it. I love the way she does that.

'I think we should help him. He's a bit weak. Not the sort of person who can do what you can – you know, things that have to be done, even if they're really hard or against the rules. I just want us to find Hope.'

Seeing the scars on her back is a reminder of her past. After I found her in the forest, I set out on a personal mission to find Bramville, to punish him for what he had done to her. I wanted to kill him. But someone else got to him first and he died a gruesome death.

But will we find Hope? And if we find her dead or damaged, how will that affect Dao?

Last year a friend of Willow's arranged for Dao to meet with two senior maths staff at Auckland University. After a couple of hours of putting her through her paces they offered to overlook the fact that she had not been to school since she was ten.

'You are self-taught and have an excellent grasp of isolated aspects of quite advanced mathematics,' said the senior person. 'I am very impressed. In some areas you are at third-year level. You have a great talent, but there are big gaps in your underlying knowledge. If you want to study here, we will assist in every way we can.'

After thinking about it for a week or two she turned

them down. Media were still very interested in her at that time. The two academics we talked to were clearly fascinated by her on a personal level, which probably influenced her decision. Too much attention makes her withdraw. She said 'No thanks' and they offered her access to the university library, which she uses all the time. Maybe they hope she will come back to them at some stage. Now I wonder how she will cope with more attention if we manage to follow through on this search for Hope.

Late morning Dao is buried in a textbook and oblivious to the world. When I tell her that Noah has called again and will drop in a USB stick on his way somewhere, she barely looks up. 'OK, that's good.' She goes back to her book.

'He says we should read what he saved on it before we see Willard tonight.' No answer.

I carry on with my proposal which is more difficult than usual. Setting up a so-called personal protection squad for an African opposition leader is nothing out of the ordinary: it's what we do. What makes this one different is the skill specifications involved – directly from the client; not based on our assessment of his needs. He went to Sandhurst and spent some time in the UK armed forces; what he is asking for is a small assault unit. Either because he thinks someone is planning to take him out or because he is planning to eliminate a rival and wants to be safe from retribution. He has informed us that he has an 'arms bunker' at his country estate; I am leaning towards the elimination of a political rival. I am having a hard time laying my hands on the required number of guys not currently deployed, people I trust to form a strong unit with the right experience.

My partner in London and I try to never send men into

situations they are too inexperienced to handle. We're not in the business of getting people killed unnecessarily.

Noah comes by a couple of hours later. He has made a detour on his way to a North Shore client and has no time to talk. He pushes a USB stick into my hand.

'I found some of these in Hope's desk drawer this morning. There are some very interesting stories on one of them, so I copied them for you. I haven't gone through everything yet. Please read the first two or three pieces before we see Willard. See you later!' And he is gone.

'How do you want to do this, Dao? Read them together on a laptop or print them?'

'Print them, please. I'm having a paper day.'

On a paper day she reads nothing on a device. Willow told her something about pixilated blue screens being bad for your eyes and she must have been convincing; Dao has had a paper day about once a fortnight ever since. I am exempt; apparently it is too late to improve my chances.

I print two copies of the first three stories, and we sit down on the sofa to read. Dao lies with her feet across my legs, so I can do one of the things I do best.

'Can you please rub my scar, Hunter?' she says. 'You haven't done it for ages.'

While we read, I gently rub the deep, dark brown scar made by the shackle she wore for years. It goes right around her ankle and it is brutally ugly, like a branding. She believes that rubbing it will eventually make it better. It looks exactly the same as it did a year ago.

THE LITTLE BOY ON THE ROAD

I was in a taxi on my way to the hotel in Parachinar when I glimpsed a tiny boy standing in the middle of the road with cars and trucks roaring past in both directions and my heart literally skipped a beat. The taxi passed within inches of him. He was so short that the top of his head did not even come up to the taxi window.

'Roko, roko! Stop!' I screamed at the driver.

I was out of the car before he came to a complete stop on the dirt verge, frantic to reach the child. With one arm held up as a signal I stepped into the traffic, terrified that I would be run over. Horns blared; cars and trucks braked and swerved. I darted between a car and a bus and ran back along the road between the lanes of traffic. The little boy was still there, just about to make a move, leaning slightly forward, poised to run. I ran towards him with vehicles nearly touching me on both sides.

'Roko! Intezar karns! Stop, wait!'

He turned his head towards me; a bus passed so close to him he was nearly swept off his feet. I was only an arm's length away when he lifted one foot off the ground. I launched myself forward and grabbed him, throwing us both to the ground.

Frantic thoughts flew through my mind; we're going to die, we are between the lanes, they can't see us on the ground – we will be run over.

I curled up with the little body clamped to my chest and tried to make myself as small as possible. Wheels were moving past my head, just a hand's breadth away; shouts penetrated the noise from engines and blaring horns. Hot dusty air and exhaust fumes swirled my dupatta around our bodies.

The traffic slowed and stopped and excited voices surrounded us. I got up on my knees, still clutching the little boy. His eyes were closed, and he was limp in my arms. A man appeared beside me and said urgently, 'Give him to me!'

I handed him the boy and got up. The traffic was at a standstill, idling engines spewing out fumes, everyone gesticulating and shouting. My hand was covered in blood.

I hope he's not dead – please let him live! He's so little, he weighs nothing.

The man stood as if frozen, staring down at the boy in his arms. The child's face was pale and still and his eyes were shut. We threaded our way through the crowd to the side of the road. I pointed, 'Come, we must take him to hospital,' I said in Urdu. 'That's my taxi just along there.'

The man did not move – I put my hand on his arm and gave him a little push. 'Come on, let's go, we need to get help for him.'

'He ran away. It's my fault,' said the man. His voice was shaking. 'He is my only son. I was talking to a friend and he ran out on the road.'

The taxi driver was coming towards us, followed by a small crowd. The traffic was moving again, and a small bunch of men crowded around us, commiserating and gesticulating. The boy's father said nothing, just stood there looking down at the boy's face.

'Please, let's go now,' I said. 'To hospital.'

The crowd escorted us to the taxi, talking and exclaiming and moving the boy's father along with them. I did not understand what they were saying, they were all talking at the same time and my Urdu was not good enough. The boy's father did not respond to the barrage of comments and questions, but he let himself be moved along by the crowd.

We got into the back seat. I was relieved to see my little backpack still on the floor and fished out a packet of tissues.

'Let me help you.'

I wadded up a handful of tissues and pressed them against the wound on the side of the boy's head. Without taking his eyes off his son's face the man said, 'Thank you, thank you. I didn't even know he was on the road. One moment he was beside me and a second later he was gone. It was my fault.'

The hospital was only minutes away on the long arterial street leading into town. I jumped out and walked around the car to help them out. The boy was still unconscious, but his eyelids were fluttering. The man moved towards the entrance and I followed him.

'I hope he's all right,' I said. 'If I give you my phone number, will you let me know?'

'I will.'

I fished in the pocket of my baggy trousers, found a pen but nothing to write on.

'Write on my arm,' said the man and stopped just beside the door. I quickly wrote my number on his arm and stepped aside for him to carry the boy inside. I saw him approach somebody and be led to one side.

I went back to the taxi and twenty minutes later I was in my room at the Shan Palace Hotel. I sat on the edge of the bed, suddenly feeling tired and listless. I unwound the dusty dupatta from my head and shoulders and pulled the tie off my ponytail. I sat there for several minutes, absently staring at my dusty feet and the rips in my trousers before I went to have a shower and to scrub the dirt from my grazed knees.

Later I ordered a room service meal to make up for the lunch I had missed. My tunic and trousers were in the rubbish bin in the bathroom, both torn and stained with blood. I had offered no explanation of my appearance when I booked in – staff stared, but they asked no questions. I rinsed the dust out of the dupatta and hung it to dry so I could use it the next day.

That evening the boy's father sent a brief message: 'My son is concussed, four stitches in his head. They say he will be OK. I am in your debt.'

'Wow, what a fantastic story! She's very brave,' says Dao. 'Most people wouldn't have done that, would they? I like her.'

PARACHINAR-PESHAWAR

I spent that last evening in Parachinar making sure I would be safe the next day at the airport. I moved everything sensitive to a USB stick and deleted the files from my laptop. I put an innocent SD card in the camera and took out the one I used for the interviews. If I got searched and they checked the camera they would only find the sort of photos a travel writer would take – and I had plenty of those, proper sightseeing photos. It says in my passport that I am a journalist and I had composed a long document about things I had seen and done but leaving out anything to do with the safe houses. Just descriptions and observations of a non-critical kind: stories about markets and children playing football on a dusty road, descriptions of towns and villages, bus rides and so on. Nothing that could be construed as being critical of their culture or religion.

Since I first went there several years ago the security measures have either been beefed up and or become more visible. There is a constant undercurrent of apprehension at the airports – or that's what I feel. There are more armed guards and soldiers and they add a sense of threat, even if they are only there to prevent terrorist attacks. Things are always dangerous in those north-west provinces next to the Afghan border; that amazing place where the Khyber Pass is only a stone's throw away. The populations on both sides of the border are predominantly Pashtu so the Taliban has connections everywhere.

I had thought it through in advance. I would have the USB stick in my pocket, so it did not look as if I was trying to hide it. If they asked me to empty my pockets, I planned to drop it on the floor and accidentally stand on it and crush it – if I could. I got on the bus to Peshawar early the next morning. The air con was out of order and I was on the sunny side; the trip was a nightmare. I wound the dupatta loosely around my head and pulled it forward, so I got some shade, but it became an endurance test. I had found some handwritten sheets of notes about one of the refuge houses in my laptop cover. I ripped them into tiny pieces and wrapped them in a tissue, so I could dump them somewhere. Even ripped up I didn't want to leave them in my hotel room.

I got off the bus at Peshawar airport terminal, which is a long, modern concrete building. I had my tickets and passport in my trouser pocket; I was still wearing local dress for comfort, so I had lovely deep trouser pockets. I had my little backpack on my back and a small, wheeled suitcase. Inside the terminal it was cool and shady. I dropped my bundle of torn-up paper in a rubbish bin and felt I had cleared the first hurdle. The line at the check-in desk was long, fifteen or twenty people in front of me. A group of children ran around, chasing each other and hiding behind the big square pillars that support the roof. Every few minutes the line moved a bit closer to the desk. I had just pushed my bag a couple of steps forward, when the face of one of the little girls caught my attention. She was staring at something and she looked frightened.

I turned my head and saw four men approaching from our end of the terminal; dressed in black, with guns held across their bodies and balaclavas covering their faces. I had never seen soldiers or police look quite like that at an airport before. They stopped about ten metres away and stood side by side looking down the length of the terminal. I should probably walk away quietly from the line and go outside. I was thinking it was good that I was dressed in shalwar kameez again; at least I looked like a local. I felt sure something was about to happen.

Just as I reached for my bag an explosion rocked the far end of the building. Something large slammed into my back and threw me face down to the floor. Clouds of dust everywhere; I was coughing and trying to get up, but I was pinned down. I lifted my head and a pair of black boots appeared in front of my face; the weight across my back was pushed to one side. Before I knew what was going on, the man grabbed my upper arms and dragged me along the floor very fast. My face was inches above lumps of concrete and debris, my legs bumped over obstacles. He pulled me around one of those square pillars and dropped me behind it. He said, 'Stay here, don't move!' He was panting, his voice urgent, nearly angry.

I was lying on my side, winded and confused. I raised myself on one elbow to look at him, but he was leaving, running and lifting the automatic weapon that he had slung across his back. He was one of the men I had noticed just before the explosion. Suddenly I became aware of the pain in my arm and shoulder. I lay back and tried to hold my arm in a position that did not hurt.

Then another explosion, closer this time and much bigger. The entire building shook. Things hurtled through the air like missiles and crashed to the floor. I huddled into a ball with my good arm over my head, terrified. When I looked around the men were gone, the floor was strewn with debris – lumps of concrete as big as suitcases, body parts and fragments of luggage. Just beside my pillar lay a pair of sunglasses, folded and undamaged. It was surreal. There was dust everywhere, I was choking and coughing.

I thought, 'Where is my backpack?' My ears were ringing and hurting; everything sounded muted. I got up and my balance was way off; I was swaying and disorientated. The backpack was still on my back. I patted my trouser pockets and the passport and tickets were still there. I got out from behind the pillar and looked back to where I had been before the man dragged me away and there was nobody there – nothing at all. Just a deep crater surrounded by blown-apart bodies and rubble.

It was a scene from hell. The blast of the explosion had felt like a physical assault and it was hard to think straight. When you know you have missed certain death by seconds it affects everything. It was hard to know what to do, where to go. Gradually the far reaches of the terminal became visible as the dust began settling. There were bodies everywhere and injured *people struggling to their feet, things dangling from the ceiling. Voices crying out, some were screaming – and everything muted by the ringing in my ears.*

To my left lay the body of a little girl, like a disjointed doll. She had been tossed by the blast and she was undamaged apart from a missing leg. I felt I should do something – but I couldn't think what. She was clearly dead: her eyes were wide open, her face covered in dust. I started making my way towards the main doors, sort of meandered through the chaos, negotiating obstacles – bodies or body parts, broken concrete and smashed luggage. I was beginning to feel nauseous and a cold sweat broke out on my face. I stood still and waited for a moment until I could move again. By the time I got to the doors, police and people in uniforms were coming in from all directions and I heard sirens. It was like a strange slow-motion dream, frightening and unreal at the same time. I made it outside, crossed the forecourt and sat down on the ground in the shade of a tree.

I put the pages down and we stare at each other. Sitting here in the quiet luxury of our house and reading about what happened to Hope is disorienting. Like entering a world of fear and threat, feeling the terror and then being suddenly snapped back.

THE CALL FROM WILLARD

This morning was full of frustrations. After knocking my hand and sending shock waves of pain up my sore wrist, I discovered there was hardly any coffee left. I mentally said goodbye to the one day this week with no reason to go out. I was still quietly fuming when the phone went. I tried to grab it fast and dropped it. The back cover popped off and the caller hung up before I had picked the pieces up.

'Shit!' I said aloud to the empty room. 'If it doesn't get better from now on, I'll go back to bed.'

The caller's number was not one I recognised, but as I stood there trying to get the cover back on it rang again.

'Hi, this is Willard,' said a deep voice I would have recognised anywhere. 'I don't know if you remember me.'

'Of course, I remember you. And you were right about the battle at Badajoz – I checked it when I got home.'

He laughed. 'That might be so, but I think we can divide the honours evenly. First time ever I've had a chance to spend hours talking about the Peninsular Wars with someone who knows the topic.'

A couple of weeks ago we sat beside each other on a flight from Dubai to Auckland. I had not been in a mood to start a conversation; I was tired and on edge, my injured arm was painful and generally frustrating. He had picked up on my lack of response and let me read in peace, but when a meal was put in front of us, he said, 'Let me help you with that. You won't be able to handle all those wrapped and sealed things.'

He checked that I was not going to protest, lifted my tray with one hand and swapped if for his own. He unwrapped and uncovered my food, buttered the bread roll and cut up the chicken.

'Thank you,' I said when he swapped the trays back again. 'What a useful neighbor you are.'

'A good engineer is always useful,' he said and tucked his book more securely between his leg and the armrest.

I glanced at the title and smiled. 'Snap!' I showed him the cover image of the book I was reading on my Kindle and he grinned. 'I wasn't expecting that!'

I was reading Wellington at Waterloo and he was reading Wellington and Napoleon: A clash of arms. We had a long and enjoyable discussion about the Peninsular Wars and a debate about the siege at Badajoz – both delighted to have found *someone who shared our interest. I gave him my card when he asked for it and had not heard from him since.*

'Would you like to go for a walk somewhere tomorrow? The forecast is good and I haven't been out of the plant in daylight since I got back. I need some fresh air.'

'It's very interesting,' says Dao. 'Are they all connected, these things and people? Or does she write a story whenever something affects her, something scary or just interesting or emotional?'

'I'm sure the incident in Pakistan and what's happened since are linked. It just can't be coincidence. The guy who rescued her at the airport is a terrorist and perhaps he's also the father of that little boy on the road. And suddenly Hope's flat is under surveillance and someone's following her around. God knows what else is going on – emails and text messages monitored? Her friends? And this Willard guy – is he really just a random new acquaintance?'

'Imagine that terrorist standing there,' says Dao slowly. 'And then he spots her looking straight at him and he recognises her, so he drags her to safety before the next bomb goes off just where she was standing.' She wriggles her foot. 'Please don't stop.'

'Enough.' I lift her feet off my legs. 'I'm going to get Scruff in from the courtyard. I think it's going to rain again.'

'But listen,' says Dao, when I get back upstairs. 'There's something I don't understand. Those guys were there – at the airport, I mean – because they knew two bombs would go off, OK? They stand at the end furthest away from the first bomb and look down the length of the building. They can see bomber number one at the far end and he blows up. Then our guy spots Hope, and he knows she's very close to the second bomber, so he saves her – to kind of pay back that debt of honour. But why were they there at all? I just don't get it. Aren't those bombers willing to sacrifice themselves? Do they need someone standing around with a weapon to see they really do it?'

'I don't know, Dao. I have no idea how they think. But from a tactical point of view, I understand it. If you let off a bomb at the end of a very long indoor space, survivors will run away from the blast. They'll head for the other end – unless they can get outside right where they are, which in this case they could not. Maybe those guys were there to shoot into the crowd and stop them escaping out of the building – trap them in place until the second bomb went off. Like that time in Paris when they bombed a café and then, when people rushed up to help the injured, another bomb went off among them. They are maximizing the impact.'

'Those people are really horrible! And now Hope is missing – which is really weird. That can't be the security people. They don't kidnap people, do they?'

8

We sit in the car just down the street from Willard's house in Freeman's Bay and wait for Noah. Today Scruff is in the back of the station wagon on his rug and Dao is talking to him to make him stay there; the latest instalment of her training program. He already knows a dozen commands.

'By the time he's five he'll be a fully trained wonder dog,' I say. 'I never taught him anything apart from walking to heel.'

'He likes learning,' says Dao. 'He is a natural student. I think I'll teach him to count.'

I lean back against the headrest and make a mental note to check the CCTV recording to see if that guy, who was on the far side of the street when Noah came the first time, has been back. Was it just chance that he was there when Noah came, or had he followed him?

Dao spots Noah walking along on the other side and jumps out. 'Hey, Noah,' she calls and he comes jogging towards us, thin and exhausted looking. He seems to have an endless supply of black T-shirts and black jeans.

'Did you read it? The stories on the USB stick? She had

half a dozen USBs in the drawer, but this one had an X done with marker pen. It's odd. She's saved hundreds of those little stories on her computer for years and suddenly some of them are saved on a flash drive.'

Dao says calmly, 'Of course we did, Noah. We think something must have happened that made her think her laptop wasn't safe – that's our guess. Not just when she went through Customs in Pakistan, but here too.'

He nods, looks slightly less frantic. 'OK, good. That's what I thought too.'

Willard is an athletic-looking guy with grey hair and glasses, about sixty. His house is a poster-pretty cottage built when Auckland was young. We sit down in a modernised interior where two rooms and a kitchen have been turned into one space. His taste is conservative, an earlier era than Samantha's, but equally consistent throughout. Maybe everyone has furniture to match the age of the house they live in, I think. I'm bang on in that case: modern house, modern furniture.

'I'm sorry I was so short with you on the phone, Noah,' he says. 'We were loading a turbine on a truck using a new cradle and we had to improvise a different way of arranging the straps to get the weight distribution right. A bit nerve-racking, so I couldn't talk for long.'

He notices our looks of incomprehension. 'Wind turbines. We make them, and this new, big model was a bit of a challenge.'

Dao looks up, instantly interested. I can read her mind: she is just about to ask if she can come and see the factory but resists the impulse.

Noah seems awkward and hesitant again. Just as I wonder if I should step in, he starts talking, abruptly and a bit too loud.

'I told you that Hope is missing. I brought some of her

journal stories to read. I think they might have a bearing on her disappearance.'

He hands the papers over and we watch silently while Willard reads them. He hands them back to Noah and shakes his head. 'I can't believe it. What happened? You must tell me more.'

'I know you saw Hope once or twice. When did you last see her?'

There is a change in Noah's voice. It is hard to decide if he is suspicious of Willard or just frustrated. Once again, I find it hard to understand him. His behaviour is erratic and sometimes his reactions are out of proportion to what others say. If he suspects Willard of something, he is doing his best to alienate him before we have got anything out of him. Dao casts one of her black looks at Noah; I nearly expect him to flinch in pain, but he is oblivious.

'We went out for dinner about ten days ago,' says Willard calmly. 'I went to Tonga to negotiate a contract the day after and took a week off. I got back a couple of days ago. I knew nothing about this until you called. Has it been in the papers?'

'No, not yet. Did you know about the explosions at the airport?'

'Yes, she told me over dinner. She said she hadn't told anyone yet, but now something had happened that worried her. She said she didn't want to tell you, because if she did, you would come back early from your holiday. It was something she thought was connected to that terrorist saving her life. We came back here after dinner and watched the video from the terminal – I knew I had seen it on the BBC website. I have it on my laptop now. I suppose you've seen it?'

I am sure my face looks just like Noah's – completely blank.

'I only just read her story about it this morning,' says Noah. 'Hadn't even thought of video being available. Did she see anything new?'

'No, not really. She wanted to know if she could have been identified from the video. And I don't think she could have, at least not from the clip we watched, but there would be other video cameras at other angles in the terminal. If anyone wanted to check who it was, who got dragged to safety, they might have identified her.' Willard gets up. 'I'll show you. Would you like a drink?'

We say 'No thanks' and sit in silence while he gets his laptop from another room, connects it to the TV and finds the video clip.

'Here it is. I saved it and fiddled around with it, so we could watch it in slow motion. I hope I can get it to work again.'

We all lean forward, as if every inch closer to the screen will reveal more. The video is from a camera mounted at the end of the long terminal, filming along the row of check-in desks.

Lines of people waiting, children running around, people trickling away towards the departure gates. The bomber is picked out in a white circle and then suddenly, an explosion. The image tilts and shakes, debris flies like missiles, people are thrown to the floor, objects crash down around them. A cloud of dust swirls up. In the distance, towards the far end of the terminal, a man runs very fast between bodies and chunks of concrete. He lifts a piece of debris off a woman, grabs her upper arms and drags her away, running backwards across the littered floor. He is looking back over his shoulder, but even so it seems like a miracle that he doesn't trip. They disappear behind a pillar and within a few seconds another, bigger explosion rocks the camera. When the dust settles there is a deep crater in the floor, highlighted by a white circle.

'Jesus, he risked his life!' exclaims Noah. 'He saved her, even though he knew he could be killed.' He shakes his head in wonder at how lucky Hope was. 'The second bomber must have been very close to where she was standing.'

Willard starts the recording again, this time in slow motion. Now that I am familiar with the scene I know where to look for the four men lined up in the far distance. I know the line where Hope is waiting. I pick her out, continue to focus on her through the haze of dust after the first explosion. I watch intently through the whole sequence, but I see nothing new.

'So that's how she hurt her arm,' says Dao. 'It's interesting. If you watch that terrorist – right from the start, the one who saved her – you can see the way his head moves just before the first explosion. You know how you can look at something, like the big picture, not with any specific focus and then something catches your eye? It's like your mind does a little jump.'

Willard replays the recording again in slow motion. The moment Dao talks about is very clear. I missed it the first time; it's a very small movement.

'You're right,' I say. 'He's just keeping an eye on the whole scene, scanning back and forth. Then he does a double take when he spots her and realises who she is. And he saves her.'

'He reacted very fast. He knew he might be blown up.' Noah's face reflects his ambivalence. Like me he is torn between admiration for the terrorist's courage and sense of honour, and the bone-chilling horror he is prepared to inflict on innocent people, some of them his own.

Willard turns the TV off and we sit in silence for a moment. What we have watched seems very immediate and personal. Noah asks Willard if he knows what had worried Hope, his tone of voice only marginally less unfriendly.

'No, she never told me. She just said something strange had cropped up and she wondered if that guy saving her had triggered something here in New Zealand. I got the impression she didn't want to tell me, and I knew she was going to discuss it with you. I didn't feel I could push her – I haven't known her very long.'

I get a feeling he is being evasive. Noah's slightly hostile approach is once again hampering progress.

'But what did you think?' he says abruptly.

'I don't know what alerted her, but something happened, and she wanted to know why and how it related to her. She said something like, "I hadn't even checked in yet, nobody could know for sure that I was there when it happened." But that's all.'

I think he has a theory but he isn't willing to be dragged into a discussion. Noah needs a crash course in how to communicate and build trust instead of alienating people.

We thank Willard and leave, briefly stand talking on the sidewalk. Dao looks cold and I suggest that Noah should follow us home instead of standing outside in the wind.

'We could go to a café or bar near here, but if we go back to the house, we can look at some more of Hope's stories from that USB stick. We've only read the first three so far. But it's a long way back for you. You might prefer to go home and read them there.'

'We could buy pizza on the way,' suggests Dao. 'It's nearly dinner time.'

'I'll come, thanks. If we read them together, we might work something out.'

In the car Dao says, 'God, he's so odd! Did you notice how he nearly made Willard angry by being so bad-tempered? Not very clever. But I want him to share everything he finds with us. I'm trying to be patient.'

9

Noah wipes his sticky fingers on a paper napkin and pats his pocket. 'I have the original USB stick with me. The one marked with X. As I said, I didn't have time to check everything on it this morning. Let's plug it into your laptop and see what else is on it. Maybe she wrote something about what worried her. It can't have been that she spotted the camera in the flat. She would have done something about it, had it ripped out or simply gone to stay with a friend, not just waited for me to get back.'

He is calm again after his tension at Willard's place. Or did he take something before he drove here?

Hope's documents are named seemingly at random. Some names are descriptive, some just the name of a person or a place name. The first one of interest is about Willard. We crowd together in front of my laptop which has a very big screen and put Dao in the middle, in charge of scrolling down the pages.

A WALK WITH WILLARD
We had an early lunch in the museum cafeteria and walked

around the Domain. My caution was justified. He is both interesting and interested, wants to take me out for dinner 'soon'. I do want to see him again; there is something about him, not just that fabulous voice or how easy he is to get on with. But I never accept anything from a new man friend unless they are prepared to accept the conditions, my Rules.

'Dinner would be nice,' I said, trying to strike a balance between casually friendly and serious. 'But I've got to warn you. I'm not looking for romance or a relationship. Just being friends.'

He took this calmly and with no change of expression. 'That's fine, but why? There must be a reason and maybe it would be a good idea to tell me what it is at the outset.

'Friends only,' I said. 'No relationship, not even a casual one.'

He gave me an appraising glance, hard to decipher. After a moment the silence nudged me to elaborate. 'It's nothing to do with you personally. It's me — it's what I have decided about my life.

'Are you going to tell me why?' In a voice of polite inquiry rather than curiosity.

I have no idea what made me say it, but I gave him the unadorned truth with no explanation. 'Because I killed my husband.'

That stopped him in his tracks — literally. He stopped walking, but his face registered neither surprise nor shock. I like him, he's very unusual.

'I see. And this precludes relationships for the rest of your life?'

This is exactly the situation I have tried to avoid for eight years. My entire existence has been built around my rules, the framework that makes me feel balanced and emotionally safe. I have never tried to explain them to anyone. I don't think I could.

'Yes, it does,' I said bluntly and walked on, and he followed. He said nothing more about it. When he dropped me off at my *flat, we said a pleasant goodbye and he said he would call about dinner. I really want to see him again, but I'll have to be very careful. At least I've warned him right at the start. He can't protest when I stick to my rules. But he won't call me – I'm sure I have scared him off.*

'I've got some questions about that story.' Dao looks at Noah clearly expecting him to offer explanations. Instead of rebuffing her he just says, 'Let's read some more and then we'll talk about it.'

'And you should arrange these files in date order,' she adds severely. 'So we can figure out how they hang together. Having them alpha-sorted is not useful.'

'OK, I'll do that.'

CALL FROM NOAH

Noah called from Australia tonight, when I was in the bath. It was lovely to hear his voice.

'What are you doing? You're not in bed, are you?'

'I'm in the bath, up to my neck in hot water with the phone and a glass of wine beside me and my Kindle, pure bliss. How is Melbourne, are you having a good time?'

He told me about the old friends he had seen and the night spots they had been to. 'I'm off to Sydney tomorrow to see Dave and Cath.'

He sounded so cheerful and relaxed. I suddenly realised how much I wanted to tell him everything. But I don't want him to come tearing home early. He deserves his holiday. I only told him about my stalker, nothing more.

'I've got a guy following me around, just the last week or so. A young chap, very tidy, good-looking.'

'What? Do you know who he is?

'I have no idea. He's not hovering outside my flat and he isn't everywhere or at all times – he just kind of turns up, very randomly. I come out from some place at night and there he is, at a distance, watching. I don't understand how he knows where I'm going to be. It's three times now. No, four. The second time I saw him I thought it was just a coincidence.'

He was thinking at the other end. There was a clicking sound, a ballpoint pen; he always does that when he's on the phone – like a nervous tic. Dad calls it the 'Bic tic'.

'If he doesn't follow you from the flat it must be that he knows in advance where you are going to be. He could have hacked your phone, I guess. Maybe he's checking your voice messages and your texts, so he knows where you are going. Check that you have a PIN on your voicemail. Your computer should be safe. I set it up to be pretty much bullet-proof, but you never know these days. And go to the police and report him. Take a picture of him next time so you have something to show them. Are you going out again this coming week?'

All this is very over the top, considering he knows nothing about my other worries, but typical of Noah, instant reaction. I promised him to only go out by taxi in the evenings and to always have someone with me and he calmed down. I texted him when I got out of the bath and told him not to mention it to Mum and Dad.

Noah runs his hand over his face, shattered. 'Jesus! Why didn't she tell me what she was worried about? She only told me about the stalker, and she didn't seem overly worried by him.'

He looks off into the distance, frowning. 'You know how she told Willard she wanted to figure out if she could have been identified from that video clip. That must be significant. God, I wish she had told me!'

DINNER WITH WILLARD

Willard is a man with many facets. We were in the Japanese restaurant he had picked (Industry Zen, amazing food and service) and out of nowhere he said, 'I hope you will let me ask one or possibly two questions. Let's say two, in case the first answer is evasive or cryptic. And then I'll shut up and leave the subject alone.'

This man is dangerous, far too appealing. I knew that this conversation would probably end badly. He was bound to try to take it one step further and then he would push a bit further still. I should never have told him. Nobody will ever understand, and it will end with sleepless nights of guilt and self-blame.

'So tell me,' he said, as casual and unconcerned as if he was asking how my day had been, 'when did you kill your husband?'

It actually made me want to laugh. The way he said it was disarming, not what I had expected. Why did he want to know when it had happened? I had been certain that he would ask 'how' or 'why'. Somehow 'when' seemed a lot less threatening.

I said, 'Eight years ago.' And for some reason I added, 'In June.'

'In June? And by the way, that was not my second question, that was just an observation with a question mark after it. So here is the second one – did you do it on purpose?'

Before I had time to control my reactions my eyes filled with tears. I blinked furiously, but a tear spilled over and ran down my cheek. I retrieved my composure with an effort of will that felt like swallowing a rock. 'No, I did not do it on purpose. But a lot of people thought I had – including the police.'

'Well, that's OK then.' He continued eating as if nothing had happened. I waited for the next question, but after taking a sip of wine he changed the subject.

'I went to an interesting lecture last month, at the museum, a visiting professor from Canada talking about the ethics – or lack of ethics – of displaying human body parts in museums.'

*He kept throwing me off-balance. Was this a diversion to lull
me into a sense of security before he reverted to the subject of
Buster?*

*'I heard someone talk about it on the radio a while ago. It's an
interesting subject. Thinking about where we draw the line. You
know, we accept that it's OK having brains and things in jars for
people to look at, but other body parts seem to be off limits. We
baulk at the thought of a head. But the Lindow man is OK, the
whole man just lying there forever, preserved after spending a
couple of thousand years in a peat bog or whatever it was,
displayed in a glass coffin like Snow White. It's interesting.'*

*Even as we spoke, I was trying to figure out what his next
step would be. Perhaps I should just cut this friendship and be
sensible. He keeps taking me by surprise. My carefully
constructed no-go zones that have protected me from emotional
involvement for years seem less secure than they used to be.*

*'Perhaps it's all to do with how old something or someone is,'
he said, and smiled. 'If it's more than a thousand years old, like a
mummy or Lindow man, it seems to be OK. We are allowed to
forget the person and regard it as an object?'*

Is it that gorgeous voice that makes me trust him?

Dao says quietly, 'She likes Willard a lot. And I know what
she means about his voice. It's lovely, makes you feel
warm.'

Noah scowls and makes no comment, just opens
another file. I am beginning to see a pattern, and file it
away to think about later.

MEMORIES

*Mum rang while I was scrolling through images of the
Pakistani safe-house women, trying to select ones to go with the*

article I have just finished. I was looking at a heart-wrenching image of a scarred neck and shoulder and remembered the girl who had let me take the photo, while I absent-mindedly listened to Mum telling me that Noah's old school friend Anna had married a TV star in the US.

'It's hard to believe,' I said. 'She was so shy at school and never dated anyone. I wonder how they met. Did it say in the paper?'

As Mum started telling me the details my mind suddenly produced a memory that made me mentally cringe. I made an effort to respond and finished the call as soon as I could. Images from the past were clear in my mind. I knew exactly where I had last seen Anna: on the courthouse steps, straight after my trial. I had come out to face a small crowd and raised cameras. Anna was there. I can picture her perfectly, a tall pale woman with thick strawberry blonde hair in a straight fringe level with her eyebrows, looking as if she wanted to say something. But she stayed where she was, on the edge of the crowd, an expression of compassion on her face. I have not seen her since.

Noah looks at his watch. 'Is that enough for tonight? We can continue tomorrow or another day. There must be things you want to do.'

'Nothing that's more important than this,' I say. 'Let's read until we drop. And then we print it all out, so we can refer to things. Hope is very deliberate with her choice of words and how she describes things. I noticed it in those earlier stories – the writing seems very simple, but there are subtle shades of meaning. I find it easier to notice things if I read it on paper. There are a lot of question marks in my head just now.'

Dao gets up. 'And in mine too. Just let me feed Scruff first. We forgot his dinner. Look how good he is, just sits there and waits. No barking or fussing.' She bends and ruffles his ears and they disappear into the kitchen.

Noah stands up and stretches, looks around the long room. 'You have a lot of alarm sensors everywhere,' he says casually. 'And CCTV all around. Remnants of the time Dao's life was under threat, I suppose.'

Is that a hint of contempt in his voice? And if so, why? Maybe he is one of those people who resent and envy others and show it by contempt. Or am I getting overly aware of his odd moods, do I read too much into them?

'Still in use.' I speak quietly so Dao won't hear. 'She's fine most of the time, but the alarm system has become a "must have". She often sets the ground-floor alarm when we go to bed. She'll get over it in her own time – possibly.'

'I went back and read the reports from before and after the trial. The whole story was amazing. She is a remarkable girl.' He sounds genuine.

'She is,' I said. 'I've never known anyone like her – male or female.'

VERY IMPORTANT – this is for you, Noah, just in case.

I am writing this and saving it on a USB stick. I will transfer some other things too and delete them from my laptop. Will text you when you are on the flight back. I'll tell you about this file and where to find it and the other things that are important for you to know in case something happens to me. What happened yesterday was terrifying. I might ask you to come and stay here when you are back. Or maybe I can stay with you.

This is what happened: Yesterday someone knocked on the door very early. I looked through the peephole in the door and saw a slightly distorted view of a middle-aged man in a blue overall. Not the tidy stalker, at least. I have been a bit careful lately – some odd things have happened.

'Sorry to disturb you on a Saturday morning,' he said, standing politely away from the door. 'I'm moving in downstairs and I've locked myself out. My phone is inside, and my car keys too. Could I please use your phone to call a locksmith?'

'Of course. I can look one up for you online and I'll fetch my phone.'

I walked to my desk and sat down in front of the computer. At the sound of wheels, I looked up. He was inside now, but with a Spiderman mask over his head. Suddenly he was bizarre and scary. He was pulling a large green wheelie bin. I leaped to my feet and he let go of the bin and rushed at me. I screamed 'No!' and pushed him hard in the chest with one hand, trying to rotate away from him at the same time, but he threw himself at me in a tackle. Out of the corner of my eye I saw something white in his hand; his arm was stretched out, away from his body. There was a strong chemical smell. I took a step backward, tried to kick him, but the desk caught against my thigh and I started falling sideways. His body was pinning me against the desk. He pressed a cloth over my nose and mouth. The world spun, I tried to struggle but my mind faded to nothing.

My first impression, when I came to again, was rough shaking and noise. I was confused and nauseous, could not remember what had happened. I was bundled up with my wrists and ankles tied and tape over my mouth. I was on my side in a dark box of some kind with my knees bent and very little room to move. My left calf was cramping. I tried to straighten my legs, but there was no room. I was terrified. I moved my cheek against the surface I was resting against, tried to imagine what it was – something made of plastic, some sort of box, with a little bit of light filtering in.

By twisting my shoulders and bending my head back I could see an outline of light. I was in a wheelie bin – and then I remembered the man in the Spiderman mask. I was on a truck or in some kind of vehicle. I felt terribly sick. If I vomited with tape over my mouth I would die. Intense fear swept through my mind.

My heart was beating too fast and uncontrollable panic was one second away. I tried to claw myself back to rational thought. I have never been so scared in my life. And this is strange, Noah, but out of nowhere the sequence of lights coming on in my flat started playing out in my mind. Objects lit up in their predetermined order and my eyes moved to where the next light would come on a fraction of a second before it did. My brain calmed, my breathing slowed, and the nausea receded. The vehicle went over a bump and something made a heavy metallic clonk just beside me. The bin rocked.

Whoever he was, he meant to harm me. I had to escape, but I could not force my wrists apart even by a millimetre. I pushed hard with my bound feet against the bottom of the bin, over and over, trying to make my head force the lid up. But it was useless – the lid was secured somehow.

I imagined looking down from above – a wheelie bin lying on its side, perhaps on a trailer or on the deck of a small truck. I knew I was on a big road with lots of traffic – perhaps the motorway. I must attract attention. If we stop or someone stops us I can make noise, I thought. I can kick the side of the bin or use my head to bang, grunt as loudly as I can.

I kicked hard against the side of the bin and it only made a dull thump, but it had shifted my body weight and it made the bin rock. I did it again and the bin rocked once more. A glimmer of hope in my mind. I was not lying evenly on a flat side; my back was across the inside of the corner. I shoved my body violently sideways and the bin tilted on its rounded corner and then fell back. I was on fire with desperation now, throwing myself against the inside of the bin over and over. Each time the bin nearly rolled on to its other side, but not quite. I stopped, *panting and sweaty, and tried to think logically of what might work better. Perhaps rocking it back and forth, as you do when a car is stuck in sand.*

I started again, this time first back and then forward, using the momentum to gain better purchase on the forward motion. Three attempts later the bin rolled over and I was face down instead of on my side. I think the bin must have been up against something, some slight unevenness under it that made it 'stick' in one position. Thank goodness my hands were tied in front of me or I might never have been able to achieve anything. I started the process again, tried to put more force into it. I felt the bin teeter on a corner again, held my breath and leant in the direction of the tilt, trying to use every little change of position to move the point of gravity. The bin rolled over once more, teetered as if on an edge and fell. Luck was with me – I had moved it in the right direction. The bin hit the road with a bone-jarring thump. My head smashed against the inside and stars cascaded in front of my eyes. The bin rolled over a couple of times. I heard brakes squealing and then all movement stopped. Men's voices were shouting.

'Let's get the fucking thing off the road before we're all killed!'

'Jeez, it's heavy. We'll have to lift it – the wheels are stuffed.'

The bin was dragged, men grunted, then a bump and the bin was upright.

'Got a knife? I'm gonna cut those cable ties and check what's inside. Stupid bastard just drove off, didn't even know he'd lost the bloody thing.'

Daylight flooded down into the bin and a man's voice, shaken and disbelieving. 'Shit, it's a body!'

I twisted my neck and looked up and his voice died away, his eyes widened. 'Jesus Christ!' They lowered the bin on its side and gently pulled me out and helped me to sit up.

One of them said, 'Call the cops and an ambulance, will

you?' To me he said, 'God knows what smashing onto the road has done to you – concussion at least. You hit bloody hard.'

They slit the strips of duct tape around my wrists and ankles. I tried to unpick a corner of the strip of tape across my mouth, but one of them put his hand on mine and stopped me. 'Wait – you'll rip the skin off your lips. Let me do it slowly.'

I nodded, and he knelt beside me and agonizingly slowly he stripped the tape away from my face, holding the skin down with his thumb as he pulled. I sat still, concentrating on not flinching. Heads turned in passing cars. My helper moved his thumb along my lips, and I smelled oil and petrol as he continued pulling very slowly. A fleeting memory from the accident when Buster died slipped into my mind, triggered by the smell. I pushed the thought aside and turned my focus to the man's face; he felt my glance and smiled. A kind man.

'My name is Craig,' he said. 'Nearly done and no blood yet.' One of the others chimed in with 'Well done, mate!'

They did not ask me what had happened, just led me to their van and sat me down in the front seat while we waited for the emergency services.

A police car arrived, and shortly after that an ambulance. I sat on a stretcher in the ambulance and told a female officer what had happened, watching over her shoulder as another cop interviewed the men. Eventually my rescuers drove off.

'OK, that will do for now. We'll be in touch later – we'll stay here until someone can come and pick up the bin.'

'I'm fine,' I said half an hour later to an ED doctor. 'I'm just sore.

'OK,' she said, shining a light into my eyes. 'Let's make sure you really are fine. We'll check you haven't cracked your skull. You're probably concussed. A scan won't do any harm.'

It was out of my control. I was a parcel being passed from one set of hands to the next. After what seemed like hours I was finally back in the cubicle with the doctor.

'No fractures, but you should take it easy for a few days. No exertions. Try not to bump your head for the next few weeks. The nurse will call someone to pick you up. You shouldn't leave unaccompanied.'

That left me with a problem. Samantha was in Wellington for the weekend, you were still in Australia, and without my phone I had no phone numbers. I had no money and no shoes. I asked for a phone directory and looked for Spencer's number, but it was unlisted. Who else was there? Calling the parents while I was in this state was unthinkable; they would worry themselves sick and drive me crazy. A lot of my friends would bandy the story around and that was the last thing I wanted. Finally, I thought of Louise Barlow, who I met at the gym and sometimes have coffee with. She knows nobody else that I know, and she works from home. To my relief she was listed.

I told her I had been in a traffic accident and needed a ride home. She turned up an hour later and I told her a fabricated story about having been in a car accident with a friend.

I said my friend (male) was being kept in hospital and she was kind and sympathetic and drove me home. The thought of walking up the stairs alone made me feel queasy with fear, but Louise took for granted that she would come upstairs with me and see me safely inside. When we got to the top my head was swimming. Thank God I remembered the hidden key. I never told you that I had hidden it, Noah. You would have been outraged at the lack of security. I have never used it, but now it was a godsend. I knelt at the far end of the landing and prised up the loose corner tile, and there it was.

Louise asked if I was OK and left to take her mother out for coffee; such a reassuringly normal thing to do. I locked the door and put the safety chain on and had a bath. I will not leave this flat until you are back in the country, Noah — only two more days now. I keep my phone in my pocket all the time. I have rehearsed what I am going to say to the emergency people if

Dao's left hand is clenched into a white-knuckled fist, pushing down on my thigh. Noah jerked several times, as if someone had punched him while he read. Now he pushes his chair back so fast it tips over. He paces back and forth, his face tight and desperate.

'Fuck, fuck, fuck! And that bastard's got her again! How the hell did he get her a second time? He must have tricked her – there are no marks on the door. And who the hell is he?'

Dao gets up and puts a hand on my shoulder as if to steady herself. She might be reliving some of her own victim trauma inside her head, but her outward emotion is rage. 'This is awful! We must find him and get her back – or get the police to do something.'

Rage is good, I think, fury will keep her memories at bay and divert her into plans and constructive thought.

Noah is like a taut wire vibrating in the wind; his distress is bordering on meltdown. 'But how? I don't get it – this happens and then he gets her a second time? If he tricked her to open the door, how did he do it this time? I wish that bloody building had CCTV. And who the fuck is he? Why did he put on that disguise? She'd already seen him.'

It is time to calm things down. 'OK, guys,' I say. 'Let's write down what we need to find out and who might be able to help us. Someone in her street could have CCTV. Can we work out anything from what else is on that flash drive? Could there be some unknown element in this that we haven't read about yet? We need to find out if people who work in the surrounding buildings noticed anything.'

Noah comes back to the table. He looks half-demented and a muscle on his temple is twitching. 'God, where do we start? It's such a mess – so many unknowns. How can we make a plan when we know nothing? It's hopeless.'

Dao looks him straight in the eye, her warrior persona suddenly coming through strong and clear. 'For God's sake, Noah, stop it. We have to do something! Nothing is impossible, nothing! We have to find Hope and punish this man. My Dad died when I was eight. If I complained about something being unfair or too hard, he used to say, "Life might give you a cactus, but that doesn't mean you have to sit on it." I'm not meaning to be rude, but all this worrying and fussing doesn't help. It makes things worse. We have to get going with this. Now!'

'OK, OK, I know. It's just that it's such a mess. Where do we start?'

'I'm going to go and see Benson,' she says decisively. 'Tomorrow, on my own. Hunter can drop me off at the station and I'll just sit there until he can see me.'

Noah stares at her. 'Benson, the cop? The one Willow talked about? Why can't you just call him and ask when you can go and see him? Is he a friend?'

'That's not how I want to do it. I want to take him by surprise, make him talk to me like he used to. I think I could maybe get something out of him that he wouldn't tell Willow.'

Noah still looks confused.

'Benson is a detective sergeant,' I say. 'He was involved in the entire investigation into what happened at the island. He has a great respect for Dao and he is also very fond of her.'

He loves the way Dao handles herself when things get dangerous, when most people would stand paralyzed with fear or run for their lives. She might be terrified, but her brain continues to work, and she acts. Like when the armed intruder smashed his way into the house or during the incident in the abandoned factory.

Gradually we work out a plan of sorts, manage to discuss options without any outbursts from Noah. After fifteen minutes we have a list of things to check, people to contact and others to inform. We divide it up between us.

Dao takes the paper out of my hand and goes through it. 'Noah, you will go around and ask people in the area if they saw the pick-up truck and the man with the wheelie bin or any disturbance a couple of days later. And you'll check if there is CCTV in the street or around the corners of Hope's block. And by the way, Hunter, your handwriting is terrible.

'I'll go and see Benson – that might take all day. Hunter is going to revisit Spencer and Samantha and see this Louise woman. He's very good at getting things out of people without asking lots of questions. And he's going to tell Willow about all this, so you don't have to, Noah. And Willow will probably go back to the cops and start making a fuss. She can argue with people and get her way without raising her voice – I've seen her. Remember that long police interview, Hunter? They didn't have a chance. Anything else?'

'Yes, I just thought of something. We must check if those guys who picked up Hope from the road noticed the number plate or anything about the pick-up truck. They might have a dashboard camera. Dao, can you ask Benson who they were? I'll ask Willow to follow up too.'

Dao turns to Noah and her tone makes it clear she expects an answer. 'And now you can tell us what happened to Hope's husband – and why.'

As usual Noah hesitates before he starts, as if he needs to make some crucial decision about how to start the first sentence. He is tapping his forefinger on the rim of his coffee cup and his legs are jiggling. Any minute now I will tell him to sit still; he is driving me crazy.

'It's a long story. The marriage was a disaster. She met him – Buster – through some friends and before you could say "snap" they were in a relationship. Everyone raved about what a great-looking couple they were. She was besotted. The family had reservations, nothing specific but we didn't warm to him. Dad thought he was self-absorbed and vain, Mum used to say he had an inflated sense of entitlement and I just disliked him right from the start. They got married in a registry office. Dad thought they got married without telling us because Buster was worried we would talk her out of it. Probably true.'

'Why didn't you like him?' I ask. 'Anything in particular?'

He hesitates, taps his fingers on the edge of the table. 'There was just something about him. Nothing obvious, but something hiding behind the good looks. Anyway, they lived in Christchurch and I was here in Auckland. I didn't see her often, but each time she had changed a bit more. She was not herself – less open, less cheerful, slightly cowed somehow. I was seriously worried about her and so were our parents. Then Mum heard some stuff about him from someone she met, a guy who used to work with him – he was a journalist too. He said Buster was a very heavy drinker, probably an alcoholic. We hadn't seen enough of him to realise and he hid it well when he wanted to make a good impression.'

He stares past my shoulder at something only he can see and sits silent for a minute. Neither Dao nor I say anything and eventually he picks up the thread again.

'Somehow, he dominated Hope in a really weird way, manipulated her mind. Everything was always her fault, didn't matter what it was – even things that *he* did. And this is the scary part – she took it. As if she actually believed she was the one causing problems or wasn't good enough. As if she made him aggressive. You know what she said once? She said, "Poor Buster. I make him so angry, even though I don't mean to." I should have abducted her there and then. It was awful, drove me crazy.'

Telling us about it is making him stressed again; his twitchy mannerisms are back, his voice takes on a higher pitch. I keep my fingers crossed that the story will not turn into anything similar to the abuse Dao experienced. Noah is too absorbed in the telling of it to think of how it might affect someone who has been victimised herself.

'Someone told me it's called gas lighting after a film called *Gaslight* made decades ago, about someone who makes his wife think she is losing her mind, but it seems to be used when someone is doing this sort of controlling thing too, playing mind games. Anyway, Buster died several years ago. They were in the car and he slapped Hope hard across the face. She was driving, normal open-road speed. The car went across the hard shoulder and hit a concrete power pole. Front left corner hit hard, the pole snapped and fell across the car. Buster's head was crushed. There were no brake marks at all, no swerving.'

He has been speaking faster and faster; he is nearly breathless. He stops and sits quiet for a moment and I wonder if this is it. But just as I am about to say something, he starts up again.

'An oncoming driver, who hadn't seen Buster hitting Hope, said she had her eyes closed and appeared to steer straight at the pole. She was charged with manslaughter. People speculated that she was so at her wits' end that she tried to kill them both, deliberately, but only he died.'

'What did you think at the time? And what do you think now?'

'In court she said exactly what she said to us after the accident. First, he backhanded her across the face and then he threw the whisky from his paper cup at her. She got it all over her face and in her eyes. He often drank in the car. Not from a bottle, but from a paper cup so it would look normal. The car stank of alcohol and so did Hope. To start with they thought she'd been driving drunk, but she had no blood alcohol at all. His was sky-high.'

He stops talking and waits. Dao just looks at him, says nothing.

'Very tragic,' I say. 'Poor Hope. It explains a lot about those stories of hers. I didn't understand her reluctance regarding relationships that she wrote about in the story about Willard. I knew there had to be something traumatic behind it.'

Dao says nothing much until Noah leaves shortly after. When we are in the bathroom before going to bed, she looks at me in the mirror and speaks around the toothbrush in her mouth. 'We have to do this, Hunter.'

I nod at her image in the mirror and continue brushing my teeth. Of course, we have to do it.

10

At half-past seven the next morning I drop Dao off at the police station where Benson works now. I hope she will get something out of him, but I am not optimistic. He is a very sharp guy who knows when to keep a lid on things. His only weakness, as far as I know, is his affection for Dao.

I'm hoping to snatch a bit of time with Willow, before her day gets busy, but it is too early. I sit in the car outside her office and consider what we know. I try to picture how the guy with the bin did it when he knocked on Hope's door. She said in her story that he stood politely back from the door. If he stood to one side, she would have looked at him. If he put his bin at the other end of the landing, she wouldn't notice it. When she went to look up the number, he had time to pull the Spiderman mask on. Then he trundled his bin inside and had the pad of chloroform, or whatever it was, ready in his hand.

What we did not discuss last night was why he put on the disguise at all. It can't have been that he wanted to be anonymous when he dragged the bin down the stairs. Wearing a mask would have drawn attention to him instead of the opposite. Anyone sane who met a man in a mask pulling a heavy wheelie bin down the stairs would run screaming for the nearest policeman. It can only be that he knew the camera was there and did not want to be recognised. So, he stood to one side when she opened the door, to be out of camera range. If he knew about the camera, he must be part of whatever organisation installed it or some other unit with close links to it. I realise I don't know the difference between the GCSB and the Security Intelligence Service; there could be others I have never heard of, not to mention those private firms Willow speculated about.

The bin man was a careful planner. So why was he so careless with how he put the bin on the truck? It could easily have fallen off, even if Hope had not rocked it to the edge. Did he leave it lying across the deck of the pick-up truck, because he suddenly had to leave quickly? I would have made it lie lengthwise, if I had loaded it. But when I replay Hope's story in my mind, the penny drops. She had heard a loud metallic clang just beside her. Perhaps bin man's truck did have a tailgate and he closed it, but he was in a hurry and didn't do it properly. The clang could have been the tailgate falling open. It would have been awkward to get the bin up on the deck; maybe it attracted unwanted attention and he wanted to get away as fast as he could. How did he manage to load a bin with an adult inside, on his own? Tilt the top of the bin against the edge of the truck's deck, I think, and then bend down and lift from the bottom edge. Lift and push, shove it sideways if you're in a hurry, probably easier and faster than pushing it further in along the deck. Then close the tailgate and drive away.

Willow drives past and turns into their underground car park. I know from experience that she takes pride in being on time for appointments and breaking into her day is easiest first thing in the morning, before she becomes busy. I give her a minute before I go inside and up to the second floor. She is talking to the receptionist in the foyer and turns around, surprised, when I come in and ask, 'Have you got any time today when I can tell you what we've found out about Hope?'

She consults the girl behind the desk. 'Right now, for about half an hour until my first client arrives. Might be a bit longer. Come along.'

First up I give her the stories from the USB drive that we printed out last night. 'Don't read them now. If we haven't got a lot of time, I'd rather tell you the basics first. You can read the details later.'

She sits absorbed and silent while I give her a brief outline of the stories and our meeting with Willard.

'Oh my God, that poor woman! What are you going to do? It's too soon to chase up that information request I filed – they can take ages. I will certainly get back to the police and point out that they already had a file on Hope, when Noah reported that she had gone missing. They never told either of us that they did or that they knew about the abduction. It's outrageous.'

I tell her what we are doing, keep the details minimal. When I say that Dao has gone alone to see Benson, she smiles.

'Can't you picture it? She'll be sitting there looking like a little Vietnamese orphan girl and draw things out of him before he knows it. Maybe he'll say no, he can't tell her anything and then she'll do that thing she does. You know, when she looks at you with her black eyes, and it's like being pinned to the wall. I'll bet you a hundred dollars he'll cave in and tell her something he would never tell me.'

I smile at the picture she paints. 'He's very fond of her. He teases her, and she likes it. There might not be any need for that look.'

'I'll ask the police about those men who rescued Hope from the wheelie bin. There's no saying if that investigation went any further – it might have been flagged for no action straight away, but if they found something out, before it got closed down, it would be useful to know what it was. I haven't come up against this kind of block before, so I'm not sure of the process.'

Her secretary buzzes her to say her clients have arrived and I leave.

I sit in the car and call Louise Barlow on the number Noah found on Hope's phone. Five minutes later I end the call none the wiser. I say nothing about the abduction but let Louise continue to think that Hope had an accident. She is very concerned to hear that Hope can't be found and wants to ask a thousand questions, but she had noticed nothing strange about Hope's behaviour.

'I did wonder why she had no shoes,' she says as an afterthought. 'But isn't that what happens in accidents? People lose some of their belongings.'

'Did she have her bag?' I know her bag was in the flat; I want to hear what Louise will say.

'Oh no, she didn't. I never thought of that. God, she must have lost that too. How inconvenient. Perhaps she called me because she had no money for a taxi. Don't you think?'

That is the sum of it. She questioned nothing, noticed nothing odd in the flat. There is no point in wasting time on her. I have no idea what her job is and can only hope she is not in charge of anything important.

Next up is Spencer, who is willing to talk, but has nothing useful to tell me. He is very upset.

'I still can't believe it! How could she disappear? It's incredible! Noah seems to think she's been abducted, but it seems so unlikely. I don't understand it – it's very worrying. Why would anyone take her? But she would never leave like that, without anyone knowing. Surely not.'

I have just started asking him something when he interrupts. 'I recognise your name, Hunter. It's unusual. You found that girl a couple of years ago, didn't you? And ended up in an abandoned factory with a homicidal maniac?'

No one from the media ever managed to sum up the vital facts of the story with so few words; it is a model of brevity.

'That's right. And now I've agreed to help Noah. We're trying to winkle out any little detail the cops might have missed.' I don't tell him the police are doing precisely nothing. 'Can you recall anything that Hope told you about her trip – anything that could possibly be linked to this? If she was asked to do something or bring something back from Pakistan for example, or if she witnessed something unusual while she was there. I don't know what we're looking for, but there must be something.'

'Let me think,' says Spencer. I hear him moving around and some noises I cannot identify. Then he says, 'No, no, wait your turn.'

'Sorry, what was that?'

'Not you, the hen. I'm dishing up the cats' food and she gets a bit pushy. But I can't recall anything of the kind you mentioned. It seems to have been pretty straightforward, apart from a few difficulties finding some of those safe houses. You know, vague addresses and street numbers not being in place everywhere.'

I thank him and ask him to call me if he remembers

something. It seems to be my day for talking to rather frustrating eccentrics.

A call to Dao confirms that she has not seen Benson, who is out on a case. 'They don't know when he'll come back. But I've got my book. I'll just wait.' She sounds quite cheerful.

Samantha's phone has a recorded message that she will be back in her office after lunch, so I call Noah and say I want to have another look at Hope's flat, if he is OK with that. He is talking to someone further down Hope's street and says to come right away; he will be somewhere close by and can let me in.

'I'll leave you here,' he says, when he has unlocked the door. 'Just call me. I mean, when you want to leave so I can lock up. I'll not be far away. I took the morning off. Trying to catch people as they arrive for work, or to go to work. I'll tell you about it later.'

The last time I was in the flat we cut the visit short when I saw the camera. It looks different in daylight: the room is huge, as big as a decent-sized two-bedroom flat. There are three very long windows at chest height, evenly spaced along the wall opposite the door. The hole in the window frame is bigger than I remembered. Why didn't Hope notice it, even if it had only been there since she got back from Pakistan? But I recall the picture Dao showed me: Hope was short compared to the others. I saw a reflection of light in the recessed lens, but someone a head shorter might not have been able to.

I go back to the front door and stand on the landing looking in. One step to the side and I can no longer see the camera hole. I picture someone opening the door and looking in my direction. They wouldn't notice anything in the other corner of the landing; the door would screen it. I walk around the long room and try to work out what the camera could see. As far as I remember the lens was set only a couple of millimetres into the wood, but the edges must have restricted its view somewhat. I search the kitchen drawers and find some tin foil, make a small plug, rub the front surface shiny smooth and push it into the hole. I try to get it just the right distance into the hole, so I can see it clearly as I move around. After a couple of minutes, I know that a wide-angle lens would have captured nearly the entire room, even with the lens slightly recessed. The corner of the kitchen, as far as the bedroom door, would be out of the camera's view and so would the corner at the other end of the room where Hope has her desk. Hope's life would have been like a shop window display for whoever put the camera there. I think of her coming out of her bedroom in the morning, possibly undressed, or sitting in her armchair watching TV in the evening – unaware that someone was watching her. It makes my skin crawl with distaste.

Noah returns a few minutes after I call him. He has finished working his way up and down the street, asking if people have seen anything.

'I'll tell you tonight. I've got to go back to work at lunchtime. I might work quite late to catch up. Had to do this first thing. I'll write up the notes I've made of people's names and addresses and send them to Willow. Not just the names, what they've told me too. She can pass it on to the cops. Not much of value so far, but a couple of things. The woman who owns the café down the block saw him loading the bin. And one of the people on the first floor here heard the bin bumping down the stairs. Nobody saw anything strange a couple of days later either.'

Samantha sits me down in one of the 1960s armchairs and gives me coffee in a 1950s cup with a saucer, and a biscuit. 'Now, how can I help you?'

'I'd like to hear about anything Hope said that might have a bearing on this. What Noah didn't tell you when we were here is that there is more to this than Hope disappearing. She was abducted from her flat while you were away, but she got away from the man who took her. Noah found a quite detailed message she had written for him – about how it happened. She said that she would stay in her flat until he returned from Australia two days after she wrote it. She was going to lock herself in and not open the door for anyone. She was very frightened. We presume the same man took her a second time, it's the only explanation – but we don't know how he did it or who he is.'

Noah had interrupted Dao when she was about to tell Samantha about the camera; I don't know why. I think he is jealous of people Hope feels close to; but why Samantha? In my opinion Samantha is a valuable person to cultivate. Hope regards her as a close friend and she might share things with her that she would not share with her brother. After she got back from Pakistan, she seems to have spent more time with Samantha than with anyone else, at least as far as we know. A trade-off is called for; by telling her more and asking more questions I might get her memory working on details.

I tell her everything we know about the bin man and describe how he got in and his disguise. When I tell her how Hope rocked the bin off the back of the truck on the motorway and how she was rescued, Samantha is visibly shocked, her eyes wide and fixed on my face. She inches forward in her chair and sits up straighter.

'My God! So, someone was really determined to get her. But why? And who is he?'

'We don't know. There is another aspect I haven't

mentioned yet. Her flat was being monitored with video equipment.'

She listens to this new revelation without exclamations, just takes it in and gets to work on the facts. She asks several questions about the abduction and the camera and sits back with a thoughtful frown.

'I can't understand how the police can ignore a thing like this – it's unacceptable! And how on earth did it happen a second time? A man takes her away in a bin and she goes through that terrible trauma trying to get away. She is locked in, but somehow, he manages to take her again. Unless she opens the door to someone she knows well, someone unthreatening – and then leaves it open? No, I can't believe she would do that when she was under threat. She would have been extra careful.'

'Exactly. She wouldn't have opened the door to him a second time. She had a peephole and could see who was outside. And if he covered it with his hand, she would not have unlocked the door. She said in her note to Noah that she was going to have the safety chain done up all the time. There's no damage to the door and the chain is intact. When Noah went there the door was ajar.'

With a promise to keep her informed I leave. I am sorry to leave her upset; she is a good person and not used to violence.

A text message to Dao gets no response, so I go to the supermarket. Halfway along the deli counter my phone buzzes.

'Hi,' says Willow. 'Just a quick update – I've told Noah already. I bullied my way to a very superior cop, by phone, and the news is not good. He said, and I quote, "The file is flagged for no action by police. A matter of national security is being investigated by another agency." End of quote. It can only mean that some Government agency has put a block on it – or possibly that Interpol is involved. I've never come up against this before, so I'm going to have a chat to a law professor at Victoria University who is a specialist in national security and civil rights legislation. Any news from Dao yet?'

With the shopping in a chiller bag in the back of the car, I return to Hope's street. Noah will be back at work now, but I can walk around and see if anything new occurs to me. The street is a mixture of activities that have evolved over decades: a little shop that sells cigarettes and magazines and chocolate bars, one café, workshops and offices of different kinds. A little micro-cosmos just to one side of the CBD. I start two blocks away from Hope's flat looking for businesses that might open early. I work my way along and stop to look up at her windows under the roofline diagonally across the street. A length of cable is still attached to the wall between two windows.

Someone speaks right behind me and makes me jump. 'That building is getting a lot of attention today.'

He is an old guy, wearing blue overalls and heavy work boots. Behind him, through a wide doorway I can see a workshop. I glance up at the sign: Electrical Repairs and Motor Rewinding.

'Oh yeah? Maybe you saw my friend Noah this morning.'

'There was a very skinny fellow here, earlier. We had a chat. And then another one, but much younger. Not that long ago, an hour perhaps.'

'Did the skinny guy tell you why he was asking questions?'

He nods. 'He said his sister has disappeared from that

building over there. He was asking about a man with a truck and a wheelie bin. Which I hadn't seen.'

'And the younger guy – what did he ask?'

'Nothing, he never spoke to me at all. He just stood looking up at the building for a while. He went inside and a couple of minutes later he came back out and walked away.'

'Did you get a good look at him?'

'Good enough, he walked right past me. I thought it was funny there was a second chap interested in the building on the same day, so I watched him. A young Maori fellow, good looking – smart clothes. Not those jeans with holes like they all seem to wear these days.'

I thank him and walk back to the car. My head is full of speculation. Was the young guy Hope's stalker? And if it was, why was he there? Or was it someone from whatever agency had installed the camera, seeing he knew how to get into the building? And how likely is it that two handsome and smartly dressed young guys are suddenly interested in Hope?

I sit in the car and wonder what I else I can do to pass the time, but before I come up with anything Dao calls. 'Can you pick me up, please? I've seen Benson – I'll tell you when I see you.'

D ao says she'd rather tell me everything when we get home, because she's still thinking about it, but we have a lengthy stop on the Harbour Bridge, waiting for a truck crash to be cleared, and she changes her mind. I turn the engine off and Dao undoes her seatbelt and sits cross-legged in her seat, leaning against the door.

'When I got there, I refused to tell them my name, I just said I had something important to tell him. They were very nice – they gave me a cup of coffee and a biscuit and at lunchtime they said they could organise a sandwich. Wasn't that kind? They probably thought I was quite young.'

'Everyone does. Be grateful – you'll appreciate it when you get to my age.'

If Benson had not moved to a different station, the desk staff would have recognised her, so at least she avoided the kind of attention her unfortunate fame has exposed her to.

'Anyway, he must have come in at the back of the building. When he got the message that someone was waiting, he came out and you should have seen his face! He was so surprised, but he's smart. He made the connection nearly straight off – Willow calling, you, me. Once we were in his office he said, "This guy, whose sister has disappeared, is he a friend of Hunter's?" so I had to say yes, kind of. He said it was just too much of a coincidence to get a call from Willow asking a favour and then me coming to see him.'

'Good old Benson,' I said. 'And knowing how suspicious he is of me doing something illegal, I suppose he refused to tell you anything.'

'Oh no, he was really helpful. He listened to what I told him and I said that I am so worried about Hope and what might be happening to her. He asked me to tell him the whole thing and I did, all about the stories she wrote and the video clip of the airport explosions – the lot. I got a bit angry after a while.'

She stops talking, looks out the window at a tow truck edging past us towards the crash at the crest of the bridge.

'But maybe that was good that he saw how angry I was. I said we feel terrible that nobody will help Noah and that I know how Hope must be wondering if anyone is ever going to find her – and that makes me really upset.'

'And then he worried about you thinking of the things that happened to you, and decided to help you?'

'I didn't do it on purpose. I wouldn't do that! It was just part of telling the story. He said he would see what he could find out. He looked up something on his computer and made a phone call. He said that someone he had known for a long time was a friend of the woman who had disappeared, and he was just trying to find out what was going on. I could see from his face that he didn't like the reply he got. Another authority – which must mean the intelligence people or something – has put a block on Hope's file and the police are being kept out of the investigation.'

'Was he able to tell you anything at all? Did he hint at what we could do?'

She frowns and shakes her head. 'I was a bit annoyed with him at first, when he told me all that. But when I was leaving, he said he hoped to see me again very soon. He had a funny look on his face, as if he was planning something. Maybe he thinks he *can* find something out, sort of unofficially? And he said he likes my hair long.'

'He's an old flirt,' I say and smile at her expression. 'Just kidding – but he's very fond of you and he has been impressed with you from the very start. Maybe he will find something out, but I'm not banking on it. Has he learnt to keep his shirt tucked in yet?'

Now Dao smiles too. 'God no, he still looks like he dressed in the dark. I don't think he cares. His tie was stuffed into a mug that says Top Cop and his desk is a mess. And he asked if your wounds have caused any lasting problems. I was really pleased he didn't ask if you still have loaded guns around all the time. I don't want to lie to Benson.'

I don't ask her if Benson said anything about the missing barrel of drugs. We know they don't think I took it, but Dao might still worry. There has been nothing in the papers about it having been found.

Samantha calls that evening. 'I've been thinking about Hope all day and wondering why on earth she opened the door for someone, when she knew the danger she was in. But I have an idea how it could have happened – it might be a bit far-fetched, but still, it probably fits the circumstances. Say he came back pretending to be a policeman. He takes for granted that she has been interviewed by the police after the abduction and that a visit from the police wouldn't be unexpected. We know he could get into her building – he did it the first time. But a cop wouldn't have the code, so this time he calls from the street and says something like, "We need to ask you some questions, can you give us the door code please." And Hope gives it to him, but he calls again and says, "It's not working, the door won't open." So maybe she says, "Go across the street so I can see you are really the police." And she looks out the window and there he is in uniform. From high up she might not recognise him as the man who abducted her, so she runs downstairs to let him in.'

'Very clever,' I say. 'And that would explain why her phone was still in the flat, and her bag. If she was just quickly running downstairs, she might well have left her door ajar and not taken anything with her. So, he grabbed her then and there, and somehow got her away before anyone noticed.'

'But why, Hunter? The only thing that comes to mind is that something happened in Pakistan, don't you think? But surely researching those safe houses can't have triggered this? Her articles haven't even been published yet.'

I don't tell her about the airport bombs, just thank her and promise to let her know if we find out anything new. Dao is dying to know who I was talking to; when I tell her Samantha's theory she nods.

'She is clever! That fits all those weird facts. Did you notice that Noah didn't want me to tell her about the camera? I was just about to and he kind of jumped in before I could say anything. Do you think there's something he's not telling us?'

'I'm not sure if he interrupted you because you were about to mention the camera. I noticed his expression when Samantha was talking about how good-looking the stalker is. I could see his mood changing – it made him angry for some reason. Perhaps he's one of those people who feel a need to rubbish anyone that somebody else praises. He didn't like it when you said you understood why Hope liked Willard's voice, either.'

'I know, I noticed that. He's an idiot,' she says dismissively. 'Like he's jealous of everyone he meets. How depressing.'

I don't mention my suspicion that maybe he is jealous of anyone close to Hope, people she feels attracted to. The kind of jealousy one mostly associates with lovers, not siblings. The idea is unpleasant; I hope I am wrong.

'It could be a serious case of low self-esteem,' I say, trying to be fair. 'It would be hard to live with self-doubt all the time. He and Hope seem to have been very close, though. The way she said in that story about the abduction that she couldn't wait for him to be back from his holiday.'

'I suppose everyone is loved by at least one person,' says Dao and gets up from the table. 'So long as nobody expects me to love him. I do feel sorry for him, but I don't really like him. He's not a bit like you.'

Just before ten Noah calls. 'Sorry to call so late. I've had a hell of a day with a project that's not going well and a boss who wants things done yesterday. I'm still at work, but I thought I'd better tell you what I found out this morning.'

I sit down next to Dao on the sofa and turn on the phone speaker. 'Go right ahead. What did you find out?'

'The guy in the flat below Hope heard the bin bumping down the stairs. He looked out the window and saw a guy loading it, he said it looked very heavy. And then he went and had a shower. He can't describe the man, but he said the pick-up truck was quite old and had no canopy over the deck. He hasn't noticed anything suspicious since then. The people in the other flat on that floor never heard or saw anything – they leave for work very early. The woman in the café was putting her sidewalk sign out and she noticed a small white truck. She saw the man lifting the bin and she said he had a terrible job getting it up – she stayed outside and watched. She described him as not very tall and a bit stocky, so at least we have one more fact to go on. She has no idea what the number plate was or what make of truck it was.'

'I went back and wandered around for a while when I was waiting for Dao,' I say. 'You remember the guy who runs the electrical repair shop, across the street and down a bit? You talked to him this morning. He said there was a handsome young guy there at lunchtime today, staring at the building and then going inside.'

It takes a good ten minutes to fill him in on everything, including Dao's visit to Benson.

'I'll be in touch,' says Noah when we end the call.

I wake up in the night and can't go back to sleep. With Dao sleeping beside me and Scruff on the floor, chasing rabbits in his sleep, I lie on my back and look up at the stars through the skylight. Being in our bedroom on a clear night is a bit like being at the bottom of a well. Dark curtains screen out all light from outside. I can look straight up and see thousands of stars that would be invisible if I went outside into the light pollution of the city. A piece of private magic.

In my head a circular process starts up and keeps going. Who put the camera in Hope's flat? Was it a Government agency? If it was, they know about the bin man – are they doing anything about it? Or was it the bin man who put up the camera? Who is the young guy and why did he go to Hope's flat? How did he know the door code? What is Noah's problem? Why the mood changes, the difference in how he communicates from one day to the next? Does he have a mental problem or a drug habit, or both? I could never rely on him in an emergency; he is far too volatile.

Dawn dilutes the darkness and the stars are no longer visible. I turn on my side and listen to Dao's barely audible breathing and wait for morning.

Somehow, I fall asleep and wake to an empty bedroom. My phone tells me it is half-past eight. The skylight is a square of blue; the house is totally silent. I never sleep in; sleeping in is what other people do. I stay where I am and wonder if my brain has worked anything out while I slept. I close my eyes and let my mind wander and smell coffee. I open my eyes again: Dao has silently appeared beside the bed with a tray.

'Breakfast in bed! We've never done this before.' She puts the tray in the middle of the bed and gets in on her side. 'Coffee, toast, half a muffin each. Isn't it great?'

'You are a treasure,' I say. 'Where is the little furry thing?'

'He's in the courtyard digging a big hole next to the wall on Nigel's side and he's totally filthy. I'll have to hose him down later.'

It is as if we have made a silent pact to not talk about the Hope affair. We do what we have done hundreds of times before Noah turned up on our doorstep: I work for a few hours, Dao studies or plays a game on her laptop, we have lunch. Early afternoon we take Scruff, still slightly damp from his hosing, for a run. We return at the end of the afternoon and Dao says she is going to call Plum while I unpack the shopping. Plum is my much younger sister, who has just graduated from university and now works for an architect in Taupo. Dao always lies on our bed when she talks to Plum. One day I'll ask Plum if she is on her bed at the same time.

The doorbell buzzes, and I run down to find Benson on

the doorstep, dressed in a T-shirt and jeans. I never thought of him as a guy who would wear jeans and it makes me smile. At least he looks tidier than he usually does with his shirt untucked.

'Hunter,' he says and returns the smile without any idea of what made me smile. 'How are you? I have a couple of days off and I thought I would call in. I hope it's not inconvenient.'

His face reveals nothing when he sees the shotgun leaning into the corner beside the stairs in the living room. 'Still there?'

'Yes, still there. It's a peace of mind thing now. Like the alarm system.'

He nods thoughtfully and looks around for Dao.

'She's upstairs, she'll be down in a minute. Would you like a beer?'

There must be a purpose behind this visit; we are not on social terms. Last time he and I met was at the conclusion of the trial of Mint, where Dao was a key witness. Having Benson back in the house revives memories from a time of threat and peril, when Dao's life and mine were under siege. We escaped injured but alive; several people died.

I get us a beer each and we sit down by the glass wall to the balcony. I say nothing, just wait for Benson to tell me why he has come. After a moment he says, looking slightly awkward, 'I'll wait until Dao gets here. I've got some news.'

When Dao comes down, she gives him a big smile. 'Hi, Benson. This is nice! You said we would see each other soon, but I didn't know if you meant it.' She sits down cross-legged in the corner of the sofa and looks expectantly at him. 'We can tell you lots more about Hope, if you like.

Hunter found out some new things yesterday and so did Noah.'

'Maybe later,' says Benson. 'But first I want to tell you something. As you know I don't like rules being broken – by me or anyone else.'

He has the uncomfortable look of a man who is about to do something he never thought he would do, as if he should perhaps leave right now.

'I've never done anything like this before in a fairly long career, so I'd appreciate it if you're totally discreet with this information until this case is sorted out.'

'Of course,' says Dao. 'I would never say anything that might get you into trouble, Benson, never!'

'I have a couple of days off and this morning I went to have coffee with a guy I used to work with. He's working in Manurewa now and I hadn't seen him for a few months. Our days off just happened to coincide. And he told me about a strange incident he attended a little while ago.'

Benson's face is neutral; he could be telling us a bedtime story. 'It was an interesting story – a woman was abducted and transported on a truck in a wheelie bin. The bin fell off on the motorway and some guys in a van hauled it over to the side and found her inside.'

He pauses and drinks some of his beer. We say nothing. 'Anyway, the truck driver kept driving, probably didn't realise he'd lost the bin. According to Bernie – that's my mate – the guys in the van didn't notice the number plate. The driver of the van, Craig, thought the truck was a Toyota, but he wasn't quite sure. Too busy watching that bin, I imagine.'

We both know that Dao already told him about this when she saw him, but we listen as if we hear it for the first time. It's a strange way of doing it, but maybe it makes him feel better about 'breaking the rules', as he puts it.

He pulls out a piece of paper from his back pocket and puts it on the coffee table. Neither Dao nor I reach out to pick it up. It looks like a single word and a phone number.

'What a coincidence that I heard about it today, Dao, just after your visit yesterday.' His grey eyes twinkle.

'Serendipity!' says Dao innocently. 'I looked that word up the other day – and that's serendipity too. Do you want to hear what we found out yesterday?'

He leaves an hour later, having declined an invitation to stay and have dinner with us. At the door Dao says, 'And please say thank you to that kind man in your reception for giving me coffee and biscuits.'

'That's nice of you, Dao, but I don't think I'll mention it. He would just be envious that I've been to see you. I think we'll just keep this visit between ourselves.'

Benson's note: *Craig 022 0250166.*

I leave a message on Craig's phone and he calls back a short while later. 'No, mate, nothing at all,' he says. 'We paid no attention until we saw that bloody bin rocking on the edge of the deck. And then all we could think of was how to take evasive action if it fell off. The traffic was wicked, mate, full on, so it could have been a real situation.'

'I can imagine. How did you manage it?'

'The bin was rocking, which was weird, and I blew the horn over and over. But he just kept going, the dozy bugger. When it was obvious it would come off any second, I braked and put my hazard lights on and started pulling over to the side. Tell you what, you've never seen three guys exit a van so damn fast. We signalled to traffic behind us to slow down and raced into the road and dragged it to the side.'

'You took a real risk,' I say. 'It must have been a shock to find Hope inside.'

'Was that her name? Hope, eh? A bin full of Hope.' He chortles; a kind man's reaction to what he thinks is good news. 'Yeah, it was a shock to say the least. Of course, we thought she was dead to start with. She was amazingly calm when you think of it, said she'd been drugged. So, how is she?'

'She's missing again. I'm helping her brother try to find her.'

'Fuckin' hell! I hope you find her. The poor woman!' It is clearly not the answer he expected.

'She kept a kind of diary on her computer,' I say, wanting to leave him with something positive. 'Her brother found it. She wrote about you helping her, she said how kind you were about removing the duct tape from her mouth.'

He makes no comment, just asks me to keep his number and let him know when we find her.

12

Two days later we're meeting with Noah in a café near his office in his lunch break. 'We're stuck,' he says despondently. 'I don't know where to go from here. It's like she's been sucked into a black hole. Mum and Dad are frantic. They've asked their Member of Parliament to make enquiries in Wellington and Dad says he'll barge into the Prime Minister's office and demand an answer if the cops don't act soon. Personally, I think some media attention might be more effective. And we still have no clue who that young guy is that she took the photo of, the one she called her stalker.'

He is thinner than ever and looks as if he has not slept in a week.

'I know! We can use Hunter's sister, Plum,' exclaims Dao. 'She's on Facebook and Instagram and all those things. Let's get Plum to put his photo on social media and ask her friends to share it, with a little caption under the photo saying, "If you know who this is please respond to xxx". I don't know why I didn't think of it earlier.'

'I'm not on social media, so I can't do it. Why don't you two do it yourselves?'

'Hunter isn't on social media and I have no friends.' Dao smiles at the look of disbelief he gives her. 'It's true, I hardly know anyone apart from Hunter's family and a couple of his friends. But Plum has over eight hundred Facebook friends, most of them in Auckland. She showed me once, all these photos most of them she can't remember if she ever met for real. So she doesn't know them all, it's just pretend. But it's a good base to start from. We could reach thousands.'

She hasn't talked to me about this, which is good. She is starting to make independent decisions a lot more these days. We're nearly back to where we were before that bloody trial. Willow said recently, 'My God, Hunter, who'd have thought it? You've developed such a range of new roles since you found Dao. Educator, mentor, lover, social worker, shopping companion, bodyguard – what next? Do you ever feel stressed by it all?'

She was joking, of course, but there is a grain of truth in it. Life with Dao is sometimes challenging, but always interesting. And much easier now that nobody is trying to kill us.

When I ask Plum to circulate the photo, she is instantly fired up with curiosity. She anticipates mystery and dramatic revelations, but she is in for a disappointment. She never could keep a secret and this would be too tempting to share with one or five or ten best friends.

'What's he done? Is he a criminal? Are you after him for something?'

'No, he's not a criminal, so don't get excited. I'm helping a friend who's lost touch with his sister. The guy in the photo is someone she knows and who might know where she is.'

'OK, I'll tell you everything I find out – but you'll let me know if he finds her, won't you?'

'I will. And please use the exact words I'm emailing. Don't add a single word. We don't want to ruin this guy's reputation.'

Plum calls the next afternoon. 'That didn't take long. Posting it on a Friday was perfect,' she says mysteriously. 'The girl who called has sent me a couple of Facebook photos to make sure it's the right guy. I'll email them to you now.'

Within twenty-four hours of Plum putting the enhanced photo of Hope's stalker on social media, and asking people to share and re-share, we have a phone number for him. The photo reaches thousands of people, by virtue of everyone having hundreds of so-called friends.

'Great result! Thank you very much,' I say. 'You'll get a finder's reward for this.'

The stalker's name is Tama Robinson. Strangely he's not on any social media himself, at least not under that name, but he has friends who are, and he appears in various group photos; some are copied into Plums' message.

I call Noah. 'Do you want to contact him? Willow can do it and make it official or I can talk to him, whatever you like.'

'I'd rather you do it. See if you can set up a meeting – my place if you like, or a café somewhere.'

'Let's record it. You know how sometimes you can hear little details in how people say things, their voice changes?' says Dao. 'I hope he won't refuse to see us.'

'OK, I'll call him now. We'll put it on speaker, and would you please sit across from me so I can see your face.' If her attention notches up at any point, I want to be aware of it.

Within seconds I know that Tama is going to be crucial, though not how. He is very guarded and I am glad we are recording the conversation.

'Hi, Tama. My name is Hunter Grant. I think you know Hope Barber.'

I don't think I have ever before made someone gasp, but that's what Tama does. An audible intake of breath, then silence. Dao's eyes open wide.

'No,' he says finally. 'I don't know her personally, but I know who she is.'

'She is missing. Did you know?

Another pause at his end. 'Yes.'

'How do you know this? It's not been in the papers.'

'I can't tell you.'

'Did you know that she had a photo of you on her phone?'

'No.'

'We found you through that photo and social media.' Now the silence lasts longer. 'So, you posted something that went viral? Did it mention her name?'

'No, it just said the girl who posted it wanted to find you, it didn't mention her at all. We made it sound a bit romantic and it worked a treat. Why did you ask if it mentioned her name?'

'I can't tell you. Who are you?'

I mouth 'Sorry' to Dao across the table, an advance apology. 'Do you remember stories in the media last year in connection with a trial about boats used in drug smuggling? The key witness was a girl who had been enslaved for years and escaped.'

'Ah,' he says. 'I thought your name was familiar. What is your interest in this?'

'Hope is the sister of a friend. I know you followed her around at times. She called you her stalker. Were you stalking her?'

'No.'

'Why were you watching her?'

'I was trying to protect her,' he says. He sounds sad.

'OK.' I try to keep my voice calm, try to hide my reaction. 'I think it would be a good idea to meet and talk face to face. Will you do that?'

'Why?'

'If you followed her to protect her, you must have known of some threat to her safety. Now she's disappeared – maybe something you noticed will help us find her. The cops won't touch it.'

'What! Why not?' This is his first unguarded reply, genuine surprise.

'They won't say. We assume there is some other involvement, beyond police. There's a block on her file. Our lawyer can't find out who or why.'

This time Tama is silent for a long time. Dao puts a finger to her lips and whispers, 'Wait.'

'OK,' he says at last. 'Let's meet – but not in a public place. Somewhere private.'

'You can come here tonight if that suits you. I'll text the address. Have you got transport?'

Noah arrives, supercharged with nervous tension and unable to keep still. Dao takes one look at him and shakes her head behind his back.

'Noah,' she says firmly. 'Will you please sit down and let me give you a drink. Have you had dinner?'

'Didn't have time.' He remains standing, moving from

one foot to the other, one hand jiggling his keys. 'It doesn't matter, I'll eat something when I get home.'

'You must eat something. Come into the kitchen with me and we'll find something you like. And a beer or a glass of wine. This guy Tama is *very* cautious. If you can't calm down this won't work. What if he gets nervous and leaves, before we find anything out?'

She walks towards the kitchen while she speaks, and he follows. I hear them talking but keep out of it. When they return, Noah carries a tray with beer and glasses, biscuits and cheese. He smells of banana and seems calmer.

'What time is it?'

'Just after half-past seven.'

'Dao, here or there?' I indicate the other end of the room. 'Maybe sitting at the table will feel too much like an inquisition.'

'Let's be comfortable,' says Dao. 'He felt threatened by our call. If we keep it kind of friendly, he might relax a bit.'

Dao has just played the recording of the conversation with Tama for Noah, when the doorbell goes. Noah is silent, digesting what he has just heard, but we have no time to discuss it or its implications.

'You stay here,' I tell Noah before I go down to open the door. 'And take your lead from me. If you can't see where I'm going with some question or comment, do *not* interrupt. I don't want any outbursts to jeopardize this.'

Dao and I have agreed on an approach and we can't have Noah chucking random spanners in the works, this is too important.

The guy on the doorstep is average height and looks as if he goes to the gym. He is also ridiculously good-looking, with wavy black hair, dark brown eyes. He could be a model. He looks calm, but I suspect there is tight self-control behind the facade. Based on how little he gave away on the phone, I imagine he is anticipating being put on the spot. There might well be questions he does not want to answer.

'Right,' I say when we are sitting down, and he has a beer in his hand. 'We know you followed Hope on a few occasions. She mentioned that she never saw you anywhere near her flat. If that is correct, how did you know she had disappeared?'

'I can't tell you. And I never went near her flat.' He pauses. 'Not until after she had disappeared.'

'Like a couple of days ago, in your lunch hour?'

I can hear how taken aback he is. 'How do you know about that?'

I smile, try to make it sound friendly. 'You'd probably be surprised if I told you just how much we know. Not about you personally, but about your movements. So tell me how you knew where Hope was going to be when she went out at night. If you didn't follow her from the flat, you could only know if you hacked her emails or her phone.'

His face betrays his conflict. He wants to help us to find Hope, but he cannot or will not tell us what he knows. He looks down at his hands and when he looks up he has made a decision. He puts his beer down and gets up. 'Sorry, I'm wasting your time. I shouldn't have come. I simply can't help you.'

He walks around the sofa, but Dao gets up and meets him halfway, blocks his way to the stairs and he is too polite to push past her.

'OK, Tama,' she says. 'You know something, but you're scared of telling us too much, aren't you? You have to trust us. We want to find her too – and you said you wanted to protect her.'

'Sorry,' he says again. 'I'd better leave.'

I must stop him leaving, once he has gone we'll never get him back. I use my old Army issuing-orders voice. 'Come back here and sit down, Tama. We haven't finished.'

He looks at me for a long moment before he returns to his chair. Dao sits down again at the end of the sofa closest to me, where she can watch his face.

'I'm not some kind of hired gun,' I tell him, intent on making him trust me. 'I'm not connected to the police or anyone else. The situation I had to deal with when I found Dao was forced on me because she was hunted by killers. The only reason Noah asked me to help was because the cops won't act. I have no personal stake in this. I report to nobody else and I am not a threat to your privacy or your job, whatever that is. I agree with Dao – I think you could help us, but you can't figure out how to do it without telling us everything you know.'

'How did you know Hope had disappeared?' asks Dao. 'Did somebody tell you? Did you know she was taken from her flat?'

'Nobody told me. But I knew.'

He is more uncomfortable than ever. He is obviously inherently truthful, which makes it hard for him to be evasive. His eyes flick from Dao to me and then to Noah.

I say quietly, 'So you were spying on her.'

A short flicker of something like relief crosses his face. 'Yes, I was.'

Not 'we were' but 'I was'. Did he deliberately use the singular to make us believe he acted on his own? Is he protecting someone? Why the look of relief? Perhaps my question was not as dangerous as he had expected.

'You knew she was taken. Either you were there at the time, or somebody told you - or you had a camera in her flat.'

'A camera.' He nearly chokes on the word.

Noah's head swings to me, his eyes tormented and he's just about to say something. I shoot him a look that stops him in his tracks.

'So, you recorded it. Do you know who took her?

'I am trying to work it out. But he must have tried again. The second time he didn't enter her flat.'

In my side vision I notice Dao's chin rise slightly. Her focus on Tama is drilling a hole through the space between them. She has noticed something I missed.

'So why don't you show the recording of the first attempt to the police?' I ask. 'If it shows who did it, wouldn't that be the smart thing to do?'

He is torn, trying to decide if he should come clean or not.

'I can't do that. It just can't be done.'

He is perspiring, very tense. We're getting closer to the truth, but also closer to the question that might make him leave. I decide attack is the best approach, now that he is unsettled and tense. Strike while the iron is hot.

'OK, let me tell you what I think. You work for some branch of the intelligence services – or someone contracted to them – and you were monitoring her. What is she suspected of?'

The relief on his face is nearly comical. You can see the tension draining away, now that I have said it and he does not have to.

'OK, yes. But I can't tell you very much. I'd end up in prison if they find out I have talked.'

'Have some cheese,' says Dao prosaically, trying to lower the tension. 'And drink your beer. We have plenty of time. Bet you didn't have dinner either, just like Noah.'

'Thank you,' he says politely. 'But I'll tell you what I can first.'

Now that he has made the decision, he wants it over and done with. And so do I, before he changes his mind.

'Could you start over? Tell it from the beginning so I don't have to drag it out of you. I'd like to have it really clear in my mind, not in bits and pieces.'

Dao gets up and returns with a cell phone. 'Do you mind if we record it?'

Tama stares at her for a moment, but unexpectedly he nods. He seems to be in the grip of some fatalistic state of mind now that he has made a decision, as if whatever happens now is out of his control.

'I first heard of Hope when we discovered that a Pakistani brother and sister, who came here as immigrants, had been in touch with her some time ago. They were being monitored. There were some things that didn't quite stack up after they came here. I actually thought we had dropped them about a year ago, satisfied they were OK, but I was wrong. They must have spoken to Hope on the phone before she went away. At that time her number was just a random phone number on one of their phones and meant nothing to us. But a short time ago they sent an email to her indicating that they had given her names of contacts in Pakistan and now they wanted to hear how she got on. She invited them to visit that weekend.' He looks at us as if expecting comments.

Noah is ready to leap in, but Dao gets in first. 'Carry on.'

'This made Hope a person of intense interest, of course. We started monitoring her phone and her emails. A colleague and I were told to put AV into Hope's flat before those two visited her. We knew from her emails that she was going to be out for several hours one day, so we went in and put AV in – that's audio and visual, sound and pictures. It was quite time-consuming – an old concrete building, thick walls, high up. We got it done just in time – she returned earlier than we had counted on. We saw her coming back as we were driving away.'

He sighs, as if the recollection of that day is something that saddens him. 'But the visit from that brother and sister gave us nothing to go on. The contacts they had provided for Hope seemed to have been a list of safe houses for abused women and nothing was said that was grounds for suspicion. But now that we had access to her phone messages and her emails, old and new, we found things of concern and she was classified as a security risk.'

Noah jerks in his chair. Dao quickly gets to her feet, ostensibly to check that the phone is still recording, but I catch the look she gives Noah. He subsides again. Tama stops talking and watches her until she puts the phone down. 'OK, carry on.'

'Hope was in that airport blast in Peshawar a few weeks ago, on her way back to Auckland. She was dragged to safety before the second bomb went off – by one of the terrorists.'

He glances at Noah, as if to monitor his reactions. He has noticed how on edge Noah is, wants to avoid a confrontation.

'And then?' I ask, as if I didn't already know this. 'There's obviously more.'

'Yeah, there is. That rescue was very unusual – unheard of, actually. There must be a link between her and the terrorist, something that overrode his normal training. They just don't do that sort of thing. We checked every single thing about her travel arrangements, her flight and hotel bookings and her Google history. She hadn't prebooked any travel or accommodation at all within Pakistan and she was there for over four weeks. That's very unusual. She must have used cash, taken local transport – she moved around leaving no trace at all. She had researched railway and bus routes before she left, all of them up in the north-west, the part closest to Afghanistan. There's lots of Taliban activity up there, camps in the mountains. That border means nothing when it comes to terrorist activity.'

He drinks some of his beer, thinks for a moment. 'There were a couple of strange text messages on her phone. First one from someone in Pakistan, who reported on the health of a child after some accident, not long before she returned to New Zealand. No response from her. Then after the airport blast, when she was back here with a damaged arm, another message from the same number asking if she was OK and if she was back at home. She replied and said all was well. And the person at the other end texted back: *"You saved my son, I saved you, now we're even"*, or something like that.'

I'm pleased with how this is going. Tama thinks he is telling us things we don't already know. He is giving us a lot more detail than I had expected, and provided I can get more out of him we will soon have a very complete picture based on Hope's journal and his information. I'm keen to know how much they managed to find out, things we don't know yet.

'Tama, what do you know about her saving a child? Anything?'

'Perhaps she saved a child, just by chance, no connection to anything in particular. Or maybe she visited a terrorist camp, and something happened to a child while she was there. We simply don't know, but there must be a link to terrorists – whatever the context. And that made her a person of top-level interest to both countries. We got in touch with Pakistan and they got what we needed from Peshawar, from the hospital and the police and the airport authority there. We got a complete set of video recordings from the airport, her X-ray from the hospital, the name of the hotel where she stayed the next two nights until they got the replacement flights sorted. We know she lost her suitcase, which flight she came back on, who she sat next to – everything. Can I use the bathroom, please?'

'I'll show you.' Dao gets up. 'Don't trip over Scruff. He likes to know everything that's going on.'

She is doing a great job of injecting little bits of trivia, reducing tension. Tama smiles at Scruff and follows Dao down the length of the room. Noah sits forward with his arms resting on his thighs, stares at the floor and says nothing. We wait in silence. Then Noah looks up with an angry look on his face and makes as if to speak; I hold up a hand. 'Not now.'

'Let's go back to what you said about her potential involvement with terrorists,' I say when Tama returns. 'I agree it seems unusual that a terrorist saves someone in a situation like that. If she was there researching terrorism, he might have recognised her from a visit to a terrorist training camp. Or maybe he knew her from when she saved his child just by chance somewhere else, completely innocently. What do you think?'

I want to hear how their reasoning went. What they based it on. I hope Willow will be able to use this information to our advantage.

'But that's not the point.' Tama is a bit more relaxed now, loosening up, open to discussion. 'Someone like that terrorist guy who saved her – God knows, he wouldn't save his own mother if she suddenly turned up. It's not what they do, not the right thing when someone else is a willing suicide bomber, sacrificing their life. Maybe Hope is involved with terrorists somehow, by chance or on purpose. But there must be a strong connection of some kind. Perhaps she's not involved with the terrorism side at all. Personally, I don't think she is, I'm not sure why. And obviously our top guys in Wellington have decided that too because they dropped the case not long ago. Just before she disappeared the second time.'

'Do they know she disappeared a second time?'

'No, not as far as I know.'

'And you are not going to tell them?'

'I can't. It's difficult to explain, but I simply can't. There are aspects to this that are outside any normal scenarios that we deal with.'

I hand my phone to Dao. 'We can stop recording now. Let's have another drink.'

I want him to relax, hope he will pay less attention to every word he says. His frank disclosure of so many details is very surprising; I expected him to be more circumspect. There are still a lot of unanswered questions, but I am intrigued by how open he has been. There is some kind of back-story here, something that will explain why he has told us so much. I wish I knew what it is.

I sit back with my beer. 'What we haven't told you, Tama, is that Hope wrote a journal about her travel and of her life in general, like short stories. Noah found them on her laptop. And some on a USB stick.'

Tama has a cracker with cheese halfway to his mouth; his hand stops mid-air. He looks confused. 'Did you know this already? Why didn't you say?'

'I wanted to compare what you told us with what she had written. You would not have told us in the same way if you knew. Some detail would have been lost.'

'You said the cops are not investigating? Why not?'

Noah speaks for the first time since we sat down. His voice is hostile, resentful. 'Her file is flagged "no action". Like Hunter said, they just blocked me every time I went.

Said another agency, obviously your outfit, is investigating and it's flagged for no police action. And ...'

'Bollocks,' interrupts Tama decisively. He has picked up the vibes of Noah's feelings, noticed my interventions. 'Sometimes there is a block on someone, because we're already dealing with it and we don't want them alerted by having cops going around asking questions. But as soon as our active investigation is at an end, the block is removed.'

'But it's still there on Hope's file,' says Dao. 'Either it didn't get removed or someone put it back. It's not just that the police didn't take Noah seriously – it's been confirmed by his lawyer.'

'Jesus!' Noah rubs his face, exhausted and depressed. His voice has taken on a higher pitch. 'I can't believe this fucking mess. Some bastard has taken her, and we can't get action! How are we going to get that block removed? It *must* be taken off, so I can go back to the cops and get them to investigate.'

'Let me sum up,' I say, trying to make eye contact with Noah. His voice has an edge of hysteria. Any moment now he'll start pacing and raving. He glares at me, frustrated and angry, but I turn to Tama and continue. 'Correct me if I'm wrong, Tama. You knew that someone had abducted her and that she had escaped and come back to her flat. But that's not when you started following her, as you put it, "to protect her". You'd already been doing that for a couple of weeks. Why?'

'There were some other things that came up, not terrorist-related – I began to wonder if she was safe. I followed her on my own initiative, nothing to do with work. Nobody told me to or knew I was doing it. And everything seemed fine. I was beginning to think it was my imagination and then the abduction took me totally by surprise.'

'You knew she had been abducted and escaped. Didn't you find it odd that the surveillance was stopped, that your bosses decided there was no need to keep track of her?'

'Things didn't happen in that order. I only knew about the first abduction after we were told to close the operation down. I did ask my boss why they had changed their minds about her status and he said that everything was taken care of.'

Dao's eyes are riveted on Tama; her chin has done its upward tilt again. 'But you didn't believe that assurance, did you? Because you continued to watch her, but now you were actually watching her flat, not just when she went out. So, you suspected that something else would happen?'

He nods and stares at his hands for a moment, then he gets to his feet. 'I have to go. I'm sorry, but there are things I simply can't tell you.'

He starts across the floor towards the stairs, stops and turns around. 'But I will see what I can do if I can give you something more definite. I'll call you, Hunter, in the next couple of days.'

He is not looking at Noah and I can't say I blame him.

As soon as he has left, Noah leaps to his feet and starts pacing back and forth, unable to sit still. 'I don't trust that bastard. He's lying, I'm sure of it. He's a fucking liar!'

'What are you talking about? Of course, he's not lying.' Dao is shocked and angry. 'How can you say that, when he's going to try and get us something that might risk his job? He wants to help us.'

Noah expression is one of stubborn resistance. He is nearly shouting. 'No way! That's absolute rubbish! He's just stalling. He'll call you and say he couldn't figure out how to remove the block on Hope's file and that he can't find out anything more. I didn't trust him from the start. He's shifty. Maybe *he* took her. He seems obsessed with her. He wasn't protecting her! I don't believe a word that lying bastard said.'

I am not going to interrupt him; I want to know exactly how furious he is, maybe get a clue to his inner demons. Perhaps this outburst will clarify what his problem is. I can't work with him if these crazy mood swings are going to make him unreliable.

Dao looks at me, dismayed. 'Hunter, tell him! He's so wrong, it's ridiculous. I totally believe Tama, don't you?'

I keep my voice calm, as if this is not really important. 'Yeah, I do. I can't understand why you call him shifty, Noah. What did he say that seemed shifty?'

'Nothing, it's not what he said. He's so smooth and he knows he can con people with his good looks – tried to impress us with what he might be able to do, which will never happen. It's a con job. You're both too gullible. He knows something – and we'll never find out.'

From the look on Dao's face, she is just about to tell him what she thinks of him.

'OK, Noah,' I say and send a silent signal in Dao's direction. 'If that's how you feel, I think we should reconsider what we do next. Perhaps a good night's sleep will put a different perspective on it. I'm not prepared to discuss anything further until you've calmed down. Let's wait and see if Tama is going to be helpful or not.'

He scowls at me and leaves nearly straight away. Even his back looks stubborn and indignant as he walks to his car. I close the door behind him and walk slowly up the stairs, deep in thought.

Dao is collecting up glasses and bottles, still seething with impatience and fury. 'That man! He's a nervous twit. And don't tell me not to say that. I know his sister is missing and I do feel very sorry for him – but he is so stupid. I'm really fed up with him.'

She looks at me for a response, but I say nothing; she needs to have her full say. 'He doesn't like handsome men! That's what it is – he has some in-built prejudice against good-looking people. I'm amazed he likes you.'

She is so cross and feisty, like some miniature avenging angel. I start laughing, and that makes her even angrier.

'What's so funny? It's not funny, Hunter. This is serious. He might have scared Tama away and he'll never tell us anything more.'

'It is very funny that you think he might not like me because of my looks, Dao. I'm not remotely handsome.'

'I think you are. Very.' And then she laughs too. 'And you know what I mean. He's jealous of Tama's looks, but it comes out as suspicion of everything he says. Instead of admitting to himself that Tama is very handsome, he kind of translates it into – whatever you call it. Sort of casting doubt on him. What do we do now?'

Noah's outburst against Tama was irrational and I doubt that he can be trusted not to do something stupid and ill-considered. Should I back out of this before he creates a mess? How will Dao feel if we don't continue trying to find Hope?

'What do you think?' I say instead of answering her question. 'We have several options. We can wait and see if Tama gets the block taken off Hope's file and then Noah can go to the police with Willow. Or we can tell Noah we can't continue to help him if he doesn't trust Tama, because we believe Tama is crucial to our search for Hope. And I honestly think he is. We can work with Tama and let

Noah muddle on by himself, maybe feed him information Tama gives us – if we can trust him with it.'

We decide to talk about it in the morning. We tidy the kitchen, set the ground-floor alarm and go up to the bedroom level with Scruff.

'Look at him, can't wait to go to bed,' I say as he runs ahead of us up the stairs. 'He's been sleeping beside the sofa the whole evening, the lazy thing.'

'He's worn out with that hole he's digging. If it gets any deeper, he will tunnel into Nigel's place.'

I make a mental note to fill it in and put some pavers over it in the morning.

13

I wake up in the middle of the night. Dao is on her back, so I know she is awake, she never sleeps on her back. 'Worried?'

'No, not worried. Just surprised at Noah. I didn't see it coming. I mean, I knew he was weak and difficult, but I didn't expect him to be so vicious.'

'He is a very strange man – and probably not someone we can depend on. What do you think we should do?'

She turns on her side and replies without any hesitation. 'We have to carry on. We're not doing this for Noah, we're doing it for Hope. I think we should do what you said before, carry on, use Tama as much as we can and tell Noah what we think he needs to know. And Willow, of course. But we can't have those two guys in the same room. Next thing he'll say those things to Tama and *he* will think it's racial prejudice or something.'

'I totally agree. Anything else?' I know that analytical mind of hers is working away, sorting information, deciding on priorities.

'Yeah, a whole lot of things. I want to talk to Benson again. Not in his office, somewhere else, private. Maybe he can see what's in that file even if there is a block on it. There are things that would be useful to know. Like, was the mask inside the wheelie bin? Did they fingerprint the bin? Was the rag that he doped Hope with in the bin? Can they DNA test the mask and rag, if they have them? Do they know what was on the rag? I think I'll call Benson in the morning.'

I suddenly remember how she reacted to something when we were talking to Tama. 'You know when Tama said he was trying to work out who it was that took Hope the first time. Did you believe him?'

'I think he was being evasive. Perhaps I should say cautious, seeing I understand him a bit better now. I think he replied in the way he did on purpose. It sounded to me as if there was a part missing.'

'How do you mean, missing?'

'Well, I just felt it was as if he could have said, "I'm trying to work it out, but I'm pretty sure I know who he is." People do that sort of "half the truth" thing sometimes, you know.'

'True, they do. I think you're right about this.'

'I love being right,' says Dao, and we go back to sleep.

I wake up again at twenty-five to six. Dao is sitting up in bed holding a phone to her ear.

That's my phone, I think, *and I bet she's looked Benson up in my Contacts list.* I hope he hasn't answered yet.

I say quietly, 'Stop. It's too early.'

She ignores me, and I lie back, waiting to hear how she will get Benson to do what she wants.

'Hi, Benson. I hope you were awake?' Short silence. 'Oh, good. That's OK, then. No there's nothing wrong, I'm fine. But can you please come here on your way to work? I really need you.'

She listens and shakes her head. 'Of course not, it's

nothing like that.' A longer silence this time; Dao is frowning.

'But Benson, that's not true. You know he only does that kind of thing when it's necessary and nobody else will do anything. I promise it's not anything bad, but you're the only person I know who can help me.'

She listens for a moment and she says, 'OK, thanks. We'll give you breakfast. See you.'

I enjoy the way she handles Benson. She turns and sees me grinning. 'Stop laughing, Hunter. We must get up right away. He's coming on his way to work and today he has to be there at seven. We have to make breakfast – he'll be here really soon, or he'll be late for work.'

By five past six Benson, who conveniently lives in Hillcrest, a fact I never knew before, is sitting at our dining table eating porridge with brown sugar. He looks as if he isn't quite sure how he got to be here. Dao leans over and puts a pad in front of him. We have agreed that there must be no mention of Tama's visit and I wonder what is on her list. Things have happened at speed this morning; she must have written it while I was making the porridge.

'You do understand how important this is, don't you,' she says seriously. 'I know you can't investigate because that other authority, whatever they are, won't let you. But surely you can just open Hope's file and look? Or is it really locked in some way, like with a password?'

Benson's expression is that of a man who has walked into a trap. A mixture of 'Oh, shit' and 'How do I get out of this?'

'I can't open that file,' he says, his finger tapping the top item on her list. 'It would be unethical because there is no reason for me to look at it. Everyone who opens a computer file in our system leaves a kind of trail. I'll never make inspector if I get caught doing something like this. I might even get demoted and have to put on a uniform and patrol the streets again.'

He is exaggerating, of course, but it has the intended effect. Dao reaches across the table and pulls the pad back. 'Sorry, I didn't realise. I don't want you to get into trouble.'

She reads her list, ticks one item and pushes the pad back to Benson. 'Can you find out this one thing?'

He drinks some coffee to give himself time to think. I am amused and feeling sorry for him at the same time. Once again it is probably something he is not supposed to do. After a moment he caves in. 'OK, I'll see what I can do.'

Dao beams at him. 'Good! And you know so many useful people. I bet you always know someone who knows something.'

Benson's expression is a mixture of admiration for Dao's tactics and slight apprehension. I imagine he is wondering if that last bit is a veiled threat referring to the information about the truck on the motorway he gave us, and how he found that out.

When he leaves, Dao takes him down to the front door and I hear her comforting him as they go down the stairs. 'You don't need to worry, Benson. I would never tell anyone what you tell us, never! You're my friend. We must trust each other.'

Good girl, I think. He deserves to know we would never do anything that harms his reputation.

We tidy up and I sit down to work and forget to ask Dao what that item on her list was. The London office has sent an email saying the contracts for the last job have been sent out and they've attached the specs for a new one. It's a simple bodyguard-cum-driver set-up that requires someone with good close-combat skills and high-speed driver training - in Central America this time. Sometimes I get a run of these simple jobs that just require the right people being assigned. I was on shared operations with quite a few of the guys who are now on our books, and having a good memory is an advantage.

Some jobs are complicated and require me to visit a client to get a good picture of what's needed. Variables like the layout of buildings, potential sniper vantage points, security measures already in place. Alternative points of egress and exit can be hard to assess from photos and descriptions.

The people, whose personnel needs I deal with, range from educated, ruthless and scary to just ruthless and scary. The men we contract out are ex-armed forces and fall into two groups: those who can't find a civilian job that pays well, and those who still yearn for conflict, danger and the feel of a weapon in their hands. And the money is good. This time it's easy to find someone suitable, so I sort it in no time, spot a name in the database that shouldn't be there, a guy who was killed doing a bodyguard job in Venezuela and red flag it for my London partner.

I go back to our surveillance video and find the bookmarked place where the man stands on the other side of the street and Noah rings the doorbell the first time. It is hard to get a definite idea of what he looks like. He is medium height, medium build and appears to be wearing a jacket of an undefined colour with the hood up. His profile is only visible for a few seconds as he steps into the shadows and nearly disappears. He has a moustache that curves down around the corner of his mouth. I snip a still from the video and save it.

I enlarge the image and stare at it for a long time, trying to imagine him without the moustache, but it rings no bells. I continue watching recorded footage.

The system is usually set to movement activation: the

sensor only detects something moving close to the front of the house. But once the camera starts recording, it takes in the full wide-angle view, across the street and out to the sides. Now and then Dao changes it to constant recording, but not very often these days. Watching the on-off clips nearly puts me to sleep, but suddenly I see something and rewind. There he is again, early in the morning a few days after Noah's first visit.

He stands for a minute on the inner edge of the sidewalk, just close enough to trigger the sensor. He looks up at the house, then walks away out of the picture. The entire scene takes seconds, but his focus is definite. He's interested in the house, came back in daylight to have a good look, noted the lights and the camera. He's wearing a cap, but I recognise the chin and the moustache. It is the same man. I save the image, the best one so far. Who is he and what is he after?

I open the old clips of the guy who came while we were in the South Island a year ago and compare them with these later ones, but it is a different man. I make a mental note to tell Benson about this renewed activity.

We have dinner with Willow and Matt and the twins, who are two years old and in perpetual motion. Dao spends half the time on the floor with them and Scruff, playing hide and seek at floor level. Plum is there on a weekend visit from Taupo and tries very hard to find out why I wanted to locate Tama.

'There's nothing to tell yet,' I say. 'No news at all, so stop nagging me. I said I would tell you and I will. When did I ever break a promise?'

She grins. 'Give me some time and I'm sure I'll remember something. Didn't you promise me a new car if I got my degree finished?'

'Good try – but no, I certainly didn't.'

She goes out straight after dinner to catch up with friends and Matt puts the twins to bed, so we can talk.

'Tell me more about this Tama guy,' says Willow. 'I couldn't ask while Plum was here, but I'm dying to know. Who is he and what does he know?'

I called Noah this morning and warned him about telling Willow too much, particularly not speculations about where Tama works. She might have reservations about acting on confidential information. But Noah is a loose cannon and I can't even guess what he might have told her. Willow is very perceptive, so I must get it right. I say briefly that Tama has promised to tell us if he comes across any additional information and we will let her know what eventuates. I mention that Noah seems to have a grudge against Tama for some reason and behaves as if he thinks maybe Tama abducted Hope.

Dao elaborates, still indignant about his behavior. 'I think there's something wrong with Noah.'

She looks seriously at Willow and shakes her head. 'He has really weird ideas about people. I mean, we knew he was kind of twitchy and nervous about things – but this thing about Tama! It was just crazy. I suppose he can't help it. Being stupid, I mean. But it's very hard to work with someone who's like that and we need everything Tama can tell us. If he does call, we'll meet with him without Noah. Hunter will explain it, just so you know, but it's the only way.'

Willow has expected this; she is good at reading people. 'I know. Noah is tricky to deal with and hard to keep on topic. But how are you going to handle it from now on if he has developed some kind of grudge against Tama? And what could he possibly base a grudge on, anyway? It sounds mad. Are you just going to keep going and leave him out of it?'

'We have to keep them separate, Willow. If Noah alienates Tama we've lost our only direct link to Hope's disappearance. He nearly alienated both Samantha and Willard already, and he's getting more volatile by the day.'

'I hope you realise that anything you tell me, any new information you give me, I have to tell Noah. I can't act for him and keep the information you give me secret. So, you'll have to devise a way of keeping things separate. The only thing that worries me is that you might come across information that could be vital, and I won't find out. Have you thought of that?'

I knew she would say this. I would feel the same way if I were in her shoes. Knowing that there might be relevant information, but not having access to it is frustrating. For Willow it is doubly hard that it is I who will find things out and withhold them from her. It is not what she likes to think of as the natural order of things. Poor Willow.

'I will tell you what I can, things that won't trigger damaging reactions from Noah. And as soon as the block is removed from Hope's file, I'll give you everything we have.'

Dao looks thoughtful now, understands the implications. I know how it is going to work from our side, but I am not going to tell Willow. She has a very strong sense of ethics and disapproves of the idea that some things simply have to be done, whether they are strictly legal or not.

She obviously has serious doubts about what I might be planning. When I was tracking down Dao's captor and trying to keep us both safe at the same time, I had to do a few things that she disapproved of. Now she wants to keep me under control, but she knows she can't, and it drives her crazy.

'That's all very well, Hunter, but I know you! I know

what you are capable of if you think the situation warrants it – and it's probably going to create problems again. Remember what a close call it was with Benson. You were so lucky he didn't charge you. And there's something you're not saying, something else about this Tama guy. Are you going to tell me?'

I deny it and Matt heroically changes the topic before it turns into an argument and we talk about other things. When we leave Willow asks, with seeming innocence, 'And how is Charlie these days? Do you see a lot of her?'

It is so transparent it makes me laugh. 'For Christ's sake, Willow, you have to try harder! If you want to know if Charlie is in any way involved in this, just ask. And no, she has never heard of Hope or Noah.'

I don't tell her that I am going to call Charlie in the morning and ask her to come over for a brain storming session. Dao doesn't know either; it will be a nice surprise for her.

When we get home, Dao turns the CCTV camera to continuous recording. She used to do this after the trial when she was a media darling and people staked out the house hoping to get a photo of her. I don't know what has triggered it this time, but I say nothing, just nod when she tells me what she is going to do. I wake up several times in the night and find her checking the tablet. The fourth time I protest, 'You'll be very tired in the morning if you keep checking the camera all the time.'

'Sorry,' she puts the tablet on the floor. 'I'm just making sure nobody is out there.'

'Why? Do you think we are being watched?'

'I don't know. I've seen the same man a couple of times lately. Not here, at other places. It made me remember last year, that creepy guy who kept coming and staring at the house after the trial. But I might be wrong. And it's not him, anyway.'

'Let's keep the camera on all the time then,' I say. 'It doesn't matter. You can check it tomorrow.'

'OK, I'll check it right through in the morning and if he's out there I'll show you.'

I don't mention the images I saved, or we will get no sleep at all. I pull her closer and shut my eyes.

14

While I make breakfast, Dao sits in front of her laptop and fast-forwards through the night's recordings. She sees nobody suspicious. No cars slow down or stop, nobody stands on the pavement on either side. 'But I'll leave the camera on permanent function again,' she says, 'just for a couple of days.'

I nearly ask her to tell me more; what he looks like and where she thinks she saw him. It is hard to strike a balance between protecting her from her worries and letting her cope in her own way. I decide to leave it for now, but I wonder if the man she saw is the guy who was outside when Noah came. I will pick my time and then show her the images I saved from the video.

When Charlie returns my message and says she can come over after lunch, I don't mention it. The doorbell goes just after one and I say casually to Dao, 'Can you please get that?'

She checks the tablet on the table and jumps up. 'It's Charlie!' and runs down the stairs at breakneck speed.

It takes at least quarter of an hour to get Charlie through the process of being greeted by Dao and Scruff. I

147

usefully occupy myself with getting a couple of cold bottles of beer out of the fridge, while I wait for my turn.

Eventually we sit down, and Charlie raises her bottle. 'Cheers, mate! So what's the problem? You didn't say much in that message. Do you need the chopper for something?'

'We just want you to check out this thing we got involved in. You might come up with something we've missed.'

First up we give her the printouts of Hope's stories to read. Dao arranges them chronologically before she hands them over. Charlie reads them in silence, occasionally she shakes her head, but she asks no questions.

'Wow!' She puts the little pile of papers on the table. 'That's some story! How did you get involved?'

Dao picks up the papers and straightens the edges, lines them up perfectly parallel with the edge of the table.

'Hunter will tell you. It's a long story now.' She sits back in her corner of the sofa and pulls her feet up.

Charlie looks at me with raised eyebrows. 'This seems strangely familiar, Hunter. This is just how you and I sat when you told me about finding Dao in the bush. The first time I met you, Dao. Remember?'

Dao grins. 'And I didn't know if you were a girl or a man, remember?'

I start with Noah's first visit and try to get it in order. Every now and then Charlie asks me to explain something and a couple of times Dao interjects with a detail. We play her the recordings from our phones and finally I describe Benson's visit.

'Shit, girl!' says Charlie to Dao. 'You know what this means, don't you? Benson is going to flip if he hears I'm involved, and Kristen will make me sleep in the spare room for a year. Talk about being in trouble. I might have to come and live with you two.'

Dao shakes her head. 'No, no, Benson won't be angry. I'm sure he won't. He just gave you a hard time because you didn't tell him before we went to that factory, but I think he likes you. Remember how he asked about your guns that night, after we got back from the hospital? I could tell he liked you then.'

She thinks for a moment. 'Do you *have* to tell Kristen? She'll be furious. Didn't you promise her not to get involved in anything with Hunter ever again?'

'I've got to tell her, chook,' says Charlie. 'If she finds out later that I'm in serious trouble. Perhaps I should get you to explain it to her.'

I watch them and smile inside. Charlie, sturdy and dressed in what looks like army fatigues, much the same as when she flew helicopters in Afghanistan a few years ago, androgynous. And Dao, exotic and feminine. Dao admires everything about Charlie; that she's a pilot, her weapons skills and her practical way of dealing with trouble. She trusts her absolutely. Charlie sometimes refers to Dao as the Warrior princess. She once mentioned the saw-disk frisbee: Dao shuddered and said, 'But I had to save Hunter!' Charlie has not mentioned it since.

'So what can I do to help?' Charlie says now. 'You know you can have the chopper any time I'm not flying clients, so long as Kristen thinks it's a pleasure flight.'

'Nothing at the moment, apart from possibly come up with ideas.' I watch the condensation from her bottle of beer make a wet circle on her thigh. 'I know it sounds a bit vague, but this whole business is full of things that don't make sense. I thought if you heard the story in one hit like this, you might come up with something we haven't thought of.'

She shakes her head. 'Sorry, mate. Can't think of anything even remotely clever. But keep me informed and if that guy Tama does come back, I'd love to hear what he tells you.'

'I'm going to clean the car,' I say when she leaves. 'I need to do something physical. It might make me stop thinking in circles.'

I reverse the car out of the garage and head back through the house to the courtyard to pick up the hose. Scruff has been trying to shift the two pavers I put over his filled-in hole; I must deal with it in a more permanent way later. When I return with the hose reel Dao and Scruff are in the open garage playing a new game they have invented. It is a floor-level game of squash played with a yellow tennis ball in two rather than three dimensions. Dao shoots it hard across the floor with the broom and Scruff runs like a demon to catch it as it bounces off the wall at an angle. I am about to start hosing down the car when she comes running out and gets down flat on the ground to poke around under the car with the broom handle.

'Watch out,' I say from the other side. 'You'll get hosed in a minute if you stay there. What are you doing?'

'We lost the ball. It's right under the middle.' She gets up and looks at me across the roof with a guilty expression. 'Sorry, Hunter, I've knocked a piece off the car.' She holds up a small black cube about the size of two matchboxes stuck together. 'What is it? Do you think you can put it back?'

I turn it over in my hands. 'I have no idea. Where did it come from?'

She shakes her head. 'I don't know. I was just using the broom handle to try to smash the ball back into the garage and that thing fell down.'

I turn the cube again and see a little catch on one side. I push it and the box opens. Inside is a lightweight black cube with 'iTrail' in white on one surface. Dao stares at it and then at me, still worried she has damaged the car.

'Stay here,' I say and hand her the two parts. 'And watch that Scruff doesn't go on the road.'

I run upstairs and get the tablet, my mind busy with uneasy conjecture. I stand in the garage where the light is not so bright, do a search for 'iTrail' and my suspicions are confirmed.

'It's a GPS tracking device. Let me have a look at the box it was in.'

I put it against the side of the car and I can feel the strength of the magnet pulling it towards the metal. 'It's magnetic, very strong. It can't have been attached properly.'

She understands immediately. 'Someone put it there to check where we go. And they can find out remotely, like that "find my phone" app you put on our phones.'

Now the significance of Dao noticing the same man 'a couple of times' and the man caught on our surveillance camera begin to make threatening sense. We put the two halves of the device in the glove box and I finish cleaning the car before we go back upstairs.

I pick up the laptop and open the saved images I snipped from the CCTV videos. 'Come and have a look at these, Dao. Do you think that's the man you've seen?'

She spends a long time going from one image to the next, back and forth, says nothing for a long time. Then she nods. 'It might be. I wish he didn't always wear something on his head. It makes it hard to see what he really looks like. The man I saw was wearing a cap, and he had a moustache, a big one like this man. He was wearing sunglasses.'

'Where did you see him the first time? And how many times do you think you've seen him?'

'I've only seen him twice.'

'Where was this?'

'The first time was at the supermarket. He was kneeling between our car and the one next to us. Remember the day after we went to Hope's flat? You were buying a Lotto ticket at the entrance and I was standing inside the big window looking out into the parking lot. I saw a man kneeling between our car and his. He must have just arrived, because the space beside us was empty when we parked. And I thought, poor man, he's dropped something, and it's shot in under our car. I nearly told you, in case you needed to move the car, so he could get it.'

'And you saw him again when?'

'When we went to the pizza place the other night. He arrived just after us and sat in his car. He was still there when we left. I never thought to check if he followed us.'

'Could it be John?'

She thinks for a while. Probably her mind has taken her back to the island. She will picture John coming ashore from his boat, touching her if gets a chance, making suggestive comments when Bramville can't hear. Perhaps her mind is playing back the time Bramville said he would sell her to John the drug runner, 'because your name is Slave, and anyone can own you'. It terrified her; she was sure John would keep her on his boat, abuse her and then throw her overboard to drown. She is very aware that for John she is a serious threat, the only eyewitness who can attest that he brought the barrels of drugs to the island.

I reach out and pull her closer; she leans into me and studies the image on the screen. 'It might be him,' she says finally. 'But I can't be sure. He never used to have a moustache and it makes such a difference. It's hard to say. If it is him ...'

'I know,' I say. 'If it is, then he's back from wherever he sailed to and he's heard that damn barrel full of drugs is still missing – and he's thinks I might have it.'

In the morning I call Benson and ask if we can come and see him. He sounds cagey, probably wary after his recent experiences of Dao demanding information. I don't tell him what it is about; I want Dao to tell him. He never goes off on a tangent and starts firing his own questions back when she is talking to him.

On the way to the station I warn Dao to be careful what she says next time we see Willow. 'The tracker on the car isn't likely to have anything to do with Hope's disappearance. If we tell her about it, she'll just start to worry.'

Dao nods. 'Of course. She'll tell you not to do anything silly and she'll say please don't do anything illegal again. I know. And then she'll ask if you have guns in the car and all that stuff. Much better not to tell her.'

When we say we have an appointment with Detective Sergeant Benson, the woman at the front desk smiles. 'It's Detective Inspector Benson now.'

He comes out to fetch us and as we walk towards his office Dao says, 'It's great you're a detective inspector now, Benson. Then if they demote you one step, you won't go all the way back to be a constable.'

He looks sideways at her and they're both grinning. I would never have dared say that; I just congratulate him politely on his promotion.

Twenty minutes later we have been through the whole saga backwards and forwards. Benson has saved the images I brought in on a USB stick and we are comparing them to the only picture the police have of John. It's at least ten years old and he is clean-shaven; impossible to relate to the CCTV pictures. Benson flicks back through the images on his screen, thoughtful and slightly worried.

'It will be well known on the street that the drug barrel has never been found. If it *is* John, we have to get hold of him. The fact that we saw CCTV images of the barrel on the back of Bramville's truck when he left the island wouldn't be widely known. *We* know he hid or sold it, but they think someone else took it.'

He goes back to the picture from a year ago. 'And this first guy having a good look at your house while you were in the South Island, just after it all happened – I bet he was after the same thing.'

He gives me a wry smile across the desk. 'And you're known as a hard man, Hunter. Maybe the gangs think you have the barrel, just waiting till the heat's off before you sell it.'

Dao is outraged. 'Hunter's never had anything to do with drugs, and he wouldn't know how to sell them.'

He raises his hands above his head. 'Sorry, sorry! I know he isn't into drugs, I just said others might think he took the opportunity to earn some cash. I know Hunter is not part of the drug world.'

'OK,' says Dao, slightly less ferocious. 'But listen, Hunter and I don't agree about the tracker. I mean what we should do with it.'

'I should have asked you. Did you put it back on the car?'

'It's in the glove compartment. I think we should put it on your car.'

'My car? Why?' It's clear he never expected this.

'Well, we can't just put it on a random car,' she says, in that way of hers, as if she is explaining to someone who is not very smart; I know it well. 'Because then this guy might hassle some poor person who knows nothing about it. We can't put it on a bus – the person tracking us would get suspicious right away. But the tracker needs to be on the move and going places, otherwise he will just put another one on – and we're back where we started. If you have it on your car, you can arrest him if he approaches you. Perfect!'

Benson and I look at each other and Dao smiles. 'And think how surprised he'll be when he discovers he has been tracking a police officer.'

'Brilliant,' I say. 'I hope your wife doesn't use your car, Benson. You wouldn't want her involved.'

'I don't have a wife any longer, so that's not a problem. She left me a few years ago – said I paid more attention to the job than to her. Not to mention that she was afraid of being alone in the house at night. It was kind of doomed from the start. Anyway, how is it that nearly every damn time I see you two, I end up doing something I have doubts about?'

He sighs. 'By the way, I checked on Noah, and the answer is no, nothing at all. Now tell me where you parked – I'm heading out, so I'll come by and pick the tracker up.'

Dao nods and says cryptically, 'OK, good to know. Thank you. See you outside.'

We walk out of the building into the humid heat and my shirt instantly clings to my back. Dao is unperturbed, as always. Heat has no effect on her whatsoever; she says she has heat immunity.

'What was that item from your list that Benson was looking into? I forgot to ask.'

'Oh, that. I wrote something like "Has Noah got a police record or is he just a bit mental, paranoid?" Because of how he always gets really twitchy when he talks about the police. More twitchy than usual, I mean. I wanted to know if he'd been arrested for drugs or something. But now we know he doesn't have a record, so he's probably just a bit crazy.'

'Or he's very lucky and never got caught.'

We wait in the car for a few minutes and then Benson pulls up beside us, leans over to the passenger window and I hand him the tracker. He drives away, and I pull out into the traffic. Time to go home.

15

That evening Tama calls. 'Hang on,' I say. 'I'll put the phone on speaker, so Dao can hear you.'

'Don't bother, I'll come and see you,' he says. 'I'd rather tell you in person. But I'm concerned about Hope's brother.'

He noticed how volatile Noah was the first time he came and how I had to keep him under control. What Tama is going to tell us must be something he suspects could trigger an explosion from Noah.

'He's very stressed,' I say, trying to keep it casual. 'His reactions are a bit over the top sometimes. I take it you're going to tell us things that will upset him?'

'Yes.'

That crisp 'yes' makes up my mind. No way is Noah going to be allowed to create a scene or start issuing threats if Tama is prepared to share vital information.

'OK, we'll leave him out of it. Come straight from work if you like – have dinner with us.'

No point mentioning that we have decided to operate in parallel to Noah without his direct involvement.

Depending on what Tama tells us, we'll share the information with him and Willow – or not.

Tama arrives at half-past six. We make small talk while we set the table and by seven we sit down to smoked salmon pasta bake from the deli and wine for Tama and me.

'Right, let's talk while we eat. Why don't you tell us what you found?'

He pushes his pasta around, eyes on his plate; when he looks up I can tell he is really troubled about this.

'It's going to either burn my career and land me in jail – or make me famous. Or infamous.' His smile is half-hearted; he knows he is facing personal disaster.

Dao is staring at him. 'Do you know who he is, the man who abducted her?'

'He's my boss, Stuart.' He looks as if he has surprised himself by saying it out loud.

'He's your boss?' I can hardly believe I heard him right. 'Do you have proof?'

'Yes, of a kind. Shall I tell you how it developed, so you get the context? It's a story of many parts.'

He takes a sip of his wine and clears his throat. He is an unusual guy; sometimes he sounds like someone much older, perhaps a grandfather. 'It started when Rob at work told me that Stuart looks at the videos from Hope's flat – repeatedly. Rob and I both have administrator status on the system. We're IT and tech people. I checked the VMS on the server and what I found made me really worried. Stuart, my boss, goes back to some of those videos just about every day. He probably doesn't know that the system records which files he has accessed and when.'

Dao jumps up. 'Let's record this too if you don't mind, Tama. If it's complicated, we'll want to go back and listen to it again – get it all exactly right.'

She puts her phone in the centre of the table. For a girl who spent more than ten years removed from IT and electronic advances, she has come to grips with things at amazing speed. I didn't even know that our phones have a recording function until she told me that first time Tama came.

'OK, carry on – and tell us what VMS is, please,' she says and picks up her fork.

'It's an acronym for video management system. Rob just thought it was a bit creepy and pathetic, he wasn't concerned about it. He came across it by chance and he mentioned it quite casually – he thought it was funny. I checked the log and it was crazy – Stuart seemed to be obsessed with that clip. I wrote a little Trojan script that grabs Stuart's log data from the VMS and pulls it together – so now I have a continually updating report of how many times Stuart accesses recordings from Hope's flat, which ones he watches and when. It also tells me which particular segments he has bookmarked.'

He glances at Dao, looks a bit embarrassed, which amuses me.

'I'm sorry you have to hear this, it's unpleasant. But there's one part that Stu looks at regularly, at least once a day, sometimes two or three. It's a segment from one morning when Hope turns the kettle on, reads her emails and then she gets up and dances around in the living room in her bra and panties – she's got Pakistani music on. Stu goes straight to the bit where she dances, five minutes and twenty-six seconds in.'

'Can you print the log report or email it to me? Just in case he starts trying to cover his tracks?'

'He can't cover his tracks – the autonomous audit trail creates itself and can never be deleted. He doesn't know as much as he thinks he does, the arrogant creep,' says Tama dismissively. 'He has no access to the server or the VMS software. He can log on and see video, but he can't access the back-end functions. And no, I can't send the log report anywhere or even print it without leaving a footprint myself.'

He thinks for a minute and eats some of his pasta. 'I can take photos of the report relating to Stuart – photos of my computer screen – because I can't even print screen grabs without leaving a trail. The log report I created is quite long now, but I can scroll through and capture it screen by screen.'

'Is there anything else that links Stuart to Hope's disappearance?'

'Not real, direct proof, no. But I know it's Stuart. I'll come to that later.'

'Can we report it to the police?'

'I doubt that they would touch it. They probably have some protocol for dealing with us. I imagine they would pass it on to Wellington.'

'Couldn't you simply report him to Wellington, then?'

'If I lodged an accusation with the top brass in Wellington, they would probably say that his obsession with Hope doesn't mean he abducted her. They've known him for years. And the process would be at a snail's pace with all the procedures they'll have in place. Stuart doesn't like me, made it very clear when I arrived. I was interviewed and security-cleared in Wellington, so by the time I got to Auckland he couldn't do anything about it. He would probably say that I'm always fantasizing and being dramatic or maybe that he never trusted me – anything to discredit what I say. He's one of those guys who can make people believe him, a creative liar and good at it.'

'Why doesn't he like you?' says Dao, without worrying about being tactful. 'Do you know?'

'He made a couple of derogatory comments when I first got there – made sure I was within earshot and heard what he said. He doesn't like me, it's a fact.'

Dao is on a mission and won't be put off by vague statements. 'What did he say?'

I hold my breath; wonder if he will tell her it is not her business, but he hesitates only for a moment.

'He said, "That new bloke looks like a damn model, probably useless and got the job because he's pretty," and then he laughed.'

'What a pig,' says Dao. 'I bet he's just jealous. But please eat your dinner, Tama – we're having a fabulous ice cream we've just discovered.'

He smiles. 'And you don't want to have to wait for it? Is that it?' The serious look is gone, and he is just a nice-looking young guy teasing someone.

Dao blushes. 'Yeah, kind of. All those years, you know, when . . . I didn't have ice cream or ...'

'And we both love ice cream anyway,' I say, to help her out.

We finish our pasta and I get up and take the plates to the kitchen. 'Keep talking, Tama, I can hear you from here. We need to discuss what we do next. Any ideas how to hold Stuart accountable? I wish we had more to go on.'

'There's a lot more,' says Tama. 'But for you to be able to use it, I will have to totally compromise myself. I will become the extreme whistle-blower.'

This is a surprise; I thought he had told us all he knew. I return to stand beside the table, waiting to hear what he will say. He takes his time; his gaze is unfocused. Is he weighing up the odds, making the final decision or is he simply deciding where to start? Dao glances at me and minutely shakes her head: 'Don't say anything.'

When he looks up and starts talking, his voice is calm. There is no hint of drama; he is simply stating facts. 'No, it doesn't matter. I have to do this, or I'll despise myself for the rest of my life.'

I sit down, consider pouring myself another glass of wine and decide not to; I want nothing to distract him now.

'Not long after Rob told me about Stuart and I looked at his record on the log, he suddenly announced that Hope was no longer suspected of anything. He said Wellington had sent a message directly to him, that all surveillance was to cease as of that day. Rob and I were very busy just then, and a couple of days later, when Stuart asked if we had removed the camera and stopped monitoring her phone and so on, we said yes. He can become nearly impossible when things back up – keeps changing his mind about what is the top priority, pulls you away from a half-finished job to start another one and loses his tempter over details. No structure and no self-discipline.'

He takes a sip of his wine. 'But we didn't actually get around to it until a few days after he first told us to do it. And when we went to her flat there was a swipe pad on the door and we couldn't get in.'

'Noah did that,' I say. 'As soon as he discovered Hope was missing.'

'Well, we had no idea what it meant. Rob wanted to tell Stuart that we had delayed taking the camera down and now we couldn't get in, but I was uneasy. I didn't want to do anything to draw attention to her case just then, even though I didn't know about either of the abductions at that stage. So I said, let's just stop the recordings and close down the link. We could do that remotely.'

He frowns as he remembers the decisions he had made at that time. 'We left the camera in the window frame,' he says, 'and the rest of the gear on the outside wall. We just stopped recording. But I was worried about Stuart and his obsession with Hope, so I continued checking her text and email messages for a short time. Which was illegal, if surveillance had really been ordered to be stopped. I never told Rob.'

The timeline seems increasingly complex; one set of events overlaps another, and the consequences are not discovered until later. I go through the sequence in my head.

'Let's see if I've got this right, Tama. This means the camera was active at the time of both abductions. Let's go with Samantha's scenario. Say Hope took the call from a bogus policeman in the bedroom, where Dao found her phone. She goes downstairs, leaving the door just ajar. The camera stops recording the moment she is out of sight – and she never comes back. So if it is Stuart, he was recorded the first time, but never entered the flat the second time. Then Noah returns from holiday and puts the new lock on. And there will be recordings of him in that flat for a day until you guys deactivated the camera remotely.'

Tama nods. 'That's right. And yes, the first abduction was recorded, but Stuart noticed and deleted it. When he went to watch the old recordings of Hope, he must have spotted the date of the abduction video. And he realised the camera had still been operational when he went in and now it was all on record. If he had taken her a couple of days later, we would never have known. The link would have been deactivated and he would have been safe. He must have panicked when he understood what had happened. But somehow, he managed to delete that recording. That should not have been possible, so there is a major flaw in the software that we haven't been aware of.'

I can't believe how unlucky this is; there had been evidence of the abduction, but it has been deleted. Tama looks from me to Dao and shakes his head as if he can hardly believe the story himself.

I decide to tell him that one of Hope's stories was a detailed account of the first abduction. I tell him how she described it, and he nods. 'Yes, that's exactly how it happened.'

He sees my incomprehension and smiles without much joy. 'I told you this was complicated to tell, didn't I? You see, I continued watching the flat on and off and after a couple of days I realised that someone else was living there – Noah, as I know now. I had no idea what this meant. Had Hope moved? Or had something happened to her? Or was she in there and never went out? I couldn't figure it out. I studied the server log more closely and that's when I discovered that Stu had deleted a video file. He knows we have a backup system, but he can't access it – it's on a separate server. The abduction video he thought he had got rid of had been backed up before he deleted it. I watched it on the back-up server and that's where I can grab it from – easier than finding it among deleted files. It doesn't show his face because of the mask, but you can see his fancy watch. It's clearly visible – his sleeve rides up as he struggles with her. The mask covered his whole head, but a big mole on the back of his neck shows in the gap above the collar of the overall. It's very distinctive, large and a weird shape.'

'If he thought the camera had been removed, why do you think he wore a disguise when he abducted her the first time?' I'm interested to hear his ideas about this; we have speculated about it more than once, but we can't make sense of it.

'I don't know. Maybe he didn't trust that we had taken the camera down and he was worried we'd wonder why, if he asked again. And then the second time he came – I can understand why he wouldn't go up to the flat. She would never have let him in, would she? So he must have devised a way of grabbing her at the street door or in the street.'

I top up our glasses and consider all the details we have now. At last we know why Stuart wore that mask, even though Hope had already seen his face. Instead of asking if the camera had really been removed, he made sure he would not be recognised. And then he was shocked to find that not only was there a recording of the abduction, but there were things on it that could identify him – the watch and the mole on his neck. So he deleted it.

Dao gets up. 'Let's have the ice cream now. We can talk about what to do next while we eat it. But getting that block removed from Hope's police file is vital – that must happen as soon as possible.' She disappears into the kitchen.

Tama sits silent and thoughtful. When Dao returns with the icecream he pulls out his wallet and extracts a folded sheet of paper which he puts on the table. With a bowl of ice cream in front of him and a spoon in his hand, he points to the paper.

'This is for you,' he says through a mouthful of ice cream. 'Shit, that's fantastic ice cream, what is it?'

Dao starts laughing. 'Avocado and honey – "with a touch of balsamic vinegar", it says on the label. We love it – their second-best is red wine and black pepper. Now, why did you only turn up at places where Hope had been in the evenings, but she never saw you follow her there?'

'Well, I'm only one person and I have a full-time job, so

I had to prioritise. I figured that the most likely time Stuart would try to get close to her – or even rape her – was in the evening. And I knew he had access to her emails and text messages. He and I both knew where she was going to be when she went out, unless she made a date by phone call, of course. So I staked out the place she was at, parked somewhere really handy and waited. Most of the time it worked. I'd follow her taxi or bus and either drive right past the taxi at her door or park and follow on foot from the bus stop, see her safely home.'

Dao and I look at each other and nod. It makes perfect sense. The time and effort Tama put into his efforts to keep Hope safe is a testament to his determined personality. We talked about it a couple of times and tried to work out firstly how he did it and secondly why it was only at the end of evenings out that she spotted him. We never quite got it right.

'Incredible,' says Dao. 'Hunter sometimes says I'm a star, but I think you are a star too.'

'I agree. Above and beyond the call of duty, as they say.'

Tama smiles. 'I don't know if Stuart left the block on Hope's police file or if he put it back, but he told us she was of no further interest. Did he lie? Or has she really been cleared, but he made sure the police file is still blocked for his own reasons? Impossible for me to tell at my level and if I ask it will filter back to him.'

'Is there some way of double-checking what the truth is about that? I don't know what – some register or database you can dig into to find out? Do you know how they normally remove a block from a police file?'

I am making random suggestions off the top of my head. There are no clear-cut answers to our problem, and I am getting frustrated. When Dao was being hunted because she knew too much, my role was familiar in a way. I used my army training, evaluated situations, prepared for trouble, left nothing to chance. It was me against them; if they tried to kill her I had to be able to kill them first. This time there are so many people involved, different considerations, having to dig and delve to find things out. Officials and confidential information, other people risking their careers and reputations, difficult personalities. I am in a foreign landscape that I must somehow navigate without a compass.

'I am trying to find out how they normally lift the restrictions on a file,' says Tama and my attention flicks back to the present. 'I don't know how they notify the police that the file is OK to use. Perhaps someone with the right level of access goes straight into the police database and takes the block off? It's not something I have experience of.'

He eats the last of his ice cream. 'God, this is the best ice cream ever! But what I can do right away is give you this.' He pushes the paper in my direction. 'As I said before, I can't copy the video file or send it anywhere without leaving a trail. And if someone in Wellington notices, then I'm toast – and we can't get anything more. So maybe starting at the Stuart end will give you something to go on while I try to work out how to remove the stop on Hope's file. And if I can't remove it, I will grab the abduction video and the log of Stuart's activities and wait for all hell to break lose.'

The note reads:

Stuart Browning, 154 Bellevue Rd, Mt Eden.

It was his parents' house, both are dead, he never left home and never married.

Drives a black BMW X1, reg FBL430.

Tama leaves half an hour later. I deliberately avoid discussing how this information might be used. His role is to get the evidence of Browning's activities documented and pass them to us. It will be safer for him not to know what we are doing, but when I say this he snorts derisively.

'Safety is an obsolete word in my dictionary, Hunter. Once I've done what I have to do, I might as well call Wellington and confess. They'll be on to it pretty fast. Maybe confessing would be a good idea, give me a better chance.'

'And when they discover, what will you do?'

I have no wish to coerce him into anything, but I would prefer some freedom of action once we have the evidence. We stand in the open doorway and Dao joins us. The summer night is warm and still and the street is quiet. I glance at the big tree across from the house; there is nobody standing in the deep shadow.

Tama turns to Dao. 'I'll say nothing about you two, of course. It would hamper you and do me no good at all. It is better that they think I just collected the evidence for myself, to use against Stuart. No breach of confidentiality, just unauthorised data capture.'

'Are you sure you shouldn't take it to the police? Or to a lawyer? It might be faster than what we can do.' Dao is worried about what will happen to him, and so am I.

He shakes his head. 'Nothing would happen very fast – investigations, interviews blah blah. It will become very complicated and meanwhile my hands are tied. Possibly yours too, if they somehow find out about you.'

He gets into his car and we watch his tail lights

disappear around the corner. Dao is probably as disappointed as I am; this has become an either/or situation. Either we do our damnedest to find Hope and let Tama sacrifice himself, or we leave it to the authorities, and it might be too late to save her. So much time has passed already; the chances of her being alive must be getting slimmer each day.

16

The next morning Dao and I discuss the pros and cons of telling Willow about Tama's job and possibly some of what he told us. Dao is against telling her anything, but I'm not sure.

'Things have changed. Now we know something quite explosive – a top guy misusing surveillance information and then committing a serious crime. Time is of the essence here, and Hope must be found.'

Dao shakes her head. 'I know, but if we tell Willow she'll tell the cops or whoever, and then we can't do anything. They'll take over and stop us working on it until they've looked into it. They might not even believe that Stuart has done anything. It will take forever! How long will that creep keep Hope alive – another week? Or two? Or is she already dead? There will be endless delays, not like when we do things.'

We finally agree that I will not tell Willow about Tama's job. We don't know the name of the organization, but he has made it clear that he would prefer not to tell us, and we have respected that. Perhaps it is some last reserve on his side; not making the final breach of confidence to outsiders. Neither will we tell her that he has evidence about Hope's disappearance. I will only indicate that he has access to confidential information and that it points to a particular person in a top-level position.

I send an email to her private address, so she gets it on her phone. Sending it to her office address would make it official and I nurse a vague hope that she will agree to co-operate with us.

When she calls, I know within seconds that there is no way she will help us unofficially. She is furious. 'Have you no idea how much you are risking by dealing with this guy? What did he tell you? If you're keeping information from me, I can't achieve anything!'

It is a long time since she was this angry with me. Not that it makes any difference. I just have to try to calm her down a bit. And perhaps not see her for some time.

'I told you the other night that this is how it's going to be, Willow. Noah is too unstable to have around when he's taken a dislike to someone. He's irrational – I think he might be on drugs. And I told you Tama might come up with more information.'

Willow is ablaze with indignation. 'I take it that Tama works for one of the intelligence agencies? He is endangering his career and your reputation! Noah told me a bit about that meeting where he was present. Tama has broken professional confidentiality by talking to you – for all I know you might be in possession of classified information. This is serious, Hunter! I don't care if they call it whistle-blowing or farting in a bucket, it's bound to end up in the courts.'

That childhood expression takes me back thirty years. I see her in my mind, aged seven or eight, after she discovered I have given her Barbie doll a crew cut and turned her into a soldier, shouting 'I hate you, Hunter. Go fart in a bucket!' If she wasn't so angry, I would laugh, but I know better these days.

'Of course, I know it's serious. I'm not an idiot. But if we're going to find Hope it will depend on speed, not on following the bloody rules. I don't give a shit if it's classified so long as the information helps us find her. Nobody else is doing anything about it, are they? And it's beginning to look as if we're well on the way now, so let's pray it's not too late to find her alive.'

I am angry too. She should understand that sometimes expediency takes precedence over following the rules. I told her we would not involve her, that we would keep anything borderline illegal to ourselves. Attacking me now seems unreasonable.

'If you want to have some classified information, just let me know.' I am on a roll now, just want to irritate her some more. 'And then you can file one of those requests for official information. By the time that's been processed Hope will have perished long ago, if she isn't dead already. But I'm not working with Noah. I don't trust him. I'll do this on my own. Let me know if you want to know what we've discovered already. It will make your hair stand on end.'

I end the call and turn around to find Dao staring at me. 'I've never heard you to talk to Willow like that before! Is she really angry?'

'Furious is more like it – steam coming out of her ears. I'm not sure what Noah has told her about our meeting with Tama. He's a bloody liability. I'm having nothing more to do with him. Let them be legal and proper, we'll just do what needs to be done.'

'Aren't we going to see Willow and Matt anymore?'

'Of course, we will. We just have to keep clear of any talk about what we're doing, things we can't tell her, and give her a bit of time to cool off. As soon as we know enough to force the cops to do something, we'll tell Willow everything.'

We sit down and discuss ways of finding out more about Stuart. When I suggest breaking into his house and searching it, Dao protests. 'If the neighbours spot us they'll call the police. And then we're stuck and can't do anything at all.'

'OK, but we can't just sit outside and watch his house – we could spend days without finding anything out.'

Then I remember the woman who came around a few weeks back doing a neighbourhood survey about playgrounds. 'That's a good idea,' says Dao. 'I'll be the survey lady. We just have to decide what the survey is about.'

We refine the survey concept to suit us, get the props together and we set out for Bellevue Road. It is new territory to me and I drive right down the length of it and then around the block where Stuart's house is and park just behind the corner. Dao has her clipboard on her lap and Scruff has his lead on; ready to go.

'Stay here,' I say. 'I'll walk back and have a look first. Just to make sure there aren't any surprises.'

The street is lined with mostly weatherboard villas, probably dating from the 1920s and 30s. A couple of modern houses have inserted themselves among the older ones; overall it is a homogenous street of well-kept properties. I walk on the far side, so I can look across and study Stuart's place without being obvious. White walls, grey windowsills and a leadlight window beside the front door; immaculate. A concreted driveway to the right of the house, a garage set well back, a glimpse of a biggish garden at the back. No obvious CCTV camera. I go all the way to the next corner, cross the street and walk back again. There is not much to see, but from this angle I can see a side door and a window on the side of the garage, which might be useful.

The plan is very basic, but there is no reason why it wouldn't work. Dao, accompanied by Scruff, will conduct a pretend survey about the need for an additional library on behalf of a fictitious community group. She will start at the corner and if someone is at home in the house to the right of Stuart's, she will keep the occupant busy while I check out his place. I position myself on the corner and try to look as if I'm waiting to be picked up.

Dao knocks on three doors where nobody is home and then she is only three away from Stuart's. I jog around the block and approach from the other direction. Dao is now having a friendly conversation with an elderly man at the house next door to Stuart's. She is explaining something, drawing on her clipboard and holding it up for him to look at.

I walk down the side of Stuart's house to the garden at the back. Clothesline, small shed, citrus trees, flower borders – nothing of interest. Through the windows that open on to the back veranda I can look into a tidy kitchen and an untidy bedroom. Through the clear glass pane in the back door I can look right down a wide passage to the front door at the other end. Rooms on both sides, all doors open.

I head for the street, walk close to the garage wall. The side door has an old-fashioned lock and on impulse I turn the handle; to my surprise it is unlocked. I have a quick look inside, close it and return to the sidewalk. Dao is still talking to the old man, he is telling her something, holding his hands out to indicate size and she is laughing. I walk past and wait in the car until she comes back.

'Well done! I had plenty of time to look around. There's a white pick-up truck in the garage. I didn't get the number plate – I didn't want to go right in.'

'Great. Let's find out about it right away,' says Dao and pulls out her phone. I wait to hear where this is going to lead.

'Hi, Benson, it's me. Dao. Oh, do you? Yes, I'm fine, thanks. Can you look something up for me in that car register you talked about the other day? Yeah, that's what it was called, the vehicle register. If I give you a name and an address? Oh, great! Have you got a pen?'

She gives him the details and ends the call, beaming. 'I'm so glad we have Benson!'

'We don't,' I say. '*You* have Benson. He would never do these things for me. And what were you and that old man talking about for so long?'

She bends down and pats Scruff who is on the floor by her feet. 'He has a little dog, very cute. Scruff liked him. We were talking about those dog houses you have outside, so the dog can get out of the rain. I've been looking at them on the Internet – you know, for when we're out and he's in the courtyard and it starts raining. He's only got the table to protect him from the rain. I might buy one for him.'

After Mint's trial I managed to persuade her to scrap her plan to clean people's houses to earn money of her own. She was deprived of her mother and much of her childhood; I want her to do whatever makes her happy, which is mostly studying mathematics, playing with Scruff and eating ice cream. Unfortunately, my relentlessly interfering mother thinks Dao is after my money. She became obsessed with the idea shortly after I found Dao in the forest, and she made sure Dao knew about it. Willow thinks her determination to try to run our lives is amusing; I find it infuriating. Dao was determined to prove her wrong, to earn her living and not depend on me. But after a lengthy period of negotiation Dao accepted my offer and now she has a bank account, her first. A set amount of money is transferred to it on the first day of every month. I tell her this is applied communism, the redistribution of wealth. A way of evening out the disparity between me having more money than I need and Dao's ten years of captivity, abuse and hard work without pay. She pays for her clothes and other bits and pieces; it makes her feel independent and we are both happy. My mother knows nothing about it; her access to our lives is now restricted.

Ten minutes later Dao gets a text from Benson and reads it out: *Two cars at the address you gave me. BMW X1, black, reg KRD418 owner Stuart R Browning. Mabel Jean Browning owns a 2003 Toyota Hilux pickup truck, white, reg BPQ190.*

'What? I thought Tama said he never married.'

While I wait for a bus to inch out from a bus stop, I think it over. Perhaps he was married at some stage and Tama never heard of it. And then the names trigger an idea. 'What did you say her names were?'

Dao looks down at the phone. 'Mabel Jean. Why?'

'Just that those are very old-fashioned names. I wonder if he registered the truck in his mother's name.'

Tama calls just as the garage door is closing behind us. 'Hunter, can you put the phone on speaker? I want to talk to both of you.' His voice is full of urgency.

'OK, Dao's just run upstairs – I'm on my way up now. We only this minute got back from checking out Stuart's place.'

Once again, we sit again at the table with the phone between us. 'Go ahead, we're both here now.'

'I think he did it once before – took a woman who was under surveillance.'

Gone is the calm self-possession; his voice is full of anger and emotion. I can hardly believe what I hear. Dao's face is frozen in shock. 'Oh no! How did you find out?'

'I only heard about this other woman today. Rob and I went out for coffee and he said something sarcastic about Stuart liking luscious dark-haired women, but never managing to find one who liked him back.'

I can hear traffic noises in the background and someone laughing. 'Where are you?'

'I'm outside – said I forgot to get something for lunch. I don't have proof, but it can't be coincidence. It was just before I started here. He had a crush on someone they were monitoring, an immigrant, an Afghani woman in her twenties. He used to refer to her as "the gorgeous Rana". She disappeared without a trace and after a year her case was archived as a suspended investigation. I asked Rob if they ever discovered where she went, and he said it was assumed she had found out she was under surveillance and left the country on a false passport. I didn't ask too many questions, but from what Rob said it sounds just like his fixation on Hope. Don't forget that Rob doesn't know about the abduction recording I found on the back-up. He still thinks Hope's case was discontinued because there was no reason to suspect her of anything.'

'Is there any way of finding out more?'

'I'm going to search the archived material and find images of Rana and any other details that could be useful. And when I print all the other stuff and steal the abduction video I'll include whatever I find on her. I'll do it very soon

– I just want to be sure there's nothing else I can achieve here before I burn the bridges behind me.'

We sit down with coffee and sandwiches; try to decide what we should do now. Our options are limited, our discussion overlaid by worries about Tama. He is risking more than anyone and there is nothing we can do to help him. He is a crucial part of the search for Hope, and it frustrates me that no physical effort or courage on my part will make any difference to the outcome for him.

'He knows that once he does this, he might be sacked or arrested or something. Hunter, what will happen to him?' I shake my head; I don't know.

And then suddenly, Dao has an idea. 'I know! We could put trackers on Stuart's cars – then we can find out where he goes. Or do you think we should break into his house first and check she's not locked up in there?'

'Of course, trackers!' I should have thought of that myself.

I describe what I saw through the back door at Stuart's place. 'If she's in the house, she is either in a wardrobe or dead, because every single door was open to that passage. I can't imagine he would dare leave her there, when he's out all day. I wonder where he goes in the evenings, if he has a flat somewhere.'

Dao is already reaching for her laptop. 'I'll do a search on trackers and find a good one.'

My phone pings. A text message from Tama:

Found photo, she looked just like H but younger. OK to come over after work? I'll leave early and beat the rush-hour traffic.

I tell him we will be here.

A couple of hours later Benson calls Dao and she puts the call on speaker again. 'I only have a few minutes. My day's gone mad,' he says. 'I didn't have time to tell you when we talked earlier on. But you'll be interested to hear that the bait got taken. The tracker guy came for a visit last night, followed me home.'

'Did you arrest him?' Dao sits up straighter, eyes gleaming at the thought that we might have got him.

'No, he wasn't doing anything I could arrest him for. I drove home and went into the house. He must have parked down the street and walked up, but he didn't expect me to come out again right away. I'd left my phone in the car by mistake. He was right up my driveway staring at the car. Probably couldn't believe he was tracking the wrong car. When I appeared, he did a double-take and ran off. But I got a pretty good look at him, definitely the same guy you had on your video clip. That Wild West sheriff moustache is pretty distinctive.'

'Do you think it was John?'

'I don't know. I never saw John in the flesh. Just that old photo of him and your drawing, Dao, from a couple of years ago, but he didn't have a moustache then. It could be him. I'll keep you informed.'

I sit there absently watching Scruff, who seems to be asleep sitting up, leaning against Dao's legs while she researches trackers online. Does the tracker guy realise that Benson is a cop? Maybe we shouldn't have moved the tracker. He might be alarmed now and pull back, and then we won't be able to get him. I have just realised how much I want to get my hands on him, particularly if it is John.

How can I trick him into a situation where I can confront him? I should get the original tracker back from Benson and put it on my car again. I would have to leave Dao at home when I go out, if I do that. I don't want her exposed to that rat. But the main thing is to get him arrested, to remove what Dao feels is a threat to her safety. I no longer think he is a threat to her. Instead of trying to get close enough to harm her, he has tried to get a look into the garage and followed me around to see where I go. Maybe he thinks I have a lock-up somewhere or a hired storage unit. I now believe that he is only interested in the getting hold of the drugs and making money. Perhaps he doesn't understand that the only evidence the police have against him is Dao's eyewitness statement; that on Dao's word alone he could end up in jail for years.

Dao opens the balcony sliding doors and the late afternoon light falls slanting into the living area where we sit with Tama. Through the balcony's glass barrier, I see Scruff in the courtyard staring at the neighbour's black cat, who sits on the courtyard wall, casually licking its front paw. The normality of it is a stark contrast to what we are involved in.

'Stuart is taking a fortnight's leave from Monday,' says Tama. 'Tomorrow is his last day at work. I only found out this morning. I'll grab all the material on Monday morning and get it to you. It's a perfect opportunity, because Rob is taking Monday off to get a long weekend. I can start first thing on Monday and just work away until I have it all. With Rob away there is nobody around who will know what I'm doing. I'll take screenshots of everything first in case my plan doesn't work – which is to email the abduction video and the rest to my private address.'

'But didn't you say you couldn't do that? Some safety thing in your system that prevents things being shared illegally?'

'That's right, but I'm going to do something totally radical. Might as well, seeing I'll be toast anyway once this gets out. I'm going to use my administrator status to hack Stuart's email account and send an email from there to my private address with one file attached. If that gets through to my personal email, I'll send the rest.'

'And it will look as if Stuart sent it,' I say. 'That will confuse Wellington for a couple of days, I suppose?'

'Not really. As soon as they notice stuff has been leaked, they'll start searching. I'm only doing it that way because Stuart can send files, which I can't, and he has no size restrictions. It will be a lot quicker than any other way of doing it. And even if someone notices right away, it will be too late. Once that email has gone, they can't pull it back.'

'And you'll give it to us?' says Dao.

'Yes. When I have it I'll forward it to you and you can put it all on a USB stick and pass it on to your sister. I'm sure she knows what to do.'

We've got one day to get something into place, before Stuart goes on leave. If Hope is alive and locked up somewhere, this holiday of his might be when something will happen. I have no idea what that something could be, but it can't be good.

'Dao has just come up with the idea of putting tracking devices on Stuart's cars,' I say, 'so we can follow him. We had a look at his house today. There's a white pick-up truck in his garage and he doesn't lock the side door. It's an old-fashioned single garage, separate from the house. We'll get the devices tomorrow. I can do the truck during the day when he's at work, but we must get the BMW done too before he heads off somewhere.'

'Get the devices in the morning and set up the app, then meet me outside work and give one of the trackers to me. He's never driven a white truck to work. I didn't know he had one until you told me about people seeing him loading that wheelie bin outside Hope's place. You do that one and I'll do the BMW. He has a reserved space in the car park under our building. I can do it easily.'

When I go down to see him out, he stops in the

doorway. 'That abduction video is pretty nasty – just thinking of Dao and how she might react.'

'Thanks for thinking of that. She already read the account Hope wrote for Noah, so she knows how it happened.'

'OK, but when Hope wrote that story, she only knew what happened until she lost consciousness. What happened next was totally repulsive – gross!'

17

In the morning we go to the JayCar shop in Khyber Pass Road. Every time I go into a tech shop I get served by some spotty-faced young guy who seems to know everything. I put two trackers with their magnetic boxes on the counter and the JayCar attendant, who looks fifteen, assures me that the app for the tracking device is 'easy as'. He reminds me of the young guy who served me when I bought Dao's phone, the same absolute confidence in his own abilities.

Dao is pottering around the displays and I catch him looking at her a couple of times. Then he glances from her to me and I see speculation on his face. I'm in a T-shirt and his eyes move from my face to the scars on my arms. I can nearly read his mind: here is a big guy with nasty scars and a tiny Asian-looking girl.

'We have a super-special offer this week,' he says. 'It ends on Sunday. You get a third one free, if you buy two of any items in this range under $60.'

Without waiting for an answer, he comes out from behind the counter and returns with another tracker.

Dao puts a little plastic packet on the counter. 'Can you buy me this please? I left my EFTPOS card at home.'

'Sure,' I say and take it from her. It is a personal alarm that claims to emit a 100 dB scream when you press the button. 'Do you think you'll need this?'

She grins. 'Not when I'm with you, but what if we get separated? You'll hear it and come and rescue me.'

I hand it to the assistant and turn to Dao. 'OK, but don't press that button near Scruff or he'll die of fright.'

She laughs and the young guy grins and visibly adjusts what he thinks about us. Who would have thought I would ever notice a thing like that?

As we drive towards Mt Eden Dao takes the tracker components out of the bag and studies them. 'I want to do this,' she says. 'You're too big, people notice you. I bet I can just open that door a tiny bit and slip in before anyone sees me. I'll tie my hair up, so the guy next door doesn't recognise me if he looks out the window.'

'OK. Put it where Stuart won't see it. Perhaps under the tray at the back – and check it's stuck on properly.'

'And you could distract the old man next door. He's never seen you, so you could ask him something and keep him busy while I'm in the garage.'

'Will you be able to lie – and lie really well, if somebody confronts you?'

Dao is nearly incurably truthful and finds it very hard to accept the need even for a social lie. She thinks for a moment. 'I'll say I've returned uncle Stuart's something-or-other that I borrowed and he's at work, so I left it in his garage.'

It makes me laugh. 'He'd be scared to death if he had you for a niece. And you need to have something with you in case you get stopped before you go into the garage. What have we got?'

We park the car at the other end of Bellevue Road from where we parked last time. Dao twists her hair into a knot at the back and uses a rubber band from the glove box to secure it. I walk around the block and up to the door of Stuart's neighbour and stand well to one side when I ring the bell. Through the frosted glass I see a man's shape coming towards the door, just as Dao slips up Stuart's driveway with my metal water bottle in her hand.

'Hi,' I say to the old man who opens the door. 'Is Gordon at home?'

He looks confused. 'There's no Gordon living here – never has been. Are you sure you have the right address?'

'Yeah, I'm sure he said Bellevue, number 152.'

'This is 152 – perhaps you have remembered the wrong number? Or could it be Bellwood? They sound quite similar, don't they? Do you know where it is? Over by Eden Park. My nephew lives there.'

Out of the corner of my eye I see a small figure walking away from Stuart's garage. I thank the old man for his suggestion and by the time I am back on the sidewalk Dao is fifty metres ahead of me.

'I put it under the edge of the tray at the back,' she says when I catch up with her. 'It's stuck on really tight and it's far enough in under the tray, so you don't notice it. I checked who could see the side door before I went in and it's only the house straight across the road. I hope nobody was watching.'

'If they did, they probably wouldn't bother to tell Stuart. And if they do he'll just check nothing was stolen.'

We get into the car and I take a proper look at her. 'What's wrong?'

'Nothing, really. There was a bundle, like a big messy roll of stuff, on the tray. It gave me a fright. You know that sort of heavy, stiff stuff – what's it called?'

'A tarpaulin?'

'Yeah, that's it. When I first saw it, I thought it might be Hope – her body, I mean. But I pushed my arm inside, and it's just rolled up loosely. There's nothing inside.'

She says nothing else for a few minutes, then she turns her head to look at me. 'That tarpaulin – he might have used it when he took her, you know. What if he had it laid out flat on his truck, and he had parked just outside the door at Hope's building. Say she opened the door and he stepped into that little space at the bottom of the stairs and knocked her out with that drug, whatever it was. If he was quick, if he did it early evening when all the places had closed, he could lift her onto the tray of the truck and wrap the tarpaulin around her – and nobody would see it.'

'You are right – that could be how he did it. That street would be very quiet by six – not too late for a police officer to call. And then he just needed to find somewhere secluded to park the truck and tie her up securely before he took her away.'

We say nothing more about it and head for Kingston Street. Dao calls Tama and we manage a perfect drive-by drop, just like in the movies. I pull in to the side in front of a double-parked courier van. Dao is ready with her window down and passes a tracker in its magnetic box to Tama, who is waiting on the sidewalk. We are stationary for no more than a second before I filter out into the traffic again.

Early on Saturday morning we are dressed and ready to leave at a moment's notice. Scruff gets excited at the unusual activity and follows us around, tail wagging, hoping for an outing.

'Do we take him or leave him in the courtyard?' asks

Dao as she fills a water bottle to take in the car. 'I'm sure he would love an adventure. We haven't been to the cabin for weeks and he loves long drives.'

'He loves long drives? He falls asleep as soon as the car starts moving. But let's take him.'

We have debated strategies and decided that it would be pointless to park near Stuart's house. We can follow him by using the tracker and if he stays at home, we haven't wasted a whole day sitting in the car. Both of us keep checking the app, even though we have set it to alert us. It is hard to settle down; we want him to make a move. I make sandwiches and pack them in a bag with some fruit, and water for Scruff, and put everything in the car.

It is half-past eleven before the tracker alert starts beeping. Dao checks her phone and jumps to her feet. 'He's moving!'

She watches the screen and gives me updates as I drive towards the Harbour Bridge. 'He's on Mt Eden Road, in the truck. He is halfway along. He's turned east into Greenlane something. Now he's on the motorway, heading south.'

We sit at a steady hundred and ten on the motorway through the central city and out the southern side, passing exit after exit.

'He's turned off to Papakura,' says Dao suddenly. 'I bet he was going to the same place when he had Hope in the bin on the back of his truck. Remember? He was on the southern motorway, heading south.'

When I turn off at the Papakura exit, Stuart is still a long way ahead on the Clevedon road. We trail behind him, slowly decreasing the distance between us, but careful not to get too close. We follow him towards

Kawakawa and then onto McNicol Road. We are way east of Papakura now, in farmland with houses surrounded by paddocks, clumps of native bush here and there and a winding stream bordered by trees.

'He's just turned left into the Otau Mountain Road. We're going to end up in the middle of nowhere.'

We are about two kilometres behind him; there are few houses, then no houses. The road climbs into the hills and follows a winding course along a ridge.

'How far ahead is he now? I don't want him to see us.'

'About a kilometre,' says Dao. 'The road is full of bends, but he might spot us anyway. Perhaps slow down a bit.'

Steep hills covered in native bush on both sides. There has been no sign of houses or driveways for some time; he is heading into the wilderness.

'This is the Hunua Ranges,' I say. 'There's a Regional Park up here, very popular. I drove through this area once on the way back from Miranda.'

Dao slants a sideways look at me. 'Was she your girlfriend?'

'No, it's a place on the coast. Lovely spot. We'll go there one day.'

'Turn left at the next road. It doesn't seem to have a name and it ends in the middle of nowhere – oh, I think it's called Mine Road.'

And then finally: 'He stopped! Slow down!'

Dao keeps her eyes on her phone as we close in on the now stationary truck. I pull off the road and park in a little space between trees, where the ground looks even. I nudge the car as far in as I can, and we get out, leaving Scruff in the car.

'Look – we're here and the truck is just there.' Dao hold

up her phone and points. 'This road ends only a kilometer or so further up. Shall we walk along the road?'

'Let's walk to that bend just before where he stopped, and then we'll continue along the edge of the bush. I want to see him before he sees us, if he's hanging around the truck.'

The truck is parked a few metres in from the road with some clear ground in front of it. We continue slowly forward, stop a couple of times, look around and listen. The truck is empty and locked. The tarpaulin is still on the tray. In front of the truck a fairly well-used track leads into the bush. We walk quietly along it, stopping frequently to listen, but we hear nothing but birds. Ten or fifteen minutes uphill the track splits into two, one narrower than the other.

We take the wider one and walk for half an hour before we turn around and head down again. At the fork in the paths Dao checks her phone. 'The truck is still there. Let's try the other one. Have you thought of what we'll say if we meet him?'

I try to imagine what he would think if he met two people walking in a place that probably has few visitors. Would he be suspicious? Could that endanger Hope? Would it be better to wait in our car until he leaves and then walk up this track and see what we find?

We discuss it and decide not to take the risk of bumping into him. I am reluctant to make him suspicious before we know what he is up to.

'Let's try to keep out of his way today. If he doesn't see us now, he won't get suspicious next time. It buys us time and opportunity.'

'OK, but we have to hang around. We can't afford to miss him. Let's move further up the road and wait there.'

We return to the car, drive past the truck and look for a good space to park off the road. Dao studies the map on her phone. 'Just making sure he has to go back the way he came – yes, it's the only way out.'

We park well in among the trees a hundred metres further up the road. Scruff wakes up and wants to go for a walk, so we take him and our picnic supplies and walk into the bush straight in front of the car. Here the forest is quite open and there is little undergrowth to hinder progress, despite the lack of paths. We sit on a fallen ponga trunk in dappled sunlight, surrounded by birdsong and have just finished lunch, when Dao looks at her phone. 'Oh, no! We have no signal here. We must have gone behind a bump or something.'

'How many bars did we have before?'

'Only two, but now we have nothing! Let's go back to the car and check – I know we had a signal there.'

He has left. There is a signal here and we can see that he is nearly back at Clevedon again. Following him back to town is pointless.

'Let's walk along to where those tracks start and take the other branch, see what we can find. He went in and came back in a bit over two hours, so we'll do the same.'

'OK and we'll take Scruff. Can you take the water bottle?'

It's cool and slightly damp under the canopy of the trees. The smell of damp earth and decaying leaves is as familiar as the smell of baking. Native bush has that characteristic atmosphere; the cool dampness and the smell of decaying leaf litter and moist earth. We follow a gently undulating course, but always heading higher. Fifteen minutes into this second track it branches into two again. We take the right-hand branch and walk for another hour but find nothing.

'Wrong again. We'll have to go back.'

'What if he ran?' says Dao. 'He could have gone a lot further.'

'OK, let's continue for twenty minutes and then head back.'

We see nothing of interest. We return to the car and head back to the city, disappointed and mystified.

Dao is annoyed. 'I don't get it. What did he do? Surely he didn't just go for a walk.'

To divert her attention, I change the subject. 'What time are we due at Charlie and Kristen's tonight? Did you say seven?'

She checks her text messages and says, 'Yes, seven. What should we bring?'

'A couple of bottles of Craggy Range Sophia,' I say. 'Kristen loves a good red and the Sophia is spectacular. She is so kind to you, taking you shopping for clothes and things – we want to take something she will enjoy. I have half a dozen in the wine cupboard.'

'What about me? Can we bring some of that lemon and lime stuff? Have we got some in the fridge?'

And then, out of nowhere, comes one of those priceless Dao moments that I store away and smile about now and then. She says, 'Why doesn't everyone have two names?'

'There's no law about it. I don't have two names. I'm just Hunter Grant – nothing in the middle.'

'No, I mean only one name – a surname.'

'I never heard of anyone who had only a surname. Where did you see this?'

She stares at me as if I have lost my mind. 'Benson, of course!'

18

As soon as we arrive at Charlie and Kristen's house, Dao is whisked away to look at something Kristen has bought. Charlie and I stay in the kitchen with a beer and I give her a brief summary of developments. It's interesting how someone can ask you a question, and through the process of explaining you come to see things from a new angle.

'Those tracks – someone made them, so there must be some purpose behind them,' says Charlie. 'If it's a popular recreation spot that could explain it. Or maybe people hunt in those hills? I don't really know anything about the Hunua ranges.'

'We'll try to find out tomorrow or Monday. I'll check the Internet for a map. The part where he went is not where the recreational people go – it's outside the Regional Park. We'll continue on standby and when he leaves, we'll follow him. He can't have gone very far today in the time he was away from his car. We can eliminate one track after another.'

'Yeah, I suppose, but maybe he leaves the track at some

point, cuts through the bush to some place where he has her hidden, or to another track. That would be quite clever – park in one area and cross to a track with a different starting point. And don't forget that other woman, the one who vanished out of sight a couple of years ago. She must be somewhere too.'

We look at each other and change the subject, but it is clear she has something on her mind. A few minutes later she abruptly reverts to the topic. 'I haven't told Kristen anything about this. I just can't get involved. I'd risk everything if I lie to her, mate. She's the only person who ever loved me. I can't risk it.'

I'm speechless. She is not joking; she really means it. I had no idea she felt like that; she has never said anything like it in all the years we have known each other.

She turns her back and peers into the oven.

I get my thoughts in order and come around the counter to stand beside her. 'I can't believe you said that, Charlie. I mean, everyone loves you. The whole damn unit loved you – every last one.'

She shrugs. 'Yeah, I suppose. But that's liking – not the same as love. You know the difference. My family can't stand me because I'm gay. They're staunch fundamentalist people, think they'll go to hell if they so much as let me into the house. I haven't been back to try to see them for years. My sister's kids don't know I exist – she told me when I called last year, just to test the waters. I've been deleted from the family, Hunter. I don't exist. Thank God we have Kristen's brothers and all their kids – and you and Dao, of course.'

I put my hand on her shoulder. 'I love you, Charlie. I'd do anything for you, just like I would for Dao and my sisters.'

She sighs. 'I know. I love you too. But I can't risk my relationship with Kristen. I just can't.'

She steps away, turns back to the oven and fiddles with the knobs. I am about to say, 'Let's forget about it, we might never need the chopper anyway,' when Kristen and Dao come back. They are both smiling, and Dao has a large carrier bag with a shop name printed on it. She puts it down and turns to me, her face alight with excitement.

'Just wait till I show you what Kristen bought me for my birthday! Lovely clothes.'

'Birthday? That's not until August. Kristen, you haven't spent a lot of money on Dao again, have you?'

Kristen looks vague; not a look I associate with her. 'Oh, is it August? I thought it was this month.'

Charlie shakes her head. 'It's a girl conspiracy, mate. You might as well give up. She loves buying things for Dao. It's like having a life-size doll to dress.'

Kristen and Dao ignore us. Kristen pours wine for herself and lemon, lime and bitters for Dao and they sit down at the table with their backs turned and ignore us.

Halfway through dinner Charlie clears her throat and says, 'Kristen, I think you should know that Hunter and Dao have one hell of a problem. And don't panic, I'm not going to get …'

Kristen interrupts, cool as a cucumber. 'You mean the search for Hope Barber?'

I hold my breath and glance at Dao. She is putting a forkful of chicken into her mouth with a dreamy look on her face. Charlie just stares.

Kristen lifts her wine glass and says in a conversational tone of voice, 'I imagine they might need you and the chopper, if things don't work out on the ground. I hope you're not completely booked up the next few days.'

I decide to keep my mouth shut. Charlie only manages to say 'How …' before Dao interrupts.

'I told Kristen all about it, because you said you couldn't have anything to do with it, but I thought she should know the story. You know, just in case she thought you *should* help. She has read Hope's diary stories too, so she understands how serious it is, and that it can't wait.'

Her gaze moves to me. 'We've made a deal, Hunter. I've promised Kristen that we won't let Charlie shoot anyone. Or do anything illegal. So you'll have to do it, Hunter – I mean, if we have to shoot someone.'

'That's OK,' I say. 'Did Dao tell you about our failure today, Kristen?'

From this point there is only one topic of conversation. Charlie and Kristen are not familiar with the place Stuart went to, but as Kristen says, 'If he wanted an innocent two-hour walk in the bush he would have gone to the Regional Park, not miles over to the side where nobody goes. Or maybe bird watchers do, and hunters.'

She has only learned about this tonight, but she pulls facts and ideas together and comes up with conclusions and theories. I bet she is good at her job; she is a paralegal in a big law firm where a highly organised mind would be essential.

'I do hope she is alive and kept up there in some hide-out, but there would be few places more suitable to hide a body relatively close to the city. I checked it on the Internet – it seems to be old established native bush – probably full of overgrown gullies and streams, fallen trees. And that part where the day trippers never go would be a safe place for him to do whatever he did without being disturbed. Dao said the tracks are good, so maybe even a moderately fit person could drag or carry someone up a track or conceal a body. If he drove up there at dusk and checked that nobody else was parked along that dead-end road – well, it would give him hours to do it and nobody around to see him.'

'Exactly,' I say, 'but if he did that, why would he return today? Unless he left her body in a temporary place and went back to conceal it better?'

I don't want to voice the thought that maybe he is depraved enough to go back to gloat over her dead body – or worse. There is no need to plant that thought in Dao's mind.

Dao says, 'Maybe he had her body in the house and loaded it on the truck this morning? There was that tarpaulin on the back, big enough to wrap a body in. No, he didn't have enough time to disappear so fast, not if he was carrying a body. We can't have been more than ten minutes behind him. And anyway, as Kristen said, why would he do it in daylight in a weekend, which is much riskier? I think he has her in a cabin somewhere up there.'

Nobody debates the point; we know that for Dao it is important to continue to believe that Hope is still alive.

Charlie and Kristen are very interested in Tama and, like us, they hope he will not end up in trouble. Kristen looks thoughtful when we tell her what we think it is safe to tell them.

'I suppose it depends on what you find out, or what the police find out, at a later date.' 'Things change according to the circumstances. If you find Hope, dead or alive, and can prove that Stuart took her, then Tama is a heroic whistleblower who unmasked a criminal and eliminated corruption within a government organization, whichever one it turns out to be. And if you fail, if Hope is not found and nothing sticks to Stuart, then Tama loses his job and might be prosecuted for leaking confidential information. And Stuart could sue him for defamation.'

A sobering summing up. We sit in silence for a moment. Then Kristen raises her glass in a salute. 'Here's to Tama – and to integrity and courage. And by the way, Hunter, this wine is fabulous. Thank you.'

At eleven we wake Scruff and leave. I have never hugged Kristen before, but today I do. 'Thank you. It's very generous of you to let us borrow Charlie again.'

She gently liberates herself and says in her understated way, 'You're such old mates. Like family, really. I know she wants to help you. And nobody else is doing anything practical about that poor woman.'

Once we're in the car I get a chance to ask Dao when Kristen read Hope's diary stories. 'You didn't bring the print version – how did you do it?'

'I was prepared,' says Dao. 'I emailed them to myself from my laptop. So after I told her the story, I forwarded them to her from my phone. We printed them out on the printer in their study. Then I tried on clothes while she read them– and there were lots more clothes than those in the bag, you know, heaps more. She takes them home on some kind of loan and if they aren't right, she returns them. I didn't even know you could do that. Are you angry I told her?'

'God, no. I'm just amazed. I never suspected you were going to do this.'

'I thought I might get a chance to talk to her. You know how Charlie said I might have to talk to Kristen, because she didn't dare to do it herself. I know she was joking, but I thought it might work. It was so lucky she took me to the bedroom to try on clothes – perfect. She totally understands that we might need Charlie.'

She sits quiet and thoughtful for a moment before she continues.

'And you know what? I don't think she really cares that Charlie might get arrested for doing something illegal. I think she's just worried that Charlie will get hurt.'

We say no more about it. I make a mental note to order a case of that red wine to be sent to Kristen.

19

The rain starts as we drive on to the Harbour Bridge; within minutes it is a downpour of tropical proportions. The windscreen is a blur of running water, cleared for only a fraction of a second by each sweep of the wiper blades. The outside security light is on at our house and a man is standing at our front door, looking in the window beside the door. He turns and starts across the street towards a car parked on the other side, head down and shoulders hunched. We are still a couple of houses away and I make a quick decision.

'Stay in the car!' I say to Dao, pull in to the side and brake hard. I turn the lights off, jump out and run towards the man, who is nearly at his car. He reaches for the door handle and I knock his hand away. 'Hang on – I want to talk to you!'

His jacket is sodden, and the hood hangs down to his eyebrows, heavy with water. He has a large moustache. He launches himself at me, his right shoulder hits me in the chest, and his left fist comes up in a fast punch. I turn my head to avoid it, but it connects with my cheekbone, hard. I grab his wrist as he pulls his fist back for another hit and twist his lower arm out sideways and back. He has two choices, relax his arm or have his elbow broken. But it doesn't work out; his right hand comes up with a knife. I manage to get a grip on that wrist too, but now we are locked. Neither of us has a hand free. The only thing that comes to me, struggling with him in the dark with water running into my eyes, is to throw him to the ground. I have the advantage of height and weight. I hook my foot around his ankle and use my weight. We fall heavily, him underneath and me across his chest. He grunts and tries to twist sideways under me. The knife is still in his right hand, centimetres from my shoulder. If he can free his arm, he will stab me.

A pair of small white trainers appear in a puddle just to the side of the guy's head and Dao says, 'I have the Glock. Do you want me to shoot him? I could shoot him in the leg, so he can't run away.'

I can barely hear her voice through the noise of rain and wind. 'Don't shoot him! Just keep the gun on him – and back off a bit.'

I don't want him to grab her ankle. I feel him slacken under my chest. He turns his head and looks in Dao's direction and then up at me. The moustache is splayed out like a small wet animal across his face.

'You are going to let go of the knife,' I say and increase the pressure of my elbow on his upper arm. 'Just drop it. And then we are going to get up and go inside and talk.'

He lets the knife fall to the ground and I let go of one of his wrists and get up on one knee beside him. The rain is bouncing off the asphalt, we are all wet to the skin.

'Keep the gun on him,' I say to Dao. 'Did you rack the slide?'

She has watched dozens of gun videos on YouTube since the armed guy invaded the house a couple of years ago, but I haven't yet taught her to use the Glock. She might not know what 'rack the slide' means, but hopefully she won't say so. The gun is always under the front seat of the car, with the magazine in, but not with a round in the chamber.

'Of course.' She sounds slightly impatient. 'I did that as soon as I picked it up. Shall I shoot him now?'

'No, thanks. Just come around to the other side and hand me the gun.'

Once I have it in my hand I get to my feet. 'You can get up now. Don't make any sudden moves or *I* might shoot you.'

He gets to his feet and I step back. 'Now turn around.' I shift the Glock to my left hand and pull his right arm right up behind his back, fast and as far as it will go. He grunts and leans slightly forward to lessen the pressure and I increase it to make sure he knows he is helpless.

'Dao, please go back to the car and lock it. And bring the garage remote.'

We walk across the street and Dao deactivates the alarm system and opens the garage door.

I push the man ahead of me into the passage and up the stairs to the first floor. Dao is right behind me. I can feel her apprehension like a current around us.

'Can you find those cable ties again?'

It's a repeat performance of the invasion long ago, when Dao managed to find the bag of cable ties in the kitchen drawer while I had our clumsy invader at the point of a Remington shotgun.

I march our guest to a dining chair, tell him to sit down and hand the gun to Dao while I fasten one of his legs to the table leg and one to the chair. As I rise, I reach over and pull the hood from his head and look at Dao. She nods;

yes, this is John. Water is pooling on the floor as it runs off our clothes. Dao is pale and shivering.

'Go upstairs and get into something dry.' I smile at her tight little face. 'And bring a towel or two. I think we're going to be here for a while.'

She might be heat-immune, as she calls it, but she gets cold very easily. We wait in silence until Dao returns in dry clothes. She puts the towels and one of my sweatshirts on the table, and I toss a towel across to John.

'Come and sit over here, Dao.'

I know she does not want to; she would rather be somewhere he cannot look at her. She loathes and fears this man. Not only did he pose a threat to her when she was a little girl, but she is also the only eyewitness who saw him deliver drug shipments to the island. She still believes he wants her eliminated, just as Bramville and the Boss did.

John wipes the towel roughly across his face and sneers at her. 'Haven't you turned into a pretty little thing, Slave. And you've got a real name, too. Aren't you lucky?'

She says nothing. I rise slightly, lean across the table and punch him hard just where he hit me. His head bounces back and his chair nearly tips over. A bright red patch outlined in white blossoms on his cheekbone; it will be a deep bruise. My knuckles ache, but I'm not going to rub them in front of him.

'If you prefer, I can shoot you. Somewhere painful.'

He is hard to shake. He looks straight at me; his eyes water in pain, but he manages to smile. 'Let's make a deal – a business deal. I know you took the barrel and you haven't a clue how to sell the stuff. I have the contacts and I can get good money for it. I sell it and we split the money.'

'If you want to make a deal, why did you attack me outside?'

'When you came at me like that I thought you were someone else. There's a lot of competition in my business.'

This is a chance to find out more. I need to make a fast decision about my approach. To gain some time and to annoy him, I turn to Dao instead of replying. 'He's pretty open with his comments. Wish I had it on record.'

She returns my look, deadpan and unblinking. 'He doesn't care.'

'Could you bring two cups of coffee, Dao? I think we need something warm. And those chocolate biscuits we bought the other day.

I hope she understands the unspoken message, but I can't make it any clearer. Making coffee gives her an opportunity to turn her phone to record. I want John to talk freely, to give the police as much detail as possible. We sit in silence until Dao comes back. She puts a tray with two mugs of coffee and a packet of biscuits beside me, walks down the length of the room and returns with her laptop. She puts her phone on the table, pulls out the chair beside me and sits down without looking at me or John.

I put one of the mugs beside her and take the other one myself, put the biscuit packet between us. She smiles briefly at me and her fingers move quietly over the keyboard. I have no idea what she is setting up, but she might need time. I pull my wet shirt over my head, rub my hair with the towel and put on the dry sweatshirt.

Dao raises her mug. 'What are you going to do with him?'

John smirks at her. 'You've moved up from slave to servant, eh? Not bad for a little slant-eye girl.'

I lean over the table again and backhand him hard

across the other side of the face before he gets a hand up to block me. 'Enough!'

'Please let me shoot him!' Dao sounds serious and the way she looks at me is hard to interpret. 'If anyone is going to shoot him it should be me. Please!'

His eyes swivel from Dao's face to mine and back again; there is a hint of fear. He is unsure of the situation now. Will I let Dao shoot him? He knows she has been afraid of him since she was a little girl; she would cringe when he touched her when Bramville wasn't looking. Having him a bit on edge now feels good.

'You can't shoot him here, Dao. Too many complications. I'll deal with him.'

John looks uncertain; are we serious? He knows Dao hates him and he can tell I want to punish him.

I slip my right hand under the table and grasp Dao's knee. 'Remember the mess it made when you killed the Boss in that factory. At least we didn't have to clean up the blood afterwards.'

A little reminder for him that she killed someone once. He has no way of knowing if she really intended the Boss to die; neither do I. I hope she will forgive me for reminding her of it. She doesn't like it being mentioned, but the look on John's face should make up for it.

'There's no need to be so fucking aggressive,' he says, trying to sound as if it is just a normal everyday discussion. 'I only defended myself when I thought you were going to attack me.'

'You've used up your chances,' I say coldly. 'Any more nastiness towards Dao and it's over. Now let's talk business.'

'For fuck's sake, don't be so touchy.' His right eyelid has developed a little tic. 'I've looked into your background a bit and I bet you don't know shit about how to sell those drugs.'

His smirk is meant to show how confident he is. 'You need to have connections to deal with stuff like this – and I do.'

He doesn't know that the police have video of the barrel on the back of Bramville's truck after he left the island, that I am no longer a suspect. This is a golden opportunity. Calling the cops was my first thought when Dao confirmed who he is, but I want more. Maybe they can get him not only on his past, but also on what he's willing to do now. Find out who he is planning to sell to – even better.

'I'm not doing some blind deal. I'm not a fool. You'd screw me if you could. I've got to know who it is you are selling to and I want half the money up front. That barrel stays in storage until I have my share.'

'No way!' His voice is full of scorn. 'It doesn't work like that. They've got to see the merchandise and check it out before they'll even discuss the price. All the gangs are the same – you can't change the rules.'

I pretend to think about this for a moment. It is what I thought he would say, but I want to make sure he comes back to me. If he sets up a deal with one of the gangs and they send some heavy type to force me to hand over the barrel, we could face mayhem. Saying I was lying about having the barrel would never work in that situation. I must create a reason for John to come back and get the police involved.

Suddenly Dao jumps to her feet. 'Oh no, we left Scruff in the car! Just wait a minute, I'll run down and get him.'

John makes as if to speak, but I hold my hand up. 'We'll wait till Dao gets back.'

We sit there in silence, facing each other across the

table, a slightly bizarre scene. I drink my coffee and eat a biscuit. John combs through his wet moustache with his fingers. It still looks like a flattened rat.

A few minutes later Dao returns with Scruff. She gives me a look I can't interpret: amused or secretive? It is sometimes hard to read her face. Something has changed her mood from fearful to assertive.

I pick up where we left off. 'I don't care what your buyers always do or what the hell their rules are. You need the money more than I do, so you'd better make it work.'

I want him to think I am prepared to drop the whole thing, that it's not important to me. 'And there's no way I'm taking you or anyone else to where the barrel is now.'

He shakes his head and starts to say something, but I interrupt him.

'Now listen to what I say. I've kept the barrel for nearly two years. As I said, call me in a couple of days. I'll have a sample for you to take to your buyers and video of the barrel and the packages. If you can't work with that, we'll forget the whole thing. I'll just leave the damn thing where it is.'

It is nearly one o'clock in the morning when I release him. He has my phone number and he's going to 'consider my suggestion' and be in touch. I walk him down the stairs to the front door and as he steps over the doorstep, I say casually, 'And just so you know, I would never use my own car to go to the place where the barrel is. You can forget about trying to put another of those tracking devices on it.'

He makes no response, just walks towards his car. It is still raining, but gently now.

Dao is in the kitchen with a tub of ice cream on the counter. 'I'm hungry. It's hours since we had dinner.'

'OK, give me some too. Now tell me what you've been

up to. That look when you came back upstairs meant something. And we must call the cops.'

'Let's call Benson,' she says, and smiles happily at the thought of waking the poor guy in the middle of the night. 'He's so going to like this – I can't wait to hear what he says. He'll know who should be told. Saves us explaining the background to someone we never met.'

I eat ice cream and listen while she talks to him; it is becoming a habit.

'Hi Benson, it's me. Dao. Sorry to wake you up. We've just had a visit from John.'

I hear his voice raised in surprise at the other end. Dao grins at me. 'I know! Isn't it great? But we have to talk to you really soon, because we've made a deal with him – or he thinks we've made a deal. And we have an idea.'

A pause while she listens; an impatient frown developing.

'Of course, he's undamaged! Benson, why do you always think Hunter beats everyone up? All he did was hit him a couple of times, but John hit him first – *and* he had a knife.'

She listens for quite a while, absent-mindedly spooning ice cream into her mouth. 'OK, we will. See you soon.'

She glances at her empty bowl, as if she wonders who ate the ice cream. 'I need some more.'

'Later,' I say. 'First tell me what you were doing. Did you record him?'

'Yes, both on my phone and on the laptop. And when I pretended to fiddle with my phone right at the end, I got a little bit of video of him too, when he was arguing with you – he didn't even notice.'

'And Benson?'

'He's on his way. He's going to park down the street

207

and walk, in case someone's watching. He's really excited. Well, as excited as he ever gets.'

While we wait for Benson I go upstairs and change into dry jeans and socks. By the time he arrives we are eating again; it's turning into a long night. We offer him a sandwich, but he says he can't face food in the middle of the night and opts for a cup of coffee.

We sit at the end of the room with the curtains drawn across the glass wall to the balcony. I am not taking any chances.

'I checked the parked cars when I came, but they're all empty. That's going to be one hell of a bruise, Hunter. Did he punch you or did he hit you with something?'

'John punched him, but Hunter still got him,' says Dao.

Benson gets out his phone and takes a photo of my face. 'Just another thing we can get him on. An assault charge is always good to add to the mix.'

'And we've got the knife he had,' Dao says. 'I must give it to you when you go. My fingerprints are on the blade, but nowhere else.'

'How . . . Oh, I know.' I smile in Benson's direction. 'She said she was going to get Scruff out of the car, but she really wanted the get the knife. Very smart!'

'No, I *really* went to put that third tracker on his car. You know, the one we got for free. But I couldn't find it in the garage. I was going to get Scruff too, of course. But then I remembered how you made him drop the knife and I looked – and there it was, in the middle of the street, so I took it. I thought he might pick it up when he left.'

'Where did you put it?'

'On the floor downstairs, just by the connecting door to the garage. I only touched the very tip of the blade, in case of fingerprints.'

'You're a star, Dao, no doubt about it.'

Benson gives me a sharp look, alerted by the mention of three trackers. 'May I ask why you bought trackers? Is there something I should know?'

'No,' I tell him. 'There is nothing you should know. Nothing that's relevant to this. Just let it go for now.'

He stares at me for a few moments and maybe he can read my face. If he starts pushing the issue, I could stall on giving him information; or that's what he thinks. I tell him why I let John go and made sure he would come back. Benson nods that he understands why I did it, but I can see he would rather I had just called 111 straight away.

'I need to get the drug guys involved. I told them earlier about someone hanging around your house and following you, and they know who we think it was. They've got the video from your CCTV system. They'll be delighted to have it confirmed. It's up to them how they proceed, but I guess they'll go all out to locate him. They've been waiting for this for nearly two years.'

'Maybe they can locate his boat? If he sailed it back from Tonga or wherever he went, he must have moored it somewhere.'

'Yeah, but it's one thirty-foot boat among hundreds up and down the coast. He's probably repainted it to make it look different. It could be in some little bay way up in Northland. They've been doing regular checks on his old girlfriend's place and his mum's, but they'll step it up now.'

Dao plays the recording of our conversation with John and the ten- second video.

'Nice!' says Benson. 'He's digging a fine hole for himself. Could you send me those recordings please?'

She promises to email them and tells him to drink his coffee, before it gets cold.

We set the alarms for the ground floor and go upstairs

to bed as soon as Benson leaves. Inwardly I sigh. Another trial coming up with Dao as the only eyewitness; another period of media fame and endless repeats of her story. Maybe more fans trying to get to know her. On the plus side there is a solid bonus: Dao will finally feel safe. Once John is convicted, she will be out of danger; the threat she posed will be defunct. I will be able to relax my vigilance; I might even give the Glock back to Charlie.

Dao is on a high for some reason and jumps into bed as if it isn't half-past three in the morning. She ought to be exhausted.

'Aren't you tired? Where did this sudden burst of energy come from? You make me feel old.'

'Don't know,' she says and burrows under the blanket to get closer. 'I feel good.'

She rearranges my arm, so she can tuck up the way she likes to. 'You know what?'

I close my eyes. 'No, I have no idea.'

'I'm not scared of him now. I just hate him. In a quiet sort of way - you know? He's just a nasty man and when you hit him, he got a bruise and he was scared when I pointed the gun at him. And he really thought you might let me shoot him. That was great. Do you see what I mean?'

And I do. She has feared him ever since she escaped from the island. Bramville threatened to sell her to John and she believed him. And she knew without a doubt that he would sexually abuse her and kill her when he longer wanted her. She confidently expects them to get John. I hope she is right.

I tighten my arm around her and fall asleep.

20

We wake up exhausted on Sunday morning, when Scruff asks to be let out. The first thing we do is pack another picnic lunch.

'We have to do it before we have breakfast,' says Dao with her head in the fridge. 'Before he takes off. Imagine spending the whole day walking around in the bush with nothing to eat!'

Her phone signals an incoming message and she dances around the kitchen. 'They got him! They got him! It's from Benson. The drug squad went to his mum's house and there he was. Yay!'

Stuart moves just as we are starting breakfast. Abandoning porridge bowls and cups of coffee we grab the lunch bag and leave.

Just like yesterday he drives south on the motorway and turns off at the Papakura exit. The frustration of yesterday's failed mission is still with me. This time we must do better.

'If only we could follow him a bit closer this time, see which track he takes at that first fork.'

Dao shakes her head. 'It wouldn't work. We would

have to be right behind him and he'd hear us.'

I know she is right, but yesterday's wasted effort rankles. We park the car in the same spot, a couple of hundred metres along the road from Stuart's truck. I take the Glock from under the front seat, feel around for the holster and thread my belt though it while we walk down the road.

By late morning we have been up and down several tracks and found nothing. The rain stopped before we woke up this morning and it's a nice day for a walk in the bush. The tracks are muddy in places, but nothing like as bad as I expected. I thought we might find footprints in some muddy spot, but there are enough dry portions to walk on. We see nothing to tell us if Stuart has walked up the track since the rainfall of last night. We find another convenient, but damp, log to sit on and have an early picnic lunch. If Stuart comes past and sees us, I hope he will assume we are harmless citizens minding our own business.

'Is there any more juice?' I ask, and Dao is reaching for the carton when we hear Scruff barking from a distance. I call to him and he barks twice, then nothing. Neither of us has realised that he is no longer messing around among the trees. A few minutes later I call again, but he just barks and stays where he is.

'Something's up. Let's go and look.'

I don't mention that this is exactly what he did when he found Dao. He barked twice in response every time I called him, but he stayed beside her, refused to move until I got there. We pack up our lunch and return to the track. When I call Scruff again, we get a bearing and continue, calling him at intervals. Suddenly his bark is very close. A nearly overgrown path branches off to the side, practically unnoticeable in the dense bush.

A couple of hundred metres in is an open space surrounded by manuka, with taller trees further back. There is a circle of ashes in the centre and on the far side of the open space sits Scruff in his guard position, straight up and watchful with his front paws together. Beside him lies a body. We walk slowly across the open space. Scruff stays where he is and watches us approach.

Hope lies on her back, dressed only in a dark blue T-shirt. One arm is flung out to the side, the other rests across her middle. Her knees are bent and folded to one side and her eyes are closed. I saw enough dead bodies in Afghanistan to know that she has probably been dead for forty-eight hours. Small leaves and dark seeds from the manuka trees are scattered over her grey skin; the T-shirt is wet.

Someone has scored lines on her body with something scalpel-sharp. Straight lines, like a drawing of a stick man. They start on her hands and feet, run along her limbs, disappear under the T-shirt. Two lines appear at the neckline and run up the sides of her neck and disappear into her hair. Another line around her face, close to the hairline and under the jaw.

I crouch beside her and peer into her half-curled left hand without touching her. There are cuts, deep cuts, on the inside of her fingers and one across her palm. At some stage she fought him and tried to grab the knife or scalpel or whatever he used. Then I notice the narrow bracelet indentations around her wrists and ankles. The cut-lines start on the back of her hands, stop at the indentation on her wrists and then continue. He tied her to something with cord or cable ties, I think. I stand up and contemplate her position. He must have kept her somewhere not too far away. Did he put her body here, or did she escape and then collapse?

The sight is disturbing. What has been done to her amounts to torture of a sickening kind. There is no doubt he cut these lines while she was alive. Some are older than others; it has been done in stages, perhaps one limb at a time. I see smears where he wiped away the blood from the most recent cut down her right shin. Dao stands silent and pale beside me, unable to take her eyes off Hope's body. I reach out and take her hand.

Her fingers tighten around mine and her voice is very quiet. 'We must get someone here.'

I get my phone out; no signal. 'Let's go back to the big track. We'll call the police as soon as we get reception.'

'I don't want her to be alone,' says Dao. 'We can't leave her alone, Hunter. We can't!'

'We have to. Nobody knows where we are and I'm not leaving you here or letting you go alone.'

We walk away, and Scruff follows when we call him. Behind us Hope's body lies in the shade of the trees, her skin grey and cold.

Back on the bigger track I tie my handkerchief around a branch. The little path is nearly invisible and might be hard to spot again. Quarter of an hour later we are in cell-phone range. Dao checks the tracking app and confirms that Stuart's truck is still parked where we last saw it. I dial 111 and Dao taps my arm. 'I'll just go and have a pee.'

I am distracted by the need to listen to instructions about which emergency service I need and I don't even notice on which side of the track she and Scruff go off.

The operator wants to know my name and address and phone number. She asks for directions to the place where we found Hope's body. I say it will be easier to show the emergency services how to find it when they arrive, or perhaps they can get the GPS location from my phone. The operator insists on following protocol, so I enter into a detailed description of the tracks and the various branch points. Finally, she has enough information. She reads back what I have told her and asks us to wait on the road by the truck. I tell her the truck belongs to someone else, but I don't mention Stuart's name or that we know who it belongs to. I tell her that my car is parked further along.

I end the call and my focus swings back to where I am standing. Dao has not returned.

At first I don't feel particularly concerned. I wait another couple of minutes and call her name, then I call Scruff; nothing. Now I am worried. I check my phone and see that I was talking to the emergency operator for eight minutes and I have stood here calling and listening for a few more. Something has happened. She could have got lost and gone off in the wrong direction; the alternative option fills me with dread. Whichever direction I take I might head away from, instead of towards her. Making a random choice is actually harder than trying to make a reasoned one. But I must start somewhere; I go downhill, back towards the road, calling out every now and then.

Nearly an hour later, after going back and forth on branching tracks, I get a call from the police. 'We've found the truck and your car parked a bit further on. Where are you?'

I explain about a girl and a dog having wandered off and describe how to get to where my handkerchief marks the little path to the clearing where Hope lies.

'Can we go through that again, please?' says the cop. 'Head up the track in front of the truck to where it forks, take the right-hand track? And then?'

We go through it again. I can do it now without thinking – it's engraved on my brain.

'My partner's taking notes as I repeat things,' he says at the end. 'Now don't you go and get lost too. Can you call us as soon as you find the girl and the dog? You'll have my number in your call log.'

I think through my options. The cops will be on the other track, so whichever one Dao comes along either they or I should meet her or hear her. I will continue up the track heading away from the road, on an angle of forty-five degrees from the track where she went into the bush. I hope she is somewhere in the V-shaped area between.

The wind has come up and occasional clouds move past the sun, the smell of damp earth ever-present in the shade. I am about to stop and call her name again, when I notice the trees thinning in front of me. I am at one end of an oblong clearing, about twice the size of the one where Hope's body lies. The track goes lengthwise through the open area. At the far side is a fence, an incongruous wooden fence running alongside ten metres of track in the middle of the wilderness.

Why would somebody build a fence along one side of a small expanse of mud? Into my mind springs the image of old men playing *boules* on hard-packed bare ground under chestnut trees in France. I shake my head and jog on, occasionally whistling for Scruff, hoping he will hear me and bark in response.

And then I hear her, a distant scream far behind me. I run back along the path; my mind constructs terrifying images of violence and danger. This was not a call to locate me, it was a scream of pain or fear. I pause a couple of times, hold my breath, listen intently. But there is nothing more, no sound apart from the wind ruffling the tree canopy above me and the pounding of my pulse in my ears. I pull the Glock out of the holster and run on with it in my hand, ready for a confrontation.

I emerge into the open area with the wooden fence and come to an abrupt halt. Stuart stands just where the fence starts at my end of the clearing with Dao beside him. Her hands are tied behind her and a black hood covers her head. He stares at me. His mouth opens, but he says nothing, just stands there. His face is red, and he is panting so hard it sounds like grunting. One of his hands is behind her back and he has a small black bag hitched over his shoulder. I need to understand more before I act. Is there a weapon in the hand I cannot see? His total focus is on the Glock; he has not moved since I erupted out of the bush. Across the couple of metres between us I see panic in his eyes.

A taut line of fear down the back of my throat; I know this sensation well. It sharpens your senses, makes it possible to see every detail, to instantly assess a situation. That intense focus can be the difference between life and death. Nothing must go wrong now.

'I'm here, Dao. Don't do *anything*.'

From inside the black hood, which looks like a jacket or a jersey, she says, 'Hunter!' with huge relief in her voice, but I know nothing is certain. The look of exhausted desperation on Stuart's face tells me there is no point in second-guessing what he might do. When there is no way out, cornered men do destructive and useless things.

'OK, mate, let her go now,' I say, trying to sound calm. 'Just let her walk towards me and nothing will happen to you.'

Dao stands completely still. Stuart is having a real problem with his breathing; sweat runs freely down his face and neck. I wonder if he is going to have a heart attack.

Just to one side and behind him a small movement catches my eye. Bubbles break the surface of the expanse of clay. My first thought is that I am mistaken, it can't have happened. I focus on it for a second and see slow ripples spreading. This is not an area of bare, hard ground; it is a weird pond of some kind with a thick layer of brown scum completely covering its surface. I have never seen anything like it.

Dao says, 'He has a knife.'

It is just the kind of composed and clever thing I have come to expect from her. The knife must be in the hand I cannot see.

Stuart drags her sideways and backs up a couple of steps. They are now on the other side of the fence, the side where the pond is. I can't see how he holds her. He could be holding on to whatever binds her hands together or he might have tied her to himself. And where is the knife? Is he holding it at her back, ready to stab her or is it in his pocket, or in the bag? Despite the scum layer being level with the ground, I think I can make out the edges of the pond. It is slightly ovoid, about the same size as an average bedroom. If he takes another couple of steps sideways, they will go into the water. If her hands are tied and I can't get to her fast enough she will drown. Does he know there is water there, concealed by the scum on top? Is he planning some desperate action if I threaten him? His eyes are still fixed on me. He knows he is trapped and whatever he does, this will end badly. I must act fast. To distract him I throw the Glock to one side; it slides along the track. His eyes swivel to follow it – and that's my chance.

I close the gap between us in a couple of long strides. He reacts by dragging Dao towards the edge of the pond. She is resisting and acting as a brake; his hand stays behind her back. She has no idea of the danger just beside them; any second now she might make a move and imperil them both. He takes another step to the side and I know his right foot is going to go into the pond.

There is no way of guessing if it is shallow or deep. His foot goes through the layer of scum and he tilts, unbalanced by the unexpected absence of firm ground. I leap forward and grab Dao's upper arm. 'I've got you Dao.'

Stuart's centre of gravity has shifted too far – the only thing that keeps him from falling in is his hold on Dao's hands behind her and the fact that I have grabbed her from the other side. I push Dao, use her as a battering ram and push once, sudden and hard, without letting go. He tilts further out. I lift her up by her arm and it takes him by surprise; he loses his grip and falls in. I step back and pull Dao away from the edge and rip the black covering from her head.

What happens next is the stuff of nightmares. Stuart's arms flail, his mouth is wide open, big slow bubbles rise to the surface around him and the stench from hell comes at us in a big wave. The scum washes over his head, into his mouth and eyes. Without making a sound he disappears.

We are choking and coughing, our eyes are watering. We stumble away, half bent over, coughing and gagging with the taste of the stench etching our throats. I have never smelled anything like it: rotting flesh and methane. I wipe tears from my eyes and turn around. The bubbles have stopped and the thick layer of scum slides slowly across and fills the gap caused by the disturbance. The ground around the edges of the pond is damp now, darker, but it will dry and there will be nothing to show that anything happened.

'Come away from here,' I say to Dao and pull her coughing to the other side of the fence. 'Are you hurt?'

'Not really,' she says shakily. One of her wrists has a bit of rope around it. She coughs again and tries to undo the knot and I reach out to do it for her. That's when I notice the cut; a long straight line, precision cut from her wrist to her elbow.

Before I can comment she says, 'When you lifted me like that and pulled – ouch, that hurt – but it made the rope break. I could feel it go.'

I replay the scene in my head and understand that disaster was a fraction of a second away. The rope breaking could have upset the precarious balance between Stuart's weight pulling on her from one side and me holding on from the other side. If I had lost my grip on her upper arm she would have gone in with Stuart. A cold shiver runs down my spine; I could have killed her.

'I bet I'll be bruised. Your fingers are so hard!' She bends over and coughs violently.

I take her hand and lead her further away. 'Let's get away from this smell. I'm sorry I hurt you, but I had to do something fast. I knew there was water there, just beside him.'

'What is that filth?'

We turn and look back at the pond and see something pushing against the scum layer, not quite breaking through.

'God, it isn't him, is it? Trying to get out?' Dao takes a step back.

I move a bit closer and she follows slowly. We stare across the fence as the scum moves aside a bit more; the skull of a large animal is partially visible. A few large bubbles are still coming up from whatever lies below, and the smell is overwhelming.

'It's awful. Every time something breaks that layer, the stench comes up.'

The skull sinks, and all is still again. I pick up the Glock and as we move further away Dao says, in a conversational tone of voice, as if we are discussing the weather, 'Do you think you could have pulled him out? I mean, if the smell hadn't been so bad and we hadn't been choking.'

I shake my head. 'No. Do you think I should have tried?'

'Oh no, I just wondered. But we can't tell anyone about this, not ever.'

She calmly accepts the situation and not for the first time I wonder what shaped her character. Was it her decade alone with a brutal man with only herself to rely on, or would she have been as ruthlessly pragmatic whatever her upbringing?

'And another thing,' she says and raises her cut arm. 'We have to decide if we are going to tell anyone he found me – and cut me. And if we do tell the police about it, then we must lie about how I got away from him. I'd much rather say nothing at all.'

'You're right. We can't tell anyone - it would make things too complicated. And if someone notices in the future, we can say you got caught in a barbed-wire fence.'

'I'll say Scruff ran away and I went to look for him while you were on the phone and then I got lost. Which is the truth, actually.'

I can't believe it. Scruff! I never even thought of him all this time.

'Where is he? Did he run away when Stuart got hold of you?'

'Don't be silly! He would never run away if someone was threatening me. I haven't told you what happened yet. He took off after some little animal while I was peeing. I don't know what it was, but he got super excited and chased after it. I called and called, but he didn't come – I got really worried he'd be lost and not find his way back. So I went after him. I did what you told me before. I turned around now and then and took note of landmarks, so I'd be able to find my way back, but I got lost anyway.'

'And you found Scruff?'

'I did, but it took quite a long time. But then, when I did find him, I had no idea where we were.'

'How long did you spend trying to find him?'

'Half an hour perhaps, maybe an hour? I didn't think of the time till after I found him. We started walking back in the direction I had come from, or so I thought, but I found a container – you know, one of those shipping things. I hadn't seen it while I was chasing Scruff, so I knew I was lost. It's in the forest and it's dark brown – I didn't even notice it till I was right beside it. It seemed really strange. I mean, how did it get there? Who would put one of those things there – no path or anything. The door at the end was open and I was standing there looking at it, when he came up behind me and threw something over my head and pulled it down hard. He had me by one arm, really tight and he said he had a knife. Scruff went crazy. It was very confusing, very noisy. I think Scruff was biting Stuart – he was growling, and Stuart was screaming and swearing. I couldn't see anything, but I think he kicked Scruff because he yelped, and that big door clanged shut. And then he dragged me away.'

'We'll say you lost Scruff and eventually found first him and then me. Nothing else at all. Don't give them any details if they ask. Just say you were lost, and it seemed to take ages. And we must hide that cut. There are no barbed-wire fences here.'

I pull my sweatshirt off and hand it to her. 'I know this is huge, but we'll say you felt cold.'

'And I've got my hoodie in the car. Lucky that you had a T-shirt underneath. Now we must find the container and let Scruff out.'

I lift her arm to look at the cut. It was done with something very sharp, but it's not deep. Blood has run along and across her arm before drying. He started another stick-man outline on Dao, like the one he cut on Hope. What would he have done next?

My grip on her arm must have tightened; she looks at the wound and then at me. 'When he did this, I was so frightened. He wasn't normal, he was mad! What's it called when people are really horrible, in an unnatural kind of way?'

'Perversion?'

'Yes! That's it.' An expression of revulsion passes over her face, she shivers and leans against me.

'I'll tell you now and then I don't want to talk about it ever again. It makes me feel sick. He pushed me down and made me lie on my front and he said, "Put your arms straight out from your body". He was kneeling beside me and he put one hand on the back of my head to stop me moving. He pressed down hard and I couldn't see anything – I still had that thing over my head. I didn't know what he was going to do. And then he started humming.'

I hold her closer. 'You don't have to talk about it right now.'

'But I want to,' she says. 'I need to tell you what happened, just this once. He was humming and stroking my arm up and down, very slowly, for ages. And then suddenly – the pain! I knew he had sliced me with the knife, like he did Hope. He stopped humming and he giggled! Hunter, he cut me with a knife and giggled like a little girl! But something happened, I don't know what it was, he just stopped. He might have heard something that I didn't hear because my head was wrapped up in that thing. He dragged me to my feet and hauled me around – I think he was trying to find something to tie my hands. I tried to pull off that cover he had put over my head with one hand, but he just kept hitting my hand away. He tied me up and we started walking. He said he had the knife at my back, and he could push it between my ribs any time, he knew how to do it.'

It doesn't make sense. Why would he walk away from the container when he could have locked her in with Scruff? Did he hear me shouting Dao's name and whistling for Scruff? Did that make him panic? And the humming and giggling – was he insane or high on something?

'Come on, Hunter! We have to find the container and get Scruff out,' she says impatiently. 'He'll be so scared. I bet it's dark in there.'

'Just wait here for a moment. I must get rid of a couple of things.'

What Stuart had put over Dao's head was a man's sweatshirt. I can't find a big rock and spend some time collecting several small ones. I lay them in the middle of the sweatshirt and hold it as far out as I can reach from the edge of the pond. Crouching I hold it by the sides and lay it on the scum and let go. Very, very slowly it sinks through and into the water. It takes longer than I expected for it to become saturated and for the weight of the stones to pull it down. As it disappears from view it tilts sideways. I hope the stones will fall off and leave the sweatshirt on the bottom of the pond with nothing to show it was weighed down.

I pick up the piece of rope from where I dropped it and hurl it into the middle of the pond. It will eventually become saturated and sink; a much less identifiable thing than the sweatshirt.

Dao has no idea where the container is. Her eyes were covered, so she has no landmarks from their trek from there to the scum pond. It takes us nearly an hour to find it. All Dao knows is that they walked steeply uphill on rough ground for only a couple of minutes and then on a track.

'Not for long,' she says. 'Maybe ten minutes – or fifteen? But we walked very fast.'

I don't mention my suspicion that maybe he knew about the pond and was going to throw her in. He must have been heading somewhere specific, else why did he take her away from the container site?

The dense vegetation with thick undergrowth shortens our line of sight to a few metres. The track is going uphill and soon we are on a ridgeline where the ground slopes steeply down on one side. I think of Dao's description of climbing a slope on rough ground. 'Could it be this slope? Let's stop here and have a good look.'

We scan the landscape, back and forth, and see nothing unusual. And then, just as I am about to suggest we carry on to the next high point, I see something you never see in the bush: a horizontal line as straight as a ruler. About half of the upper edge of the container is visible, but only as a line. The brown box shape is camouflaged by vegetation and blends into the background.

Slowly, carefully, we make our way down the slope. There is no sound from the container. Dao wants to run forward to get to Scruff, but I put my hand on her shoulder and hold her back.

'Let's be very careful. If this is where he kept Hope, he might have cameras set up and we can't risk being recorded. It might be best if the cops don't know we found it. Stay here.'

'I might already be on video,' says Dao. 'I never had time to look around properly before he grabbed me.'

I do a long slow circuit among the trees around the

container, looking at it from all angles. In my head various scenarios play like video clips: Dao and Stuart recorded, how to explain how she got away from him, how to avoid discussing the scum pond.

Photovoltaic panels, mounted on the roof, angled north. No sign of a camera on the outside. A plastic supermarket bag on the ground: I crouch to peer into it without touching it. One of those clear triangular sandwich boxes and what looks like the inside tube from a roll of toilet paper.

'I can't see a camera,' I call to Dao and she comes forward.

I take my T-shirt off and wrap it around my hand before I twist the handle up and out.

'Stand back so the door screens you.' I wait until she has moved to one side. 'It just occurred to me that there might be a camera inside aimed at the door. When Scruff comes out, don't run towards him, just stay where you are and let him find you and keep him there.'

I walk backward pulling the heavy steel door with me and Scruff explodes out, barking like mad, looks briefly at me and heads straight towards Dao. They move further in among the trees and Dao sits down on the ground. Scruff is ecstatic with joy, licking her face and squirming onto her lap. I walk to one side and then to the other, so I can study the interior from all angles before I go in. There is a plywood partition right up to the ceiling a short distance in, with a door in the centre. I can see no camera aimed at the outside. The interior door is half open.

I step into the container, open the inner door wider by using the back of my hand. I look as far in as I can without going right in. It is very dark in there. There is a small square hole in the metal wall halfway down the left side, but very little light comes in. All I can see is a camping lantern in the corner, what could be a bunched-up sleeping bag, and a bucket.

I take a step back and study the area I stand in. At the top corner of the partition is a small white box screwed to the plywood; beside it a cylinder shape in a dip cut out of the top of the plywood wall. A perfect position for a wide-angle camera's view of most of the inner room. The box will be a hard drive where the recordings are stored, maybe with a battery charged by the solar panels outside.

Draping the T-shirt over my head, I wind it around to leave only my eyes exposed and poke my head through the door. My eyes have adjusted to the low light. I check the camera first. The lens is recessed, so the T-shirt is unnecessary. There is a camp-stretcher along the wall and an apple on the floor beside it. One of those workshop lamps with a metal cage around it hangs from a hook on the plywood wall. The cord exits through the hole in the metal side. I turn my head and look into the corner to my right and my heart misses a beat. Slumped in the corner, legs out in a V-shape, with her chin resting on her chest, sits a woman with long dark hair. I keep my eyes on her, try to focus as hard as I can in the dim room. She is clearly dead, emaciated, but there is something odd about her. I can't quite decide what it is. I remain there for a couple of minutes and use the bad-light trick of looking just to one side of her to get a sharper focus. She is not only dead, she is air-dried, mummified. There appears to be a thick layer of dust all over her, but it could be mold. I move aside and lean in around the doorframe. With less of my body in the way, slightly more light filters in; she is fully dressed and wearing shoes. I can't make out what is in her lap, but she might be holding a bunch of very dead flowers.

When I step through the external door the daylight blinds me. I stand there blinking, feeling dazed. Dao sees me from where she and Scruff are playing catch around the trunk of a cabbage tree.

'Can I come and look? Is it safe?'

'In a moment.'

My expression sends a message, and she looks closely at me. 'What's in there? What's wrong?'

'Let me tell you before you go in.'

We sit down in the doorway, on the edge of the container floor. The sun has come out again and the feeling of warmth on my bare chest is comforting. 'He built a wall in there with a door in it. He probably held Hope in the inner room – there is an apple that looks quite fresh on the floor. There's a camera mounted in the top left corner of the wall – you can see it from the outer room. There is a dead woman in the inner room.'

Dao sucks in her breath and stares at me. 'Is she like Hope?'

Is she asking if the corpse looks like Hope or if she has been cut?

'I couldn't see. It's quite dark in there and I couldn't risk going in and being captured on video. You can have a look if you want to, but you can't step into the inner room. Just poke your head through far enough to look around.'

I stand close behind her with a hand on her shoulder as she leans forward and looks first one way and then the other. The grey misery of that bare space and the thought of Hope being held there is heart-breaking.

Dao is very still. She stands looking into the right-hand corner for a long time before she steps back.

'That man was a *monster*,' she says with great emphasis when we are outside in the bright light again. 'I'm glad he's in that horrible pond. I bet that is the other woman, the one Tama told us about.'

21

We debate our options as we clamber back up through the trees. Keeping Stuart's capture of Dao out of the story is relatively simple; all we need to do is never mention him. We can say that Dao chased Scruff, got lost and then eventually found me – or I found her. If nobody knows about Stuart grabbing her, we have eliminated any trace of direct contact. The container requires more thought.

'You can't let the police see the Glock,' says Dao suddenly. 'Now that I'm wearing your sweatshirt, they'll spot it straight away.'

She is right. I take my belt off and remove the holster, but now I have a new problem. I have nowhere to put it. I can't carry it in my pocket and my T-shirt is too tight to conceal a gun.

Dao reaches for it. 'Give it to me. This sweatshirt is like a tent, I could hide several guns.'

She sticks the gun and its holster inside the front of her T-shirt, tucks the shirt into her jeans an lets the sweatshirt drop.

'Like this – if it starts to slip, I'll put my arm across my middle – perhaps I'll hold my phone in my hand, so it looks natural. What do you think? Can you see it?'

It makes me laugh in the middle of this ghastly situation; my sweatshirt reaches nearly to her knees and you could fit three of her inside it. 'Not a sign – plenty of room to hide a lot more.'

We continue along the track. Scruff is being particularly well-behaved and keeps his position right beside Dao.

'Dao, we must tell them we found the container,' I say, after some thought. 'Not that you found it on your own or that Scruff got locked in – and certainly not that you ever laid eyes on Stuart. We'll just say we found each other, and on the way back we came across the container. I promised I would call them as soon as I found you. Let's keep it simple.'

'I know. If we don't tell them where it is, they might not find it – or not for ages. It's so well hidden down there. And the sooner they know what he did, the easier it will be for Tama.'

The policeman I spoke to earlier is relieved to hear that I have found Dao and Scruff. He asks us to go down to where Stuart's truck is parked and wait; someone will come and talk to us.

Near the bottom of the big track we meet three people heading up, two carrying cases and one with a dog. The humans nod, the dog glances briefly at Scruff and Dao takes a tight grip on his collar.

Down by the road there is a tidy line-up of four police cars and a van parked nose-in, filling the open off-road area behind Stuart's truck. A lone constable stands beside it. He asks who we are and has obviously been told to expect us. I say Dao got cold and is it OK if we walk down the road to my car to get her jacket, so I can have my sweatshirt back.

'I'd like you to stay here for now. The boss is coming down from the site to talk to you,' he says politely. 'I mean, Detective Inspector Sinclair.'

We wait for what seems like ages. I wish I had some water and wonder where we left the picnic bag. While the constable talks to someone on the police radio in one of the cars, I quietly ask Dao if she can remember where we last had it.

'You put it down when we found Hope. I only realised that we had left it much later, when I got thirsty while I was chasing Scruff.'

DI Sinclair turns out to be an efficient-looking woman with blonde hair in a bun and the most startling blue eyes I have ever seen. She has our picnic bag inside a clear plastic bag in one hand and Dao exclaims, 'Oh good, you found our bag!'

Sinclair holds it up and asks politely if Dao can tell her what is inside.

'Of course,' says Dao. 'One nearly empty carton of orange juice, two bottles of water, one left-over peanut butter sandwich and a dog's blue plastic drinking bowl. And a really squishy banana.'

'It's obviously yours,' says Sinclair. 'Here you are.'

We give her our full names and address details and I see the exact moment when she realises who we are. While we have stood here waiting a whole chain of consequences have played out in my head and I make a snap decision without warning Dao. We have to tell the police who Hope is, so family can be notified. The downstream effect will be closer scrutiny of us and speculation about our involvement. We will instantly be persons of interest, rather than just chance bystanders who found the body. Once Sinclair starts asking questions, protecting Tama will become very difficult.

'We know who she is,' I say. 'The dead woman.'

As I expected, Sinclair's face undergoes an instant, subtle change. Her expression remains neutrally pleasant, but there is a tightening around the eyes. 'Really? You surprise me.'

Dao looks at me and shows nothing of what she might be thinking. I recognise her blank look, the one she uses as camouflage when she can't get an instant grip on a situation. Behind the mask her mind will be performing rapid assessments and deciding how to react. It has stood her in good stead in various situations since I found her, most of them police or court related. Most people would think her mind is idling, when she wears that blank look. Dao's mind does not have a setting called 'idle'.

'Her name is Hope Barber. She disappeared from her apartment and her brother Noah reported it to the police. There were some very worrying circumstances. Her apartment door, for example, was left ajar and her bag and cell phone were left behind.'

I stop talking. Now it is her turn. Does she already know any of this and maybe more? After a short pause I am just about to tell her that the truck belongs to someone of interest, when she says, 'Would you mind waiting another couple of minutes? Sit down in one of the cars if you like.'

We remain where we are, and she walks a short distance to one side and gets her phone out. The call goes on for some time; she is pacing back and forth, listening more than she is talking. When she returns she looks frustrated.

'We have Noah Barber's contact details and we will inform him. But there are complications, and some aspects are confusing. I would like to know how you got involved.'

She walks us over to the two police cars parked side by side behind Stuart's truck. She perches sideways on the front seat of one car with the door open, so she can make notes, and we lean against the side of the car alongside it.

'Now then, what can you tell me?'

I have mapped out what to say and where I will draw the line to protect Tama. Noah is bound to tell the police about him, probably with toxic comments, but for now I will leave him out of it.

'A short time ago Noah Barber turned up on our doorstep and asked me to help find his sister. I can tell you the exact date later. I told him I couldn't help him and sent him away. He came back a couple of days later, in a terrible state. Hope was a journalist who wrote in-depth investigative articles, mostly relating to India, Pakistan and Afghanistan. She also wrote short stories that are like diary entries – just for herself. Noah found them on her laptop and on USB sticks when he was going through her things.'

Dao nods; she stands there, leaning against the car with her arm bent and her phone loosely held in her hand; no visible sign of recent trauma or stress, but inside her all sorts of emotions will be churning. I put my arm around her, and she gives me a little sideways smile.

'Those stories explain a lot,' she tells Sinclair. 'Hope was actually taken by someone not long ago, but she got away and she wrote a story about it, just before she disappeared the second time. But there is no story about that, of course. I have the most important of her stories attached to emails on my phone. I can send them to you. It's really important that you read them.'

Sinclair looks bemused. 'Didn't Noah give these stories to the police?'

'Of course not, *they* weren't interested,' says Dao with

great contempt. 'He went back several times and his lawyer did too. But they didn't want to know, just pretended they didn't think it was serious! Said they couldn't investigate and told him to go away. Useless!'

'But somehow you found out something that made you come here to look for her. Tell me about that.'

This is where it gets tricky. I have to think on my feet; I don't want to look as if I am struggling, but I must keep Tama out of it.

'The most important thing is the fact that she actually was abducted once and got away. The police attended an incident on the motorway, when some guys in a van reported that a wheelie bin with a woman inside had fallen off a truck – and that was Hope.'

Another subtle change on Sinclair's face. She knows this; probably the person she just talked to on the phone told her.

Dao points at the vehicle in front of us and says, with no particular emphasis, 'And that is the truck the wheelie bin fell from.'

The connection between what she had been told over the phone and the truck in front of us has not yet occurred to Sinclair. For the first time her face reveals exactly what she feels: first utter surprise, and then excitement. She gets up and calls across the roof of the car to the constable, 'Has anyone touched that truck?'

'No, not since I've been standing here,' he says. 'I was told to call someone down from the scene when the owner turns up.'

'Well, now it's evidence,' says Sinclair. 'Get some crime scene tape out and make sure nobody touches it until forensics can go over it. You will stand a little bit closer to the start of the track and if the owner comes down you call me. I'll be here to assist if necessary.'

She turns to us. 'Excuse me again, but I'd better radio in and get some more crime-scene people here and a vehicle recovery truck.'

We wait while she makes the call; Dao looks at me with raised eyebrows and I shrug. This could go anywhere now. It's out of our hands.

'Right!' Sinclair is back on the job. She sits sideways in the seat again and looks carefully at us both. 'I checked the ownership and it belongs to a woman who lives in Mt Eden.'

'It might have done,' I say. 'Or it might not. She is dead, and her son uses it. His name is Stuart Browning and he lives at the address where the truck is registered.'

'How do you know all this?'

'We were told in confidence that he was acting suspiciously, that he was interested in Hope. Her flat was monitored by CCTV and it was assumed that he had set that up.'

'Who is he? How could he secretly set up surveillance in her flat? Did he know her?'

More questions line up every time I tell her something. Perhaps I should just fire my last shot and let her get on with it.

'Personally, I think he must be working for an intelligence service.'

I can see the cogs moving. She has obviously been told that there is a file on Hope already and that there is a block on it. But the leap from there to accepting that the file might be blocked because someone in an intelligence service is a killer, who wants to make sure the police can't investigate? Too much to accept all at once, too far-fetched to happen in real life.

'Listen,' says Dao suddenly, 'I can email Hope's stories to you now, if you give me your email address. As I said, I have them on my phone. I think you'll get a much better idea of what has been going on, if you read them first and then relate them to what we have told you.'

'We probably need to go back to the station and get all this on tape. It's far more information than I expected from you and I want it documented while it is fresh in your minds.'

'I can send you the recording, if you like.'

Sinclair stares at Dao; slow to get the meaning of what she is saying.

I decide to help her out, try to keep a smile off my face. 'I think Dao has recorded this interview on her phone. I noticed she's had it in her hand the whole time we have been here. She often does this – she's very organised.'

Sinclair's face is a mixture of interest and suspicion. She looks hard at Dao. 'Why did you do that?'

'I record things sometimes when people talk about things that are new to me,' says Dao innocently. 'I just like to get my facts right.' She looks at Sinclair without guile. 'Just like you do.'

Even I, who have lived with Dao for close on two years, can't tell if she is being sarcastic. There is nothing in her tone or expression to indicate sarcasm, but that means nothing.

To my surprise Sinclair grins. 'Oh my God! This is something else again. I know your story, Dao. I never quite understood how you coped with things all those years and how you have adjusted since. I remember you giving evidence in that trial last year – I went along to a couple of the court sessions. I have rarely seen a better witness. You're one of a kind, all right. Please send me those stories right away and if you can give me the recording later on it would be useful.'

While she scribbles her email address for Dao, I drink

some water and think of what I should tell her now. She is bound to ask how we came to follow Stuart. That will require a complete explanation but leaving out the role Tama played.

Dao takes the slip of paper from Sinclair. 'I think I have to stop recording if I send an email.'

'That's OK, I'll talk to Hunter while you do it.'

My turn to be opportunistic. I start in on the story without prompting, so I can tell it the way I want to instead of responding to Sinclair's questions.

'We are convinced that Stuart Browning took her both times,' I say, never taking my eyes off hers, determined not to let her butt in. 'The rumours we picked up about him were disturbing. Another woman had disappeared a couple of years ago – and he was connected to her too. We gradually came across more information that suggested the involvement of some form of intelligence service – the concealed camera in her flat, the block on Hope's police file and the mention of "another agency" investigating. Hope wrote about events that might be the reason she was surveilled, as you will see from the stories Dao is emailing to you. It all fits. I don't know how many intelligence branches there are – or who they sub-contract to – but I'm sure Browning works for one of them.'

Sinclair looks silently at me, waiting for more. No change of expression at all. Either she has thought of this possibility herself or she is very patient.

'We found out where he lives and put a GPS tracker on his truck. We thought he'd use that rather than his good car to go to wherever he held her. Dao can show you where the tracker is – she attached it. We followed him here yesterday and lost him. This morning we followed him again and our dog found Hope's body – completely by chance, I might add. He's not a search dog, but he took off while we were having lunch. We didn't expect to find Hope dead. We thought Browning might have a cabin up here or that he rented a place – we were hoping to find her alive. After we found her, I called 111, which took a while, and Dao and Scruff went off the path and got lost.'

'I did *not* go off the path just like that,' says Dao. 'I know better than that. I needed to pee, and Scruff came with me. We were only a few metres in from the path, and then he took off after an animal. I don't know what it was, some little oblong thing. And he didn't come back, so I went after him, calling for him to come back, but he didn't. And *then* we were lost.'

'OK, I apologise. I didn't mean to imply you just carelessly wandered off. But we eventually found each other, probably an hour or two after my 111 call. And on the way back we spotted a shipping container in the bush, way off the path.'

Sinclair's eyes are riveted on mine. 'A shipping container?'

'Yes – it seemed very strange, so we went and looked at it. There's a dead woman inside.'

If this whole thing wasn't so tragic, the expressions that flit across Sinclair's face during our talk would be highly entertaining. Some are so subtle you would miss them if you blinked, but this time her face goes from stunned to excited. Is she imagining the media attention and the possible benefit to her career that this complex story will generate? Admittedly most of it so far has been given to her pre-packaged by us, but still, it won't do her career any harm.

'So you went inside it? Did you touch anything?'

'The door was open,' I say untruthfully, not wanting to explain that I had wrapped my T-shirt around my hand and why they won't find my fingerprints on the door.

'We went in and I don't think we touched anything at all inside. There is a dividing wall with a door, which was open. The inner space is very dark, and we just peeped around the edge of it and saw a corpse. She's been there a long time – looks nearly mummified. We didn't go in and we came straight out.'

'Why didn't you mention this earlier? It's pretty significant.' Her eyes move from my face to Dao's and back, watchful and focused.

'I don't know,' I say slowly, as if I am thinking, not just following my own script. 'I suppose we started by telling you we knew who Hope is and that led down a track of how we knew her identity and how we came to be here. It's taken a bit of time. And now we're getting to the rest of it.'

'Fair enough. Just hold on a moment.'

She walks around the cars, gets her phone out and stands on the edge of the road for several minutes. When she comes back, she has made a decision. 'Take me to the container now and then you can leave. I'll be in touch about a formal statement tomorrow.'

Dao asks if she can run down to our car and get her hoodie. 'It's cooling off,' she says innocently, 'and I have Hunter's sweatshirt. I'll leave Scruff in the car when I get the jacket.'

Sinclair says OK, so I give Dao the key and she runs down the road with Scruff. I move out between the vehicles and stand on the far side of the road, where I can see her until she reaches the car. I can feel Sinclair's eye watching me; she understands why I do this. Dao comes back with her jacket and hands me the sweatshirt. There is no gun bulge in her T-shirt.

Sinclair tells the constable that she will send someone down so there are two of them looking after the truck and then we walk up to the clearing where Hope's body lies. The scene is now like something out of a TV drama. People in white overalls and with covers over their shoes are picking things up and putting them into plastic bags. They have erected a square tent over Hope's body and crime-scene tape runs across the clearing close to where the path enters it. They are setting up spotlights on collapsible stands and running cables along the edges of the bush.

We stand quietly watching while Sinclair talks to a man, who digs around in a couple of cases lying open on the ground and hands her things that she stuffs into her pockets.

She comes back to where we are waiting, pulls off a long tail end of the tape tied to a tree and rolls it around her hand while she walks ahead of us back to the main track.

'And now I want you to show me where the container is, so we get a GPS location for it.'

We go back down to the fork in the track and start up the other branch. We talk sporadically while we walk, but it's nothing like an interview. Sinclair is interested in what Dao is doing; she has heard about Dao's aptitude for mathematics and asks if she is studying. Dao replies in a friendly way, but she is beginning to flag. We got little sleep last night and have spent a long day walking in hilly terrain, not to mention today's traumatic episodes. She needs to get away from here.

It takes time to find the exact location where we spotted the container. There are several places on the high ridge where the landscape opens up; we stop several times and scan the downhill slopes. When I spot that distinctive straight line, I point it out to Sinclair, but she can't see it in the fading light.

Dao goes to stand right beside her and points. 'Look to

the right of that very tall ponga tree down there in the little gap – the one in a group of three. See the straight horizontal line behind the bushy things? That's the top edge of the container.'

Sinclair takes pictures of the scene below us and in both directions along the track. Before we start down the slope, she gets the crime-scene tape out of her pocket and ties it around a tree at the point where we will leave the track to descend the slope.

The trees block the late slanting sunlight and it is darker under the trees as we slowly make our way down. Dense undergrowth fills the spaces between tall trees, supple-vines and air roots dangle and catch on our clothes, a fallen tree trunk makes progress laborious.

'I think we might have come down slightly further on,' I say to Sinclair. 'I don't remember it being such a struggle.'

Suddenly the shape of the container materialises a few metres ahead of us; a moment ago we could not see it. Sinclair holds out her arm like a barrier. 'Let's stop here for a moment.'

This late in the day the slanting light does not reach the dark bulk of the container. The outer door is half open, and we can just make out the inner wall and the black outline of the open door inside.

'Stay here, please.'

She fishes around in her pocket and pulls out a pair of white shoe covers before she disappears into the dark box. Light illuminates the outer space and then dims as she goes through the connecting door. She comes out and takes the device the forensics guy gave her from her pocket. Its little screen lights up and she writes the GPS fix on a slip of paper from her notebook and hands it to me.

'Can you call this number when you get up to the high point of the track? You'll be talking to Allan. Give him the coordinates I have written down and tell him we put the tape up on the track as a marker. Ask him to send a man up here, two if he can spare them, with flashlights. I have to stay here now in case Browning comes back. I'll be in touch tomorrow about a formal statement.'

'I bet he won't come near this place,' says Dao. 'If it was me I would avoid all the commotion as soon as I noticed and cut through the bush to the road and walk out. Have you got a light, or was that your phone you used?'

'I borrowed a little torch from the chap who gave me the GPS locator,' she says. 'I'll be fine, Dao, but I can't leave until we can secure this place.'

We struggle up to the ridge and Dao stops to look down; dusk is setting in and the container is now invisible. '*We* know he won't come back and harm her,' she says and pulls her hood up. 'I just wanted her to know we were worried about her safety. I mean, she's been very nice really, don't you think? Just walking away would feel a bit mean.'

The dichotomy between Dao's pragmatic ruthlessness and her kindness is as interesting as ever.

I make the call from the top of the ridge before we trudge down to the road again, tired and hungry. Five minutes uphill from the point where the tracks join, we meet a police officer. He carries a case in one hand and a torch in the other. 'I'm on my way to that container you found,' he says. 'I hope I won't walk right past the place where I have to go off the track.'

'You can't miss it. That strip of police tape is really visible and if you call out from there Sinclair will hear you,' I say. 'You probably won't spot the container in this light.'

He thanks us and continues uphill; it gets rapidly darker and we make ever slower progress. Now there is another police van and yet another car parked on the road; it's getting crowded.

We walk along the road and Dao looks up into the bush on our left and stops for a moment and shakes her head. 'Isn't it strange? We know what's going on up there, all those people working and bringing in equipment, but you can't see a thing. It just looks like a dark hillside. Only the police cars on the road back there show something is wrong.'

I reverse out from between the trees and drive away, relieved to be leaving this place. The interview was a mental balancing act and we both know that the formal statement tomorrow will be more thorough and harder to handle.

'She'll have a lot more questions then,' says Dao tiredly. 'She's sure to want more detail about everything, particularly where those rumors came from. What are we going to say?'

'I don't know. We have to talk to Tama. We can't refuse to answer – and we can't avoid the issue either, like we did today. Call Tama and see if he can come around tonight. I need to talk to Willow too.'

Talking to Willow is urgent. The police will tell Noah they have found Hope's body and she needs to know what has happened, but not the details of how we managed to find her. I stop in Papakura and call her. It takes a good twenty minutes; she keeps asking difficult questions and seems to sense when I am leaving something out. This conversation is as much a balancing act as our talk with Sinclair. I am glad that Noah never heard what Tama told us during his second visit. Willow has no idea that he is contemplating a serious breach of confidentiality.

'Noah will try to paint Tama black,' I say to Willow. 'Try to tone down his viciousness a bit. Tama doesn't deserve any hassle from the cops. Without him we would never have found Hope.'

I can see her in my mind; she will be running her free hand through her hair, as she always does when she is working something out, eyes narrowed in suspicion. I end the call and think of tomorrow's interview. Can it get any more difficult than this?

Dao has stood outside the car talking to Tama, but she gets back in again long before I finish talking to Willow. The moment I end the call, she fills me in, the relief in her voice obvious.

'He is going to tell them everything. He said we can tell the police where the rumours came from. He doesn't want us to get into trouble and he's going to hand over all the evidence he has now – the access log from their system and the deleted video of the first abduction, everything. He said if he gives it all to them now it will make everything easier and they won't have to battle through the red tape to get to the confidential stuff. I'm sure he's right. If they get the lot right away, they'll accept that Stuart is the one who took her. It will save a lot of time.'

'Great. Much easier for everyone, including us. And he can tell them the details about that other missing woman too. Is he coming over tonight?'

'No, he said he'll come and see us another day. He's going to spend tonight writing a statement for the cops, absolutely every detail of how he monitored Stuart and how he followed Hope around. He wants Sinclair's phone number, if we have it.'

'It's at the bottom of that note she gave you with the

email address. Stick your hand into my sweatshirt pocket, it's in there somewhere.'

He is doing the right thing, I think, as we drive onto the motorway and head north. I hope they don't penalise him in any way. They should reward him instead. But I know from experience that the authorities don't work by the same principles of practical justice that I do. We sit in silence until we are nearly home. The car is warm and Scruff snores beside Dao's feet.

'Did we kill him?' she says suddenly. 'I can't make up my mind how it happened. I couldn't see anything, and things just happened – you grabbed my arm and he pulled from the other side. Did you know the water was there?'

'I had just realised what it was, a moment before he stepped sideways, dragging you with him. When I took hold of you, he was already overbalancing – his foot was going into the water and he was about to fall sideways. I'm really sorry I hurt you, but the only way I could make him let go of your hands was to use you to push him hard, take him by surprise.'

'Thank you,' she says politely. 'That was very clever of you – he had such a grip on the rope around my wrists. I tried to pull away from him earlier, but he just hit me over the head and told me he could stab me any moment. I suppose you could say he nearly killed himself. We didn't save him, but that's a bit different.'

I will not tell her of my suspicion that he probably knew the pond was there and meant to drown her. We need no more material for Dao to have nightmares about.

We sit by the balcony window and eat left-over pasta and ice cream. I remember seeing missed-call notifications when I called Willow and pick up my phone to check them. Two calls from Benson and a voice message. I play it on speaker, so Dao can hear it: 'I tried to call a couple of times. You must be out of range. John will not get bail – we regard him as a serious flight risk. He's in a police cell over the weekend and by tomorrow night he'll be safely behind a locked door in prison. And there he will stay until a trial gets under way. Sorry, Dao – we'll expect you to be our star witness again.'

'Oh well,' says Dao tiredly. 'I'd rather go through all the court stuff again than have John on the loose.'

But a few minutes later she looks up from her laptop, in a burst of energy. 'It's marked on Google Earth – the pond! Come and have a look.'

And there it is, with one of those photo markers to indicate that someone uploaded a photo of the place. It is the only photo for that whole area of the Hunua ranges. On the satellite image you can't see much detail; uninhabited areas seem to have lower resolution. The open area is just a narrow, pale streak in the bush and the fence is not visible at all, but the uploaded photo is perfectly clear. It shows the fence and the flat surface of the scum-covered pond behind it. The person who uploaded the photo has given the place a name: 'The Scum Pond'.

'I bet it's where hunters dump parts of animals – heads and carcasses – if they cut them up where they shoot them rather than carry them out. If it's been there for years, there might be a lot of stuff slowly rotting on the bottom.'

'And that's why it stinks, and all the scum has formed. Horrible!'

I stand beside her vacantly staring at the screen and try to imagine how that pond works. Perhaps someone drove a little digger up there years ago and dug an offal pit and it has filled up with water from rain and run-off. That clay would make a nice lining and stop the water from draining into the ground. But there is no water leaving it in the form of a stream, so probably it just overflows when there is heavy rainfall.

'Imagine what's down there,' says Dao with ghoulish glee. 'Bones and skulls, everything covered in slime.'

'And now Stuart is there among the bones,' I say. 'Not a great place to end your days. And think of those poor cops, if they have to drag everything out of the pond.'

'They'll have to use those suits, like in England when they were looking for the nerve-agent poison.' She points to the photo. 'And look, when they took that photo there was a sign on the fence.'

By increasing the size of the image, we can read it. Handwritten on a piece of board and tied to the fence with twine are the words: *Warning – dangerous pond!*

It is not until we go to bed that I remember the personal alarm gadget I bought for Dao in JayCar.

'You could have used that when you were lost with Scruff. I would have heard it from miles away.'

'Yeah, I know. I thought of it at the time, but it was in my jacket pocket and I left the jacket in the car.'

'Sod's law, just like when I came out of the pizza shop and those heavies jumped me. The Glock was in the car and all I had to defend myself with was a pizza box.'

She shoots me a black look. 'That's not funny!'

22

Very early in the morning Dao's phone buzzes. We both sit straight up in bed before we even register what the sound is; our level of alertness still on the maximum setting. Dao grabs the phone.

'Text from Tama - *Are you awake, can I call you*? I'll say yes.'

He calls immediately, and Dao holds the phone up so I can hear.

'I'm going in to work early, at seven.' He sounds energetic and decisive. 'I'll get all the material together and email it to myself from Stu's account. Once I have it in my personal emails, I'm calling DI Sinclair to say I want to see her. I wrote the statement last night, every last detail of how I got alerted to Stuart's obsession with Hope and what I did. It nearly turned into a novel, took hours to get it right. And then we'll see what happens.'

Dao pulls the phone a bit closer. 'We are supposed to make a proper statement today some time. Do you want to come over tonight?'

He says yes and asks what he should bring. 'Icecream,'

says Dao decisively and Tama laughs. 'Do you mind if I bring someone? A friend?'

Dao make a question mark face at me and I say, 'No problem.'

Dao lies down again and tucks the phone under her pillow. 'Do you think he's got a girlfriend?' She is delighted. 'I wonder what she looks like. Do you think she'll be as gorgeous as he is? But we can't tell them about Stuart or the pond. We need to be really careful when we talk about yesterday. Not just with Tama, with everyone. We must remember that we never met Stuart and we don't know what he looked like or how old he was.'

'And you have to wear long sleeves until that cut has healed. Let me have a look at your arm.'

She holds it up; the cut is healing, but the edges are red.

'Does it hurt when I touch it?'

'Just a little, not too much.'

'OK, get into the shower and clean it really properly and we'll get some antiseptic cream on it. God knows what he cut you with – could have had a million bacteria in it.'

Dao shakes her head at me and makes a face. 'It's only a cut! I washed the blood off last night. I'm sure it's fine. You're being fussy.'

'No, I just want to make sure. You have the first shower and we'll get it tidied up.'

She sings in the shower. I lie in bed and listen to her lovely mezzo voice, thinking how surprising it is coming from such a small body. It's a relief that our troubles are behind us, at least the difficult and dangerous ones. There will be tedious interviews, another court case when John comes to trial – and probably more media attention, but at least the worst is over.

I have never been so wrong.

One of Sinclair's people calls and asks us to come in

tomorrow afternoon. 'Things are very busy, but DI Sinclair wants to conduct the interview herself,' he says. 'She can see you any time after half-past one tomorrow.'

I say we will be there at two and end the call, wondering if something she has just got from Tama has raised alarm signal about our role.

Midmorning I get an email from Tama with the statement he sent to Sinclair attached.

'I've got Tama's statement,' I call upstairs to Dao, who is trying out some complicated hair style she saw on YouTube.

She comes racing down the stairs with an intricate braided effect on one side of her head and her normal dead-straight hair on the other. 'I'll finish it later. Do you like it?'

'It's very clever,' I say diplomatically. 'Is it hard to do?'

'Very hard and I'll probably never get it to look the same on both sides. Do you really like it?'

'I'm not sure. I think I like you best with your hair down.'

'I knew you'd say that, but I don't mind. I think you're right. It isn't me, makes me feel I'm pretending to be someone else. Could you please print Tama's thing? I decided to have a paper day.'

Dao reads it on paper and undoes the braiding one-handed while she reads. The statement is long and very detailed. He has set it out chronologically, entering dates, times and locations and what he did or found out. Either he has a fantastic memory, or he started making notes as soon as he got concerned about Hope. In some places he has added quite long paragraphs of explanations, the technical details of what he did and where the police will have to look for the evidence, if they manage to get access to the IT system. There are paragraphs about his colleague

Rob's comments that started him on his personal surveillance of both Hope and Stuart, and how he knows about the second missing woman.

It reads like a thriller; one thing leads to another. The final paragraphs are about the young woman who disappeared earlier, Rana. Tama has included details of her identity and connections and the date when she was last known to be alive. He has in fact put together a perfect case for the prosecution, but that will not happen, of course. When he relates things we found, there is an asterisk and a footnote: 'Refer to Hunter Grant for details.'

On the last page is a note about a USB stick he is giving Sinclair. He lists what it on it: screenshots from his work computer of the report he set up in their server to record how often Stuart watched that video clip of Hope dancing. At first, I don't understand why he bothered with this; all of it is detailed in the statement already. I think it is probably his way of making doubly sure they believe his evidence. A printed report of Stuart's video-watching could be a fake, compiled 'by hand' so to speak, but the screenshots prove where it came from. His thoroughness is impressive. Once again, I worry about his future: he should have a great career, provided this doesn't ruin his prospects.

We have just finished reading it when my phone goes. I look at the screen; it's Noah. I wish I didn't have to take this call, but I might as well get it over with. I've been steeling myself to call him since I woke up this morning.

'Hunter,' he says in a voice dulled by sadness. 'They found her. She's dead.'

'I know, I am so sorry, Noah.'

'You knew? How did you know? Her name hasn't been released yet.'

Oh shit, I think, I shouldn't have said that, but I

thought he called because the cops had told him we found Hope. He will find out sooner or later; I might as well tell him now.

'Dao and I found her.'

He explodes into instant fury. 'What! You knew where to look? And you didn't tell me? The police said they think they know who killed her and they're looking for him now. Do you know who he is?'

I try to sound reasonable and sympathetic at the same time, possibly not my best performance. I understand his anger and his grief, but as always with Noah it is difficult to predict his reactions.

'It's a long story, and I don't know how much the police want me to say. Tama came back with some information and we worked out who he might be – and I say "might be" deliberately, Noah. Nothing has been confirmed yet, as far as I know. Dao and I put a tracker on this man's car and when he headed into the ranges yesterday, we followed. We probably broke several laws, but we have told the police what we did. It wasn't something I had time to call you about. We were tracking him and lost him in the bush and then we found Hope by chance. It all happened just like that, one thing after another. There was no way of alerting you in advance.'

Thank God he wasn't with us, I think. I can imagine how out of control he would have been, touching her, destroying evidence, impeding the police. I could never have constrained him in that situation. I don't want him to know exactly how the timeline played out. Adding to his feelings of anger and frustration will do him no good at all. But he surprises me.

'Thank you. I should have trusted you.'

This is generosity of a kind I have not come to expect from him, and it makes me feel slightly guilty. 'I am very sorry, Noah. I did hope we would find her alive. How are your parents?'

'Devastated, and so angry. They can't stop thinking that we might have found her much sooner and saved her, if only the police had acted when I first told them she was missing.'

Should I point out that even if they had acted then, there are many factors that the police might have taken a very long time to pull together? Or should I let him rage and grieve and maybe come to the same conclusion himself? Sooner or later he might acknowledge the important role Tama played in this drama. I have told Willow that Tama came back with crucial information, so Noah knows that. If the police had acted and Noah had not come to me, Tama would not be involved now and Hope's disappearance might never have been solved. I want Noah to see that the person he should give credit to is Tama, but he will have to reach that conclusion himself. I think of his parents who have heard everything up to now through the filter of Noah's jealousies and obsessions. There is nothing I can do to give them a more balanced overview.

The conversation becomes increasingly difficult. Noah wants to know every detail: what Hope looked like, how she lay on the ground and what she was wearing. What was the expression on her face? Were there any visible injuries? The cops have told him very few details and now he is fixated on trying to find out more from me.

I interrupt him after a couple of minutes, having told him nothing much. My focus is on avoiding saying anything the police might not want immediately known. I have no experience of how much they share with a victim's family while they still think they have a suspect to track down and evidence to protect. Eventually the police will tell him what they think he needs to know.

'Have you met with the police?'

'Yeah, this morning. I've just been to the morgue to formally identify her. She looked so dead, Hunter. So cold.'

He starts to cry, and I wait; after a couple of minutes he calms down. 'Can I come and talk to you? I want to know more, so I understand what happened to her, why she died. And how.'

I have to make some sort of decision very quickly or this will get out of hand. If he has already seen her body, he either knows about the cuts or they were covered up somehow. And if they were, was it because the police did not want to upset him? Or because they did not want him to see what had been done to her and talk about it?

'We haven't had a formal interview yet, Noah. I can't discuss anything until the police say I can. I'm very sorry. I know it's hard for you. What I can say is that she looked completely peaceful and there was no sign of why she died.'

Dao is sitting up straight, staring at me as I talk. She has understood most of the conversation and the expression on her face is agonised. As soon as I manage to end the call, I text Tama and warn him, in case Noah manages to find out his number. It is unlikely, but I give him Noah's phone number, so he can ignore the call if it comes. Talking to Noah is hard enough for me; I am used to him and have some understanding of how to divert him from a topic, but Tama might find it harder.

Dao and I spend some time discussing how to deal with future conversations with Noah without lying, but without revealing too much. I don't want to deceive him, but there are details that will only make things harder for him, things he does not need to know, at least not yet.

Later on, when the inquest takes place, a lot more will emerge; for now we can spare him the worst.

'He doesn't know where Tama works – well, let's face it, neither do we,' says Dao. 'And I don't think we told him Tama's surname. I hope the police won't tell him who he is. And he won't find out later, because there will be no trial to make Tama's name public. And that's another thing we must remember not to say! Particularly not to Willow. Imagine having to explain that one away. Did you finish reading Tama's statement?'

'Yes, literally seconds before Noah called. It's very impressive. Imagine Sinclair reading it and then she reads the log report and watches the video of the first time Hope was abducted. An amazing amount of evidence handed to her on a plate.'

'I'm glad we've read it before our interview, so we know exactly what he told them, much easier.'

I hope Dao won't ask Tama if we can see the video evidence he gave to the police. He warned me that something disturbing took place after Stuart knocked Hope out. After thinking about it for a moment I text him, hoping I am not being overprotective: *If Dao asks, please imply cops don't want you to show the video to anyone. Thanks.*

He replies: *No way am I showing it to her. As I said, it is totally gross. Sinclair has already asked me not to talk to anyone about the details. See you tonight.*

'Lunchtime!' Dao gets up and so does Scruff. 'No, Scruff, I said lunch. You don't have lunch - you only have breakfast and dinner.'

I am just about to join them when my phone goes again; now it's Willow. This will take another half-hour, I think, and nearly don't answer. Then I remember all the things she doesn't know yet and relent.

It takes a long time. She has talked to Sinclair on

Noah's behalf and now she is fired up with questions about our involvement. By the time we finish I am sick of talking about it. She is smarter than Noah; she knows how to draw things out of people. She also knows how to draw conclusions from what you leave out, which is disconcerting and nearly trips me up once or twice.

Dao abandons the idea of lunch and sits down again to listen to my end of the conversation. Willow is very persistent; not because she suspects anything as dramatic as the Scum Pond incident, more that she senses I am hiding things from her.

'You're not telling me the full story, Hunter. It makes no sense. You can't possibly expect me to believe you went to the Hunua ranges on a hunch and just happened to find Hope's body! You say this Tama fellow told you of certain rumours about the killer – but how did *he* know? I hope to God you're not going to lie to the police, Hunter. If this comes to trial and you lie, you risk a perjury conviction and prison.'

Ever since I had to bend the rules a bit to protect Dao a couple of years ago, Willow is convinced that I will go too far one day and end up in jail.

'I don't think so, Willow. There are things I haven't told you – the cops have asked me not to talk about some of it. And you are Noah's lawyer – you told me yourself that if I tell you things, you can't withhold them from him. You just have to live with the fact that there are some things you might never find out, unless the police tell you.'

We end the call on reasonably good terms. There has been no mention of the intelligence services and she has no idea how we knew to go to the Hunua ranges. I know she appreciated the detailed debrief I gave her and Matt after the final chapter of the 'saving Dao from being killed' saga. Then we had nobody else to consider, no slightly unbalanced relative who might feel a need to apportion blame or demand retribution. I am well aware that, despite her protests, she actually enjoyed hearing the blow-by-blow tale of what happened that night in the abandoned factory. But this time it's different.

Eventually we have lunch and go for a walk on the beach with Scruff. We don't mention yesterday's events and return to the house feeling more normal than we have for some time. Tama calls and says he will be with us after dinner. We are in the kitchen making dinner, when Dao suddenly says, 'Why don't we argue?'

'Are we supposed to?'

'You know, how people on TV and in films argue – or they talk about people arguing. And that book I just finished - those people argued all the time. I mean, other couples argue. Even Matt and Willow sometimes. And you argue with your mother. But we never do.'

'It's because you can't argue with me.'

'Why not? What if you said something and I argued about it?'

'Because I won't argue with you and you can't argue on your own. It doesn't work. When did we ever have a situation that could have caused an argument?'

'Oh, probably never. Or maybe when I refused to use your money and wanted to take a cleaning job. I don't *want* to argue, I just think we seem to be unusual.'

'We are unusual, Dao. And lucky.'

Just before eight I go down to answer the door and find Tama outside with a ginger-haired giant beside him. 'Hunter, this is Tyler.'

I open the door wider. 'Nice to meet you, Tyler. Come in.'

Dao is going to be disappointed: not a girlfriend after all. And then I notice the white cane.

'One step up,' says Tama. 'Now flat, seven steps towards one o'clock, then a staircase.'

Tyler's cane feels for the bottom step and they make their way up. Tama watches Tyler's feet.

'One more' – and Tyler walks onto the floor or the living area without hesitation. They have done it many times; no words wasted and no hesitation from Tyler.

Dao has been standing at the top of the stairs watching, eyes wide.

'Dao, this is Tyler. We are flat mates and he wanted to meet you and Hunter.' He hands her a bag. 'Ice cream as ordered, home-made.'

He watches Dao take the bag to the kitchen and says casually, 'If we are trying the ice cream now, we should sit at the table. Much easier for Tyler.'

Conversation is on hold while we taste the ice cream. Dao has no idea what it is, but says it is 'super amazing' which makes Tyler laugh.

'Think of vegetables,' he says, and turns his head towards Dao at exactly the right angle. 'Something red, obviously.'

Dao and I look at each other. We have played this game before; Dao sometimes picks something in the supermarket and conceals the packaging and makes me guess.

'Beetroot!' I guess after another mouthful. 'And

something else. I should have guessed earlier – that intense red colour. And beetroot is sweet.'

'Beetroot and a little bit of sweet basil. Tama told me about the fabulous ice cream he had here, and we bought an ice-cream maker. We've been experimenting.'

When the ice-cream tasting is over, I tell them to go and sit in comfortable chairs while I take the bowls to the kitchen. I put nibbles and drinks on a tray and listen to their voices from the end of our long room. From the kitchen I can't hear the words, but their voices sound happy and relaxed. It is a striking difference from recent evenings in this room with tension and worry colouring everything.

'Don't worry about Tyler, he knows all about it,' says Tama, when I join them. 'He works from home and I used to come home and start raving about things before I even closed the front door. First it was how hostile Stuart was, and then the strange goings-on with Hope and it escalated from there. Tyler's like an oyster, he's kept all my secrets since we met at school when we were ten.'

'Have you been flat mates for years?' asks Dao, looking at Tyler. He hears her voice coming directly towards him, knows she is talking to him and answers. He doesn't need people to use his name to alert him. I never thought of it before, but it's obvious now I sit here and listen and watch.

Tyler nods in Dao's direction. 'Since we left high school and went to university in Wellington. We both studied computer technology, but I didn't complete my degree. I was hit by a car in Courtenay Place one night in our second year and landed on my head, which made me blind.'

'Then I got the job up here,' says Tama, 'and Tyler came with me. He's a trained counsellor and does phone counselling for a youth crisis charity, so it doesn't matter where he lives. He had to get used to a new neighbourhood, of course, but he thought it was worth it.' Tama grins at Dao. 'People sometimes think we're a couple, but believe me, Tyler is a demon for pretty girls. I tell him they're pretty and he does the rest.'

They both laugh; it's an old joke between them.

Dao is fascinated. 'Do you lie to him sometimes? Do you say someone is really pretty when they're not?'

'He did once,' says Tyler and raises his big fist in Tama's general direction. 'Once!'

'How did you know?'

'By touch,' says Tyler straight-faced. 'If they feel pretty, it's all good.'

We spend a couple of hours discussing all that has happened since we last saw Tama. The fact that Scruff found Hope is of great interest. Tyler has not realised there is a dog in the house and Dao brings him over for Tyler to pat.

'You should have a dog,' she says. 'You can train a dog to do all sorts of things. I'm going to teach Scruff to count soon – he knows everything else. Didn't they offer you one?

'I could have had one, but at the start I was determined to cope on my own. Well, with Tama as a flat mate, of course. I suppose I could trade him in for a dog.'

'Tell me how you found that container, Hunter. Sinclair said it was miles away from the place where Hope's body was.'

'It is a long way and through difficult terrain too, if you don't stick to the tracks. We've been discussing how she got there, but we might never find out. She had nothing much on, no shoes. I guess she must have walked down the track, which is pretty smooth, or her feet would have been more damaged. They were just dirty. But how did she get away? I'm sure he didn't let her go.'

'Perhaps she didn't walk from the container,' says Tyler. 'Perhaps there is another hide-out up there, closer to where you found her.'

I tell them about the fresh apple in the container and the plastic bag outside with what looked like fresh rubbish.

'Someone has been staying there recently. The cops might find out from the recordings. I think that perverted creep locked her up with the other woman and went up there at intervals. Perhaps he left the door unsecured and she got away. And then she died for some reason.'

Tama stares at me. 'What other woman? Was there another one?'

'Didn't Dao tell you? Yes, a dead woman. She was in the container. She had been there a long time.'

'Rana!' he exclaims. 'Well, Sinclair knows about her now, so they'll be able to confirm that.'

'Did I forget to tell you? Sorry! I was so tired,' says Dao. 'I can't stop thinking of her, the other woman. It was so strange. She looked dusty. It was very dark in the inner room and we didn't go in, of course. But she looked as if she was covered in a layer of dust. Hunter thinks she looked kind of mummified. You know, dried out. Not something Stuart did.'

We describe how she sat in the corner, as if she had been overcome by exhaustion and sat down to rest. 'Like you would put a doll down, leaning against something with her legs straight out. She had something on her lap', says Dao sadly. 'It might have been a bunch of very old dried-up flowers. Perhaps he put them there after she died, like you do on a grave.'

We say nothing about our encounter with Stuart or the Scum Pond.

When I tell Tama how impressed I was with this statement he shrugs. 'It got a bit too long, but I thought I should give them every single bit of evidence, including my reasoning at various points. The more they see how many details confirm it was Stuart, the better it is. We listened to the news in the car coming over, but they haven't found him yet. Sinclair said they've had people up there all the time and no sign of him. He never returned to his truck.'

'He wouldn't, not with the police there,' says Dao, straight-faced. 'I suppose he could have walked away and got a lift, but he's probably still up there somewhere.'

When they leave, we say we must get together again, and Tyler promises that Tama will cook us dinner one night. I walk up the stairs, thinking of the police searching that big expanse of hilly terrain covered in bush. Would they use a helicopter with heat-sensing equipment? Will they find out about the Scum Pond – and if they do, will they search it?

24

At two o'clock the next day we sit in an interview room and wait for Sinclair. She arrives fifteen minutes late and sends a constable away to get coffee for us all.

'Busy day. There's a lot going on. We haven't found Browning yet. He's not at his home address and his other car is still there, so we assume he's either hiding in the ranges or he hitchhiked out. We have a man posted at his house. It's going to be a big task searching that area.'

She opens the folder in front of her and looks at me. 'I imagine Tama Robinson has been in touch with you? And that you know he gave us a statement and came in for an interview?'

Gently does it, I think. Unless she asks, I'll not tell her we have read his statement. Dao and I decided on the way in that we will answer questions, but only volunteer information if it seems vital to the investigation.

'Yes, he told us he had given you an account of what he did and what he found.'

'He has been very helpful – and very honest. A lot of what I was going to ask you to explain is perfectly clear now. Like how you heard of Browning and found out where he lives and so on. And Mr. Barber told us about the camera you noticed when he took you to Hope's flat. Why did you go there?'

'It was his idea. As I said earlier, he came to us and asked us to help him, but we sent him away. Then he came back and after some hesitation we agreed. It's not what I do and not what I want to do either. Then a couple of days later he invited us to come and see the flat. His lawyer was there too.'

She nods and looks at her folder again. 'He said you all went there because he thought seeing it would convince you she must have been abducted. Is that what you thought at the time, before there was any other evidence to back that theory?'

Dao looks steadily at Sinclair across the table. 'Of course, we did! Can you imagine going out and leaving your door open, and leaving your bag and your phone behind? Even if we thought she might just have gone off somewhere, those things just didn't fit.'

'Quite true,' says Sinclair. 'And you located Mr. Robinson very cleverly via a photo on Hope's phone and social media. I must say I'm impressed. But putting trackers on Browning's cars – it could be construed to be illegal surveillance. What gave you the idea?'

Dao and I look at each other. Telling her the whole story is a tedious prospect and neither of us wants to do it. Then Dao takes the initiative. 'Do you know Benson? He's a detective inspector too.'

I know the moment she says it that Sinclair has been in touch with him; her eyebrows rise a fraction.

Dao has noticed it too. 'I see that you do know him, or you've talked to him? Did he call you or did you call him?'

I nearly laugh out loud. Here we are being interviewed

and now Dao is interviewing Sinclair. She goes a step further before Sinclair has a chance to reply. 'I bet he called you. We asked him to help us find Hope, but he said he couldn't because her file was blocked. It said on the news that a woman who had been missing for some time had been found dead and he would have guessed it was Hope. Benson is *very* smart, you know.'

Sinclair has met her match and she knows it. A tiny smile lifts the corners of her mouth. 'Right. He called me this morning and told me exactly what you have just said. And he told me that you had some trouble recently when you found a GPS locator on your car. How long had the tracker been on Browning's truck?'

I step in here; I don't want to open the door for unnecessary questions and trouble. 'Only since Friday. He leaves the truck at home and takes his car to work, so it wasn't difficult.'

I don't want to say he kept the truck in his garage and give her another reason to warn us we've done something illegal.

Sinclair takes us back over all the things we talked about on Sunday, more detailed questions this time, but nothing that is hard to respond to. We describe again how we had a picnic lunch and Scruff wandered off and found Hope's body. She brings out an aerial photo of the clearing taken from a drone.

'This is the scene from the air. You can see how far it is from any major track. We want to work out if Hope could possibly have walked there from the container or if she was brought there. When we spoke the other day, you seemed to assume she had walked. Why did you think that?'

Dao and I look at each other; if I look as blank as she does, then Sinclair has her answer.

'I don't know,' says Dao. 'She was bare-foot and her feet were filthy, but that doesn't mean she walked there. I think it was more the way she lay, as if she was really tired and just fell asleep.'

'I thought she looked relaxed,' I add. 'Neither arranged nor just tossed down. Do you agree?'

'I do, but I also know that sometimes victims are put down somewhere when they are dying, but not yet dead – they can move, sometimes they don't die until hours later. Maybe he took her there and left her, before she actually died.'

'Those cuts,' says Dao. 'That was horrible, perverted. We thought he must have had her tied up to do that. She must have struggled. Hunter showed me the cuts on her palm – she tried to get the knife off him'

'I know, it's distressing to imagine it. I'm sorry you had to see that, Dao. Was there anything you saw there, or at the container site, you would like to comment on?'

'No, not really. But I should tell you that you might find dog hair inside the container because Scruff ran in before we could stop him. I don't think he touched anything. We called him to come out right away because we didn't know what might be in there.'

'Do you think she was drugged?' I ask. 'He had something with him when he abducted her the first time – she wrote about seeing a cloth in his hand then going unconscious – so he had access to some chemical substance, whatever it was.'

'We don't know yet. Not all the lab reports have come back from the autopsy. They will test for a range of things and look for needle marks. We need to find out what actually killed her.'

Sinclair gets another paper out of her folder. 'This is a map of the tracks – it's on the Internet, but we got a bigger version from the tourist information office, so we can see all the tracks. As you can see there are probably hundreds of kilometres of tracks up there and it's a very popular spot for walking. Some walks are short and easy, and some are more demanding. Where you went is outside the Regional Park area where families go. You were in what is called a remote tramping area, not recommended for inexperienced walkers.'

Someone has marked where the truck was parked and where Hope was found, but not the container. We lean forward over the table and I know this is the perfect opportunity. Various things from the events on Sunday have been sitting in the back of my mind. I know that we must make sure that they find Stuart; his death must become known. I keep thinking about the Scum Pond: can we give Sinclair a hint without risking repercussions? We can't tell her what happened, or next thing I'll be charged with manslaughter. How to go about it seems at first nearly unsolvable. How can I bring it up without exposing myself to risk? If they find him there will never be a trial. That will take pressure off us, as potential witnesses, and enable us to talk more freely, for example with Willow and Matt. It is only during the last few minutes that a solution has developed in the back of my mind.

I point to the first fork in the main track. 'We went up both these branches and then we tried the smaller ones further in that don't show here. Some of them peter out and seem to disappear. I wonder if they are used by hunters. Presumably people are allowed to hunt here.'

Sinclair frowns and studies the boxes of text on the pamphlet. 'It doesn't actually say. I'll find out. We know the area is popular among bird watchers and they conduct a species count up there every year. Only the two main tracks are maintained, the others are there by usage – if nobody uses them nature takes over. Like that one which leads to the clearing where you found Hope – barely a track any longer.'

I run my finger along the path that I know comes closest to the container. 'Somewhere along this ridge is where we spotted the container.'

Sinclair points with her pen and makes a small cross slightly off a track. 'About here, I think.'

'But who put it there?' says Dao. 'They must have used a big helicopter. And why would anyone bother? Do you think it was Browning?'

'Someone we talked to yesterday said that the Department of Conservation had it airlifted in years ago, when they were thinking of creating an inland island for kiwi conservation. You know, one of those areas with predator-proof fencing? I suppose they wanted somewhere secure to keep equipment. But their funding was cut, and it never happened. How Browning found out about it I don't know.'

I continue to study the tracks while they talk then casually nudge Dao, keeping my finger on the map. 'This smaller track here isn't that far from the container, but on the other side from where we spotted it. It angles away from the main track. I think it's where we saw that mysterious fence.'

Dao doesn't show it, but I can sense her tension. She is very alert now, not sure why I am bringing it up.

'I think it might be,' she says. 'Wasn't that weird?'

'Bizarre.' I turn my face towards her and smile. 'Someone's idea of a joke, perhaps. But what a lot of work just for a joke. Think of carrying all those fence posts all the way up there.'

Now we have Sinclair's attention. 'Someone built a fence way in there?'

'Oh, not a big fence,' says Dao casually. 'Just a straight length of wooden fence, about ten metres long. Do you think that's right, Hunter?'

'More or less. We thought it was a bit mad, because it doesn't fence anything in. The track goes across a little open space and the fence runs alongside the track from about halfway across, and then it ends. There's nothing there at all. Just the track on one side and an expanse of bare ground on the other.'

We look at each other in silent agreement that some things are too strange to explain and carry on with the interview.

Right at the end Dao leans forward in her chair and looks at Sinclair in a way I am very familiar with. 'I have some questions,' she says, and she clearly expects answers. 'People have asked us about things and we have said nothing so far, apart from stuff they will find out anyway. Do you want us to keep quiet about everything we have discussed with you? It's not that we mind, but Noah wanted a lot of details about Hope and Hunter said we couldn't discuss it.'

She adds as an afterthought, in case Sinclair thinks I am unfeeling, 'He was very kind about it, but he said you had asked us not to discuss it, just in case. And anyway, some things are so horrible it's probably best he doesn't know.'

'Like the cuts?' says Sinclair. 'I know. It's often hard to decide how to handle these things. We didn't tell him about the cuts, and he didn't see them when he identified her. I think it's best to keep everything you don't see in the media to yourselves for the time being. That mutilation is evidence and the less it is talked about the better.'

On the way home, I explain why I brought up the track with the fence. 'And the way you stepped in, that was great. I only made up my mind in the last minute to bring the subject up, but Sinclair provided the perfect moment. If they look at that particular path, they might find the pond and then they might find him. And if they do find him, there won't be a trial and we will no longer be of interest as key witnesses who can give evidence against him.'

'I knew you had a reason, but I couldn't work out what it was – not until you mentioned that mud area. Then I figured it out. You wanted them to find the pond. That was clever.'

When we get home, Dao goes to let Scruff in from the courtyard. I hear a shout of laughter and turn around halfway up the stairs to investigate.

'Look!' She points through the glass door. 'I can't let him in!'

Scruff is peering at us over the edge of a hole as deep as he is tall. He is covered in dirt, his tail wagging like a dusty flag.

'He's making a tunnel!' Dao can't stop laughing. 'He's making an escape into Nigel's place.'

'Bugger! Now I'll have to find a way to stop him doing this. He's started a new one beside the pavers I moved. I'll go and change into shorts and hose him down.'

25

The next little while is devoid of drama. The days are getting noticeably shorter and as usual the Auckland weather alternates between rain and sun. Despite this it feels like spring instead of the onset of autumn. When I mention this weird thought, Dao instantly nods agreement.

'It's done, that's why. All the hard stuff is over. Apart from the funeral, I suppose. You know how you said, "when we get our life back"? I think that's where we are now, we've got our life back.'

We buy a dog deterrent and spray the concrete border along the high walls in the courtyard and Scruff starts a new hole more or less in the middle of the lawn instead.

Dao reads about why dogs suddenly start new behaviours, like digging large holes, but none of the reasons seem to fit. 'I think he just discovered he likes to dig,' she says. 'Like when I discovered I like to climb. And when are we going to Clip'n Climb again, anyway? We haven't been for weeks. I double-promise I won't try to get you to do it – I know you don't want to.'

A double promise can never be broken; it lasts even

after death according to Dao, whose father told her about it.

Last year, just after Mint's trial, Matt suggested that it might be good for Dao to do something totally new. 'I know everything she has come across since you found her is new,' he said. 'But I mean a fun activity that challenges her a bit. She is so resilient and so good at coping that it's hard sometimes to remember how damaged she is. I was thinking of something like kayaking or rock climbing.'

Matt is one of that rare breed who observes more than he interacts and never says anything that is not worth listening to. After some research I took Dao to an indoor rock-climbing place in Dominion Road and it has been a favourite recreation ever since. Dao climbs ten-meter high walls like a monkey, with hand and footholds sometimes so far apart she can't reach them, and she has to jump and grab. Thankfully she is roped and can't fall all the way down. She climbs, and I watch and send video snippets to Matt. Once I sent a couple of shots to Charlie with the result that she and Kristen came with us one weekend. There's going to be no prize for guessing who is going to join in, I thought, when they arrived. I was totally wrong. Charlie said she could think of few things she was less likely to do, and Kristen spent an hour climbing with Dao and has joined us there since.

Having a few days of beach walking with Scruff and climbing in Dominion Road is like doing a factory reset. We feel normal again. Not that we can ever forget the events of the last couple of weeks, but now we look forward.

Benson calls in and stays for a drink on his way home one afternoon. 'I thought you'd like an unofficial update,' he says. 'Sinclair seems to think that I have some special connection to the Browning/Barber case, and she's called a couple of times to fill me in on progress. I told her my only interest was because you came to me for help at the start, but whatever – she called today.'

Dao gives him a speculative look and he says, 'What? Why are you looking at me like that?'

'Oh, no reason really,' she says, and I don't believe a word of it. 'I just want to know what she told you.'

He takes a swig of his beer and shakes his head. 'She didn't have a lot to tell me, but a few things are coming together. They found hairs on the tarpaulin on the back of the truck and they are Hope's. They found Browning's fingerprints on the camera unit in the container, but nowhere else, so presumably he used gloves but forgot when he put the camera up. They got a lot of prints from his house and the truck and they match the prints on the camera. They're still searching the ranges for him. His phone and bank accounts haven't been touched and he hasn't been sighted since the day you found Hope. Unless someone's hiding him, he must be still up there.'

'I think he's lost,' says Dao and avoids both lying or being devious. 'Sinclair said that part of the ranges is called a remote tramping area and you need to be experienced to go right into it. It's proper wilderness. And look how I got lost with Scruff – just a few minutes and I had no idea where I was.'

I reach over and hand Benson the bowl of crisps. 'He might die in there and never be found, I suppose. You read about it now and then – someone goes hunting or tramping and comes across a skeleton that's been there for years.'

'Well, at the moment they've got a very unpleasant job. Sinclair said they are draining some kind of water-filled pit that stinks. They've had searchers out combing the area where the container is, and one group came across a fence

– apparently you had mentioned it? This offal pit or whatever it is, it's behind the fence.'

'Can't be the same fence,' I say mendaciously. 'There was only a flat area of mud behind the fence we saw.'

Benson makes a face of disgust. 'Yeah, she said that's exactly what it looks like. Imagine walking on the far side of that fence and stepping onto what looks like mud and finding yourself in a scum-covered pool of putrid water. She said the scum on top is exactly level with the ground and it's so thick and brown you can hardly make out the edges of the pool.'

'But how can they drain it?' asks Dao. 'Are they using buckets?'

'They've brought in a diesel generator and a pump – which keeps stopping because it gets blocked with all kinds of smelly bits.' Benson laughs. 'Poor guys. They're wearing masks, but Sinclair thinks they're going to need breathing apparatus if it takes much longer. The deeper they go the worse it gets.'

'That look,' I say to Dao, when Benson has gone. 'What did it really mean?'

'I just thought he sounded kind of pleased with himself when he said that Sinclair has rung him a few times. Do you think he likes her?'

I try to imagine Sinclair and Benson side by side and feel a grin spreading over my face. 'Can you picture it? There she is with not a hair out of place and not a crease anywhere and Benson's got his shirt half untucked and his tie hanging undone, and his pockets are full of God knows what. They would be the most unlikely couple I can imagine.'

Now Dao is smiling too. 'As unlikely as you and me?'

She is right – unlikely has nothing to do with it. I head

for the kitchen. 'I never think of us as unlikely, but probably others do.' I know damn well they do.

'Oh, yes, they do. I see the way people look at us.' She sounds amused. 'It doesn't really matter where we are, expensive restaurant or a pizza shop, someone will stare, but it doesn't worry me.'

She gives me a wicked look. 'They probably think you bought me from one of those websites. You know, like a mail-order bride.'

'Hunter, phone for you.'

Dao stands in the bathroom door with my phone in her hand. I dry my hands and take it from her, make a face meaning 'who is it?' and she shakes her head.

'Hunter, my name is Will. We haven't met, but I have heard a lot about you.'

It is the kind of call I don't like. When people say they have heard a lot about you it can be good or bad; when this guy says it, the words have an undercurrent of menace.

'OK,' I say, keeping my voice neutral. 'What's this about?'

'I think we can do business together. You have something I want, and I have the money to pay for it. No strings attached. You get rid of an embarrassment and I can use it.'

'I have no idea what you are talking about. I have nothing that is for sale.'

He chuckles, as if he is genuinely amused. 'Ah, but you do. You have a blue barrel that you don't know what to do with.'

'Are you connected to that maniac who came around here a few days ago? I tricked him into believing I had the barrel and said I would provide a sample, but that was just so he would come back here. I told the cops all about it, so they could come and get him when he returned, but it was a wasted effort. They got him anyway – they knew where he was. I never had the barrel in the first place.'

'We know you have it, you and your mate with the chopper. You picked it up from Bram's place on the coast when he ran off. And you've been holding on to it all this time because you don't know how to sell it.'

Now I am getting angry. 'I'll tell you something that you obviously haven't heard. The cops have CCTV footage of that barrel on the back of Bram's truck from when he left his place. He was caught on camera at a supermarket in Whangarei, but a couple of days later he was filmed somewhere in the city and the barrel was gone. He either sold it or he hid it. Ask a cop called Benson. He was the one who told me how they know that I didn't take it.' I end the call.

A couple of hours later we are sitting on the balcony having lunch and watching Scruff investigate his new doghouse in the garden. 'He loves it. Look, he's gone inside it again. Do you know what he's doing?' Dao looks at me, hoping I'll say no.

'I have no idea. Maybe he's trying to work out what it's for?'

'He's making his bed! He's moving the blanket and the old towels around to get it just the way he wants it. He's so busy.'

The doorbell goes, and I check on my phone. There's a tall, fat guy in a suit outside, not someone I recognise. A black SUV is parked behind him. 'Stay here, I'll go down,' I say.

'Hunter,' he says jovially and holds out his hand. 'I'm Will. I thought we should have a chat.'

I don't take his hand and neither do I let go of the door

handle. 'You're wasting your time, Will. We have nothing to talk about.'

I close the door and go back upstairs.

'Who was it? Was it the man who called?'

'He doesn't believe me when I say I haven't got the barrel. I'm getting really fed up with this bloody barrel saga.'

'Did you get angry?'

'I tried to keep it civilized. Did you expect me to get angry?'

'Of course,' she says, as if I should have figured it out for myself. 'When you're angry you look really scary – dangerous. That night when John came, and you got so angry – wow! No wonder he got a twitch in his face.'

She laughs; apparently this is either hilarious or deeply satisfying.

'OK, next time he comes I'll show him I'm angry.'

26

We go to the Depot for dinner with Charlie and Kristen, and a dozen of their friends, to celebrate Kristen's promotion to head paralegal at her firm. One of the women in the group turns out to be a fame vulture and corners Dao before the meal. I can see Dao getting uncomfortable, but before I can intervene Kristen moves sideways and says something, and the woman moves away.

Dao sidles between two men and comes to stand beside me. 'I got a text from Tama a little while ago. I went to the toilet, so I could reply and ask him a couple of things. It's really weird. He and Tyler are visiting Tyler's uncle in Forrest Hill and he said he's got the tracker he put on Stuart's black car! He's going to put it in our letterbox on their way home. He got it back – isn't that funny?'

'I wonder why he did that. And how did he get access to the car? That property must be behind police tape.'

'I texted back and asked how he got it. He went to Stuart's house as soon as I called him – you know, when we were on the way home from the Hunuas. He said he thought it was better to remove it. The car was parked on the driveway, so he just took it off and put it in his car and then he forgot to give it to us when they came the other night.'

It's a pleasant evening, but groups of new people make Dao uneasy and I prefer smaller parties. We are the first to leave and I ask Dao what that woman had said.

'She said she wanted to know what it was like living on the island, but it wasn't true. She was asking all sorts of questions about what Bram was like and I didn't want to answer.'

'Did she ask what he did to you?'

'I think that's what she wanted to know, but she didn't ask directly. She was hoping I would tell her. I didn't like it.'

'I was just coming over to rescue you when Kristen noticed. When you meet people like her you don't have to say anything. Just say that you prefer not to talk about it and walk away. It's not rude to walk away from people if they ask rude questions.'

'Two rudes make a right,' says Dao, who is developing a disturbing talent for bad puns.

I press the remote to deactivate the alarm and wait for the garage door to open. Dao jumps out. 'I'll check the letterbox.'

Just as the door has opened, I hear her shout. I look towards the letterbox and there is a large man beside her. I reach hurriedly under the seat for the Glock and feel it sliding further in, so I leap out of the car without it. Will, the fat man, still wearing a dark suit and looking as if he is off to a formal meeting, has Dao by the upper arm. They are on the sidewalk now and his SUV is just beside him with the engine running; both doors on the driver's side are open.

'Now then,' he says in that irritatingly reasonable

voice, 'let's stop playing games. I'll take this little girl with me and give you a day or two to think about my proposal.'

'What the hell will it take to make you realise you're wrong? It doesn't matter what you do, it won't change the fact that I never had the barrel. Did you talk to Benson?'

'Don't be silly,' he says, still jovial and friendly. 'Of course not. He would never tell me anything and you knew I wouldn't call a cop and ask questions. We'll do it this way instead. I'll look after your little friend and you can call me on the number you have on your phone when you want her back.'

Dao's face is hard to read. She is frightened, but she doesn't look as scared as I would expect. Perhaps Will's calm and reasonable manner makes her feel that she won't be harmed. I curse the fact that the Glock was out of reach. I am ready to rush at him, force him to let go of Dao. As if he can read my mind Will lifts his other hand. He has a gun.

'Don't do anything dramatic, Hunter. We'll leave now. You just call me when you want your girl back. OK?'

There is nothing I can do, apart from get a bullet through my foot or wherever he is planning to shoot me to enforce the lesson and stop me grappling with him. Dao is silently mouthing something I can't understand. Will shifts his grip on her in one swift move. He lifts her one-handed and lets go; snake fast his arm catches her around the waist and swings her into a horizontal position. Now she is tucked under his arm like a parcel. Her head is hanging down beside his thigh and I can no longer see her face. She is trying to kick him and punches his leg as hard as she can. He laughs and shakes her, and her phone falls out of her pocket.

'Behave yourself, little girl.' He sounds like a kind uncle. 'If you're naughty you'll get no cake.'

Fast on his feet for such a bulky man, he runs around the back of the car, throws Dao into the back seat, slams the door and they are away in a matter of seconds. I leap into my car and reverse across the sidewalk, press the garage-door button on the remote and drive away without looking to see if the door is coming down. There are two sets of rear lights further down the street, but I can't see what kind of vehicles they are. If he turned at the first corner, he is already out of sight.

I follow the cars I originally saw, closing in fast. One turns left, and I see by the profile that it is a sedan; now the other one is fifty metres ahead of me. At the T-junction I get held up by traffic and wait, impotent and impatient, my eyes going back and forth between the red tail lights disappearing and the crossing cars.

I slip into a gap between two cars and speed up. Now there are four cars between me and the vehicle I am following. I am still not sure that it is Will's car. I catch up and overtake two by using the turning lane where a side street branches off. Against the lights coming towards me I can see that the car two places in front of me is big enough to be an SUV. The car between us turns left and now I am directly behind the SUV. It is impossible to tell if it is the same car; it has a spare wheel mounted on the back and I can't see enough of the interior to count heads. I pull back a bit and follow at a distance. I want to find out where he is going without alerting him. He indicates right and turns into East Coast Road without slowing down. At the apex of the turn the left rear door opens and Dao literally rolls out and hits the road. His brake lights come on for a second, then he accelerates away.

Braking hard I flick the hazard lights on and jump out as soon as the car stops. A driver coming the other way only just manages to stop. I run forward and get down on my knees beside her. More cars arrive; we are surrounded by headlights and brake lights. Questions and suggestions come from all directions. I hear a man calling the emergency services. A woman kneels beside me and together we turn Dao over; she is unconscious. The woman carefully straightens Dao's legs.

'I'm a nurse,' she says. 'We'd better not move her – we don't know what might be broken.'

I pull my sweatshirt off and put it under her head and my hand comes away with blood on it. Someone hands the nurse a rug and she tucks it in around Dao. She turns to the crowd, raises her voice. 'Can someone sort out the traffic? Get the cars on that side to move on and ask the ones on this side to put their hazard lights on.'

Out of the corner of my eye I see feet moving away and hear cars starting up. The nurse bends down and checks Dao's pulse. 'Did someone hit her and take off?'

I realise she has no idea what happened, that possibly nobody apart from me saw her falling. 'She jumped from a car that turned into East Coast Road. I was immediately behind it.'

A man's voice says, 'I saw it too. I was coming towards you. An SUV turned right and she kind of fell out to the left. Lucky I wasn't going faster, or I would have run her over.'

Sirens are coming towards us and I must make a quick decision about what I am going to say and when. Starting in on the complex story about the barrel and Dao being taken hostage will take up too much time and might result in having to go to a police station to make a statement.

Two police cars and an ambulance arrive, and the situation resolves into a state of orderly chaos. Paramedics tend to Dao; the nurse stays beside her. I don't tell anyone that I know who she is. A policeman asks those who witnessed the accident to come over to the side of the road and another tells the rest to move on. One sets out road cones and directs traffic past the scene.

I stand on the sidewalk with two others and we tell the cop what we saw. He takes our names and contact details then he asks if anyone noticed the make or number plate of the SUV. I curse myself for not memorizing the number.

'Black, Isuzu Rodeo,' says the man beside me. 'Definitely.'

While we talk to the cop, my eyes are on the group surrounding Dao. The nurse is still there, talking to the paramedics as they slide the gurney into the ambulance. I walk forward to pick up my sweatshirt and the nurse turns to me. 'Poor little thing. Head injuries are always tricky – you don't know how they'll turn out.' She has no idea I am connected to Dao; she thinks I am a concerned first-on-the-scene bystander.

As soon as the cars behind me have moved, I head for the North Shore hospital, which is only ten minutes away. I sit in the car in the ED car park for a few minutes and work out how to handle this. They need to find out who she is, and I must somehow cut through the red tape with the cops, who will surely turn up shortly.

Benson is the only one who can help me now. The poor man, we are using him as a personal emergency assistant, but I know he feels connected to us. As luck would have it he is on his way home after working late. I tell him the whole story and add that I have not told anyone who she is.

'OK, you go in and tell them who you are and who she is.' His voice is very calm, and he sounds as if this is nothing out of the ordinary. 'Just say you were told she had been in an accident. No need for them to know you were behind the car she fell out of. I'll be with you shortly, twenty minutes or so. If any of our guys turn up, stall them till I get there.'

Benson arrives before the police and sits with me in the waiting area. Dao has been taken away to have her head scanned and her arm X-rayed.

'What did you tell them?'

'Nothing apart from her name and her date of birth so far, and that she is my partner. They didn't ask how I heard about it or got here so fast. The police haven't arrived yet, but I've got to tell them something. If it's the same guy who talked to me at the scene, he'll recognise me. It would be difficult to explain why I didn't say anything then, but how could I? They would have asked why I was just behind the car she jumped out of and did I know who the driver was and why she jumped. Too complicated.'

'OK, I get it.' Benson's phone buzzes. 'After you called, I talked to Chilton, the Organised Crimes guy who's now in charge of the drug-barrel issue – and he's just sent a text.'

He reads the message out: *I have a couple of ideas. You sort out the immediate situation and I will meet with Hunter tomorrow. Please send his phone number. Might be useful to have you there.*

'I'll hang around until the local guys arrive and sort it out.'

'Thank you. I can't say how grateful I am.'

I know I am getting special treatment thanks to Benson. Not that I can imagine what Chilton can do, but it's a kind offer.

'I'm as concerned as you are, Hunter. I feel I have a stake in this too.'

He asks me to look after his briefcase and heads for the men's room. Two policemen come in and talk to a nurse at the reception desk; she points and they both turn to look at me. Benson appears from the other side of the waiting room and they all converge on me; thankfully Benson takes charge before I have to say anything.

Halfway through his explanation of the background, a nurse appears and asks me to follow her.

Dao is lying on a bed with a blue blanket over her. She is wired up to machinery with computer displays. Her eyes are closed; she looks very small. The nurse pulls the curtain behind us and checks the equipment.

'She will be taken to the Assessment ward, but they won't let you in tonight. They will contact you if anything changes and you can come back tomorrow. Would you wait here, please. Doctor Carlyle wants a word with you.'

She gestures to a chair in the corner and I pull it closer to the bed. Dao's breathing is barely noticeable. I study the monitors and begin to make sense of them. I take her hand and say her name; her heartbeat goes up a bit and then drops back. I put my face right next to hers and say her name again, still holding her hand, keep my eyes on the monitor; the same thing happens again. When I straighten up, I notice a chubby middle-aged woman standing just inside the curtain watching us.

'I saw that,' she says. 'That's encouraging – she's waking up. I'm Doctor Carlyle, Maria. Are you her partner?'

Her voice reveals nothing, but her eyes move from me to Dao and back again. It is a familiar reaction.

'Yes. What did the scan show?'

'She's concussed, but no haematoma, no skull fractures. She woke up when she first came in. She went straight to radiology for a scan and fell asleep while she waited. They sedated her, so she wouldn't wake up inside the machine and panic. It looks promising, but we'll keep her in the

Assessment Unit overnight until she wakes up properly, so we can do some tests. We have to make sure there is no risk of the intercranial pressure rising. But she has no broken bones, which is a bit of a miracle from what I hear about her fall. Her arm is OK. Scratched and bruised, but it's not broken. She has a pre-existing cut that is healing well.'

Benson pushes through the curtain behind her and introduces himself before he walks up to the bed. He takes Dao's hand and stands there holding it and looking down at her. 'Poor little Dao,' he says. My eyes move to the monitor. Once again, she reacts, but her eyes remain closed.

27

Benson uses his rank and commandeers a room they use for doctors to talk to families. The two cops don't question his right to be in charge. He outlines the background and says he will talk to their boss in the morning and then he turns to me.

'Hunter, tell us what happened, right from the start. I mean from the first time this man contacted you. You said something about a phone call earlier.'

I tell them everything I can remember about Will and his car and promise to send them a CCTV image of him when I get home. I know there is a very clear image of him standing outside when he came for a chat, as he called it. 'I'm staying here now, so it won't happen directly.'

One of them gives me a card with an email address and says to send the image with Dao's name on the subject line. They thank me and leave, and Benson picks up his briefcase.

'Are you going to just sit here? They won't let you into the ward tonight. Why don't you go home and have a sleep?'

'I don't want to sleep. I'll go home and feed Scruff and

turn the alarms back on and then I'll come straight back here.'

He nods, his hand lifts a fraction and then it drops back.

'OK. Let me know if anything changes, please. I'll see you tomorrow. Oh, by the way, Sinclair called and said it will be in the papers tomorrow that they found a body in that offal pit. Not formally identified yet, but it's Browning. So at least Dao won't have to face appearing at another trial.'

As he turns to leave, I realise I have completely overlooked something. I can't believe I missed something so obvious.

'Benson, wait! The whole thing tonight will have been recorded. Dao will have triggered the camera by walking to the letterbox and it takes in a wide-angle image and across to the other side of the street. I'll send it to you and you can forward it to your mate who's looking for the barrel.'

The garage door is closed, and the alarm is off, just as I left it. Scruff is in the courtyard in his new doghouse; he doesn't come out when I turn the lights on in the house. I put some food outside for him, refresh his water and go back inside.

The camera has captured the whole scene, lit by the security light on the wall and the light spilling from the open garage door. I watch it twice, hoping to understand what Dao tried to communicate without using her voice, but the camera is filming from an angle and only shows part of her face.

The way he threw her into the car makes me furious. I send the two videos to Benson and to the address on the card I was given. The daytime picture of Will from his first visit is very clear and the car is in the picture, but side-on; the number plate is not visible.

What can I bring that will cheer her up? Apart from Scruff, what will make her smile the moment she sets eyes on it? And suddenly I know: the red-and-gold Vietnamese-style jacket, the first present Kristen gave her. Dao loves it and often wears it when we go out for dinner.

There is no way to get into the Assessment ward via the main entrance in the middle of the night. I go back to the Emergency Department. The nurse at the desk tells me I can't get to the unit at this time of night 'unless it is an urgent emergency'. I take this to mean 'if someone is dying'.

I wander around the public areas and find a passage leading to various areas, including the Assessment Ward. The doors are locked, and you need a swipe card to get in. I lean against the wall and after a while a man with a trolley comes through from the other side. I manage to get my foot in the gap before the doors close behind him; he doesn't look back and I go through. The doors to the ward are locked. I sit down on the floor in a corner and wait; the bag with the red top lies on my knees.

Sometime later, a doctor comes out and spots me sleeping in the corner. 'Are you waiting for someone? You shouldn't really be here, you know.'

'I know, but I can't go home. My partner is in there. I have to be here in case she wakes up.'

'Who is the patient?'

'You probably have her under her proper name, Susan Johnson, but she's usually called Dao.'

'OK, let me check.'

He goes back into the unit and is away for longer than I expect. I get increasingly nervous, my mind tormenting me with images of Dao dead or being kept alive by a ventilator. I am on my feet now, ready to push past him if need be, but he opens the doors and beckons.

'Come in for just a moment so you can see she's all right. I'll give you an update here before you see her. There's probably nothing much to worry about. She is sleeping, all her obs are fine. She was unconscious, woke up in ED and was sedated lightly for the scan. She has woken since and talked to us, but she's asleep now. We have her hooked up to monitors, so we'll know if anything changes. She'll be moved to a regular ward later this morning, just for a day or two.'

Dao lies on her side, her normal sleeping position. They have washed the blood from her hair, but there is no dressing on it. The grazes are not as bad as I thought. I touch her hand and her eyes open, she says, 'Hunter, my head hurts!', and closes her eyes again. I put the red top on the rail at the end of the bed; the doctor makes no comment.

'It's a good sign that she recognised you right away,' he says on the way out. 'I don't think you need to worry. You'll have to make sure she doesn't get any more knocks to the head for a few weeks. Repeated concussions aren't good, even light ones. She will probably have headaches for some time.' We part at a side door and I drive home, mentally compiling a plan.

My alarm goes off at half-past eight and I call the hospital. A nurse with a Welsh accent tells me that Dao is awake and will be moved to a medical ward straight after breakfast. I send an unalarming group message to my sisters, to Charlie and Kristen, Benson and Tama: *Dao seems to be OK after a concussion yesterday. Will be in NS hospital for a couple of days. Update later when I have seen her.*

They all get back to me while I'm having breakfast. Matt is home on five days' leave between flights, so I ask if he can have Scruff for a couple of days. I promise him that I will send a proper update to everyone as soon as I've seen Dao.

Next, I call Charlie, who is polishing her helicopter.

'No flights today or tomorrow, so I'm doing the housework,' she says. 'What happened to Dao – did she fall down the stairs? It scares me stiff the way she runs down those wooden stairs in her socks.'

I say, no it's a bit more complicated than that and I'll tell her later. I ask her to meet me and she says there's a café just by the main entrance at the hospital. She promises to be there no later than eleven.

Dao is sitting up in bed. She grabs my hand and her voice is urgent. 'Did you get him?'

'I don't know where to find him. I brought your PJs.'

'Isn't he with his car? Did you check?'

I have no idea what she is talking about. She is getting agitated, which can't be good for her.

'I don't know where to check, Dao.'

'On the app. Check the app, of course!'

Is she talking about Stuart? Has she lost track of what has happened? You hear about people who have been concussed and can't remember the period leading up to the accident.

'Don't worry about Stuart. He drowned.'

'Oh, not him!' She is frantic now. 'I mean the man who took me. Did you check the app?'

My blank face tells her everything. 'Oh no, didn't you check? I told you I left the tracker in his car.'

'You what?'

'I told you in the middle of the night!' Her face creases in concentration, then doubt. 'Or maybe I was dreaming. I picked it up from the letterbox and then there he was, right beside me and I screamed. I had it in my hand and when he chucked me in the car, I put it in the pocket on the back of the driver's seat. I thought I told you. Have you got my phone?'

I get her phone out of the bag and watch as she finds the app. There's nothing wrong with her brain. Her right arm is deeply bruised and scratched. In my head I see her throwing herself from the car, landing on her right side, where the grazes on her scalp are. Thinking of her sliding along the asphalt makes me cringe. I wonder what the doctors made of the cut on her other arm; the one in the night mentioned it, but nobody has asked me about it.

'Your poor arms – they've taken a beating lately. Did they ask about the cut?'

She pays no attention, just holds up her phone for me to see. 'Here, look! You'll be able to see it on yours too.'

'Who would believe this?' I say, elated. This changes everything; it's perfect timing. I need to think fast. 'My God, Dao, this is great. I never thought of that tracker after he took you. I didn't even check the letterbox. Now, I'll get him!'

I ask her to text those I messaged earlier, to tell them she's all right. It will be far better coming from her – they will all relax if they see she is well enough to send a message. They will ask how she is feeling, and she can tell them herself.

It feels as if I have only been there a couple of minutes when a nurse comes in to remind me the ten minutes are up. She says I can come back after lunch during proper visiting hours. Dao kneels on the bed, so I can hug her properly before I leave. I go for a walk around the parking lot to get some fresh air and clear my tired brain. The hour I spend in the café waiting for Charlie seems like minutes; my mind is in overdrive. The tracker Tama left in the letterbox was the one he took off Stuart's BMW and it shows on the app on my phone too. Now I know exactly where Will's car is. I order a second coffee and sit back and work through possible scenarios.

Charlie arrives on time with a bunch of red and yellow flowers that don't look real, but she assures me they are. She also has a shiny yellow carrier bag and a silver balloon on a stick.

"I hope they'll let me in even though it's not visiting time. I promised Kristen I would deliver these personally first thing.'

'They might. I'll let you go on your own – they're sick of sight of me trying to get in when I shouldn't be there. Can you take her phone charger? I forgot to get it out of my pocket when I saw her. She'll want to keep her phone operational.'

She takes the charger, puts it in the yellow bag and leaves. I watch her walking away and smile. The combination of her usual army-like appearance and the shiny, yellow bag is incongruous enough; the addition of a silver balloon on a stick makes it perfect. I am still deep in thought when she comes back.

'Look at this – I just sent it to Kristen. She's going to love it.' She holds up her phone. The picture is of Dao sitting in bed with three little parcels on her knees and the flowers and the balloon on the bedside table. The red-and-gold jacket hangs on an empty IV stand beside her bed.

'I asked why that top was there and she said she didn't know, but it was on the end of her bed when she woke up, so she knew you had been there. Did you bring it with you?'

'I did, in the middle of the night – I wanted her to see something she loves as soon as she opened her eyes. And she would know I had been there. They wouldn't let me stay.'

Over coffee and chocolate brownies I tell her what happened and how I have just found out that Dao planted a tracker in Will's car. For a moment she stares at me in disbelief and then she bursts out laughing.

'What a damn thing! They say timing is everything and it certainly was. If she hadn't had time to get that thing out of the letterbox, we'd have nothing to act on.'

I tell her what I want to do, she asks a couple of questions and nods. 'Sounds good. But we might need a plan B, so we don't have improvise in an emergency.'

Willow calls and wants to know exactly what happened. It takes ten minutes; she wants the whole sequence of events in minute detail. At the end of the call she says, 'And I've just heard that they are releasing Hope's body for burial in a couple of days. Sinclair called and told me the lab results are back.'

'That sounds unusual. Is it so you can tell the family?'

'No, they do that. They and the victim support people are meeting with the family as we speak. She said she thought you would like to know, but it felt better doing it via me. They found needle marks on her body and traces of a drug called propofol in her blood. It's a powerful drug – used in surgery to sedate people, I think. I must look it up. I wrote down what she read out to me. Hang on.'

There is a brief pause and I hear her turning pages. 'Here it is, and I think she quoted from the forensic report: "a steep dose-response curve makes it a very dangerous drug, as it suppresses breathing and can lead to death". Did you know they found that Browning guy? In some kind of nasty pit where hunters dump the remains of animals, way up in the wilds. He must have been trying to get away from all the police activity and fallen in. And by the way, the forensic details are not for public consumption.'

I end the call and try not to think of that pervert injecting women with drugs and cutting them and God knows what else. The Scum Pond seems like fate punching back.

I have a voice message from a number I don't recognise and for a moment I wonder if it is from Will, but it's Benson's colleague in the Organised Crimes unit:

'Hi Hunter, just a quick call. Something urgent has turned up and I can't meet today. We have filtered out a rumour on the street that the barrel of drugs has been voluntarily surrendered. The person we used is sure to share this widely. We have used him before – he owes us a few favours. I hope that will prevent any further problems. They will either think that you got the wind up and handed it over to us or that someone else did. Please let me or Benson know if you have any further problems.'

I reply and thank him; surprised at how helpful he has been.

Charlie and I get in her car and drive to the place where the app tells us the SUV has been since seven this morning. Canaveral Drive in Albany is lined with large modern buildings housing various businesses. The one we are looking for has the initials GBA in stylish white font on the grey metal cladding, with no indication of what kind of business it is. There are no cars outside, but the app tells me the tracker is there. It must be inside the big sliding doors. There are only two windows facing the street, one each side of a door near the corner, probably an office.

Charlie parks at the back of the block and gets out. 'I'll be back in a minute.'

I fall asleep, but wake up when she gets back in, panting.

'Jeez, I haven't jogged that far for a while,' she says. 'It's a very long block – I'm getting unfit. There's no sign of life. CCTV cameras and lights both at the back and the front and only one entrance you can drive a vehicle through. There's a loading dock at the back, but it's a platform at truck-loading height. He can't drive out that way.'

We have already discussed what the options are. He might not be alone in the building, so we won't go in. If he has another car, he could have left the SUV locked up and gone off somewhere else; we will wait until the SUV moves. Charlie drives me back to the hospital for visiting time.

Dao looks a lot better than she did this morning. The moment I walk in she asks if we have found him yet. I tell her what we are going to do, and she gets her phone and checks the app while we talk.

'I wish I could come – I'd like to be there. Promise you'll let me know what happens – straight away!'

On the way out, I meet a nurse and ask if she knows when Dao will be discharged. She's the one I talked to this morning, the Welsh one, who let me sneak in for ten minutes.

'I don't know for sure,' she says, 'but possibly late afternoon when the doctor has had time to read the notes and check her over again. Do we have your number?'

I steal a roll of wide elastic bandage from a trolley parked in the hallway and manage to squeeze it into my back pocket. I get a text from Dao as I walk towards Charlie's car: *Check app!* The SUV has left Canaveral Drive and is heading in our direction. I run to the car and tell Charlie to start driving. We catch up with him on Forrest Hill Road and stay three cars behind.

'He's indicating right,' says Charlie suddenly.

He swings across in a gap in the traffic and parks outside Forrest Hill Physiotherapy.

'Turn at the next corner,' I say. 'We'll go around the block and park outside the physio clinic and get him when he comes out.'

'Did you bring the Glock I lent you?'

'It's in the holster, on my belt.' I'm very uncomfortable, with a gun behind my right hip and a roll of elastic bandage in the back pocket on the other side.

'I brought the other Glock just in case. It's in the glovebox.'

We angle park one space along from the SUV and wait.

28

Will comes out forty minutes later and Charlie is ready. She hails him when he is nearly at his car; leans out the driver's window and starts asking for directions. I come up behind him while they are talking and stick the gun into his side, just below the ribcage.

'Stand very still, there's a gun in your ribs, level with your liver. Do not turn around.'

He stiffens and turns his head very slightly. 'Well, well, I wasn't expecting that,' he says, still jovial and seemingly unconcerned.

'We are going to step away from this car, two steps back.'

I don't want him to make a run for it, so I add, 'And don't think I wouldn't shoot you here in broad daylight, because I don't give a fuck after you killed Dao.'

We checked the media while we were having coffee this morning and there has been nothing about anyone falling out of a car. Charlie listened to the radio while I was visiting Dao and heard nothing. Telling him she is dead will make him believe I mean what I say, that I am so furious I won't hesitate to kill him.

He says nothing more, no reaction at all. We take a couple of steps back and Charlie gets out. She holds her gun down alongside her leg and makes sure he sees it. Between us we get him into the back seat. Charlie closes the door and stays beside it while I get in next to him on the other side. Both rear doors are set to 'childproof'; now neither Will nor I can get out without help from the outside. Charlie pulls out and heads towards the nearest motorway access. Nobody is staring or pointing; the whole thing took no more than a minute and there was no disturbance.

We cruise straight through Auckland, out the other side and peel off one stop before the Papakura exit. Charlie pulls over in a quiet spot. While she covers him with her gun from the front seat, I wind the bandage around his head, round and round. Now he can't see a thing; he looks like a mummy on his way to a film set. Charlie laughs and says, 'Shit, Hunter, this is the most fun I've had in ages.'

I hope nobody will report us as suspicious. If we get stopped, I'll say we are taking him home from hospital after surgery and keep the gun in his ribs while I say it.

I get my phone out and text Dao: *Got him. Heading off into the wilds now. Tracker still in his car, will pick it up on the way back. Love you, clever girl.*

I direct Charlie to the Hunuas by using 'left' and 'right' only. By the time we have wound our way through a couple of suburbs and out into the country he will have no idea where we are. Charlie is humming quietly to herself and glances at me in the rear-vision mirror now and then. There is no conversation in the back seat.

We stop on a gravel road as far as you can go by car into the north-eastern corner of the ranges. As the crow flies it's not far from the Scum Pond.

Charlie lets me out first. I shut the door behind me

before we walk around to Will's side. He stands like a monolith beside the car; his eyes are covered; he has no idea what is in front of him. He has said nothing, not a single word, since we got into the car. You have to give him full credit for being cool.

'I've got you covered. Just stay as you are,' says Charlie pleasantly and I search him. He has a wallet, a phone, his car keys and a handkerchief, nicely ironed; no messy collection of random junk in his pockets to ruin the lines of his suit. I chuck his possessions on the back seat.

'OK, Will. We're going to leave you here. You might be able to walk to the nearest house before it gets dark, if you walk really fast. We won't tell you which direction is closest to civilization. This way it will be more of an adventure for you. We'll take your shoes and leave them with your car – somewhere. What I want you to think about is this. You took a blameless girl and scared her so much that she jumped from your car and I will never forgive you – so I am punishing you. The police have the drug barrel now and you will never contact me again. If you do, I will kill you. I hope you understand that I mean this?'

He nods his mummy head and says a muffled 'yes'.

'Now stand absolutely still until you can no longer hear the car.'

Charlie bends, undoes his shoelaces and taps his ankle. 'Lift your foot.'

He steps out of his shoes. She puts her plastic water bottle beside him. 'We're leaving you a water bottle that is more than half full as an act of kindness. You'll find a stream or a ditch somewhere to fill it up as you walk.'

While she makes a five-point turn on the narrow road I get out my phone and take a photo of Will standing there with his head covered in bandages, shoeless and helpless in the wilderness. I pick up the shoes and get in beside Charlie and we drive away.

I send the photo of Will to Dao as soon as we are in cellphone range, then hold the phone up so Charlie can see the picture. She laughs so hard she has to stop the car and wipe her eyes.

'God, Hunter, isn't this the greatest? If someone had asked me to come up with the most awesome revenge I could think of, I'd never have thought of this. He'll never get to those houses down on the flat before it gets dark. It's a hell of a long way.'

'Oh no, not a chance. It's miles away and he's got no shoes. And if he starts out in the wrong direction he'll get nowhere, because the road ends a bit further on, which I didn't tell him.'

Dao reacts with total enthusiasm; her text reply is full of exclamation marks.

Dusk is falling as we make our way back to the North Shore. The physio clinic is empty and dark. Charlie waits while I unlock the SUV and we drive in convoy to Castor Bay, where we leave Will's car at the beach with his wallet, shoes and handkerchief inside. I take the tracking device out of the seat pocket, lock the car and put the keys on the ground below the driver's door. Before we drive away, I take a photo of the car showing the number plate, which is nicely lit by the headlights on Charlie's car.

'Why did you take his phone?' asks Charlie as we head back to the hospital carpark. 'Are you going to keep it?'

'I might give it to Benson if I can figure out a way of doing it anonymously. His mate in Organised Crime might be interested in what's on it. Or I might chuck it out the window on the way home. I don't know yet.'

Visiting time is over, but I wangle my way in and manage to see Dao for five minutes. She loves the description of Will standing on the road not knowing which way to start his long, shoeless walk. Which is exactly why I did it this way. It gives her a nice feeling of having been avenged, and it makes Will seem ridiculous and less dangerous.

Matt answers the phone and says not to worry about Scruff, he is fine and the twins love having him there, so I go home. The house feels empty without Dao and Scruff. I turn lights on and check my laptop for emails, turn the TV on. Nothing engages my interest. I don't feel like making a meal; I am at a loss.

When the phone buzzes I pick it up without checking who is calling. Unfortunately, it is my mother. If I had checked who the caller was, I wouldn't have answered. I try to be nice, but when she starts in on Dao again, with veiled suggestions that she is freeloading to avoid having to work, I lose it.

'Listen carefully, Mum. I am very serious. This might be the last time you and I speak, much less meet. It's up to you. And I mean that. I have put up with your nasty comments and innuendoes for nearly two years now and I've had enough. Either you accept that Dao is my partner and that nothing you say or do will turn me against her, or you and I have no further contact. Willow and Matt and Plum all love and admire Dao. Dad thinks she is marvellous. So learn to accept her or I will never pick up a call from you again. You can send me an email if you feel like telling me, sometime in the future, that you will treat her as part of the family.'

I press the off button so hard my finger nearly goes right through the phone. Somehow or other this burst of anger is exactly what I needed. I have been snapped out of my strange mood. I turn the sound up on the TV to have some company and make myself a late meal.

Halfway through making a toasted cheese sandwich I have an idea.

While I eat, I research police stations and their addresses. In my head I replay the conversation I had with Benson about his colleague who helped with the drug-barrel media statement, try to recall his name. I have his number on my phone, but no name attached. It comes to me as I'm getting ice cream out of the freezer – his name is Chilton.

I print the photo of Will standing shoeless on the road with his head wound with the elastic bandage and the one I took of his car at Castor Bay. There are no envelopes in the house, but I make one out of a brown paper bag and Sellotape it together. I wrap Will's phone in several layers of paper towels, put the lot in my home-made envelope and tape it shut. No way is anyone going to prove I sent this unless they do it with fingerprints. I type the address to the central police station in Auckland, add 'ATTENTION: CHILTON', print it and tape it to the envelope.

I sleep like a log and wake when Dao sends a text at 5.58 the next morning.

Are you awake? I miss you. I'm going to have a shower now so I'm ready to go home as soon as they let me.

I reply and say that I am awake, and I miss her too.

At midday I walk into Dao's hospital room with a complete change of clothes and her hairbrush in an otherwise empty bag.

'Is Scruff in the car?'

'We're picking him up on the way home – Matt's been looking after him. We've been invited for lunch. It's Sunday and Willow is home. I'm glad I brought the bag – you've managed to accumulate a lot of stuff while you've been here.'

'Amazing,' she says. 'Presents from Kristen and Charlie and flowers and my ripped clothes and the red top – thank you for bringing that, it made me feel good when I woke up and saw it. That giant box of chocolates is from Tama, he called too – the chocolates have black pepper and chilies and all kinds of strange things in them. They were delivered by courier, right to my room. He arranged it specially – the nurses were so impressed!'

'What did you tell Tama?'

'Nothing much. He called to see how I was and to talk about having us for dinner. Remember they invited us? I told him I'd fallen and got concussed. I didn't tell him any details, but he's calling later, so we have to make something up. I got out of it by saying I had to stop talking because the nurse wanted me for something. God, it gets so complicated with all these secrets. We should go and live somewhere nobody knows us and have no more secrets.'

Lunch at Willow's is a repeat performance of keeping track of what we can say and not say. We discuss what happened at the house when Will took Dao, and our experiences in the Hunua ranges. I manage to keep to the basics about how we tracked Stuart and found Hope's body. Willow tries to ferret out more; as usual she can sense when I am hiding something. I stall her successfully, with some help from Dao, and divert her attention by asking her to let me know when a date has been set for Hope's funeral.

'Have you seen Noah since she was found? How is he coping?'

'I've only talked to him on the phone. He's not good. I honestly won't be surprised if he has a breakdown. Those poor parents must be going through hell.'

On the way home, I stop at a Post Shop in Takapuna,

buy stamps and mail the envelope. We get home late afternoon; Scruff is ecstatic to be home again, and Dao is exhausted. She lies down on our bed to have a rest and falls asleep; I lie down beside her and watch her sleep. The house feels right again.

Three days later, Dao has her first day with no headache and Benson calls and asks if he can come by on his way home. We are sitting on the balcony with coffee and black-pepper chocolates when he arrives carrying a bunch of flowers nearly as big as Dao.

'This is nice,' he says and sinks into a wicker armchair. 'I've never seen you use the balcony before.'

'We couldn't – not while one of those murdering bastards was still on the loose. We're like sitting ducks in a shooting gallery here. Now that John's been caught, we can relax. There's no one left that Dao can ID.'

We talk about how Dao is feeling, and he tells her to be careful not to knock her head. She smiles and says I keep nagging at her not to run down the stairs, so there is no way she can do herself any harm. He looks like a man with a secret, but it's hard to tell with Benson; I wait patiently. When he is leaving, he pretends to remember something. He's a lousy actor.

'Oh yes,' he says casually. 'I know what I meant to tell you. Something really weird happened today. Chilton called. You remember Chilton? Someone sent him a cell phone and a photo of a guy with his head wrapped up like a mummy standing on some deserted shingle road without any shoes. And another photo of a car parked at a beach.'

His is looking at me for a reaction. I hope I look

vaguely interested, nothing more. 'What a weird thing. What do you think it means?'

Benson shifts his focus from me to Dao, but she is doing her blank look. Her face reveals nothing.

'We don't know.' The corners of his mouth twitch slightly. 'The car belongs to a company called GBA. The sole director of the company is a William Scott. One of Chilton's men identified the beach where the car photo was taken from a sign you can see just in front of the car – it's Castor Bay. Chilton is visiting Scott tomorrow. He sent someone to check if the car was still at the beach and it was. They were concerned in case someone had drowned. There was a wallet and a pair of shoes on the driver's seat and the keys were on the ground. The wallet belongs to this guy Scott. The whole thing is very strange. The car is the same model as the one you fell out of, Dao. Chilton says he's going to dig deep into this. He thinks someone's trying to tell us something.'

He's having a hard time keeping a grin from breaking out.

A couple of weeks later Dao has fully recovered, the summer heat is fading, and we spend a lot of time walking on beaches with Scruff. Somehow small pleasures seem more important than ever. We try interesting ice cream flavours, start learning chess together and discuss going on holiday.

One evening we arrive for dinner at Charlie and Kristen's place and Tama's car is parked outside and Dao grins at my surprise.

'When Charlie invited us, she asked if I'd give her Tama's number. She said they wanted to meet him and Tyler after all we told them last time we came.'

Over dinner we tell them everything they don't already know; how we used the trackers to find Hope, how Dao got lost and stumbled across the container, how Will abducted Dao and what Charlie and I did to punish him. We make no mention of the Scum Pond.

Dao sits silent and thoughtful while the others talk and exclaim about what we have told them. I study her face and wonder what she is thinking.

Then she looks up and says, 'Isn't it sad? If Hope hadn't risked her life and saved that little boy, maybe none of this would have happened. I keep thinking about it – that one single thing started this series of events – and she died. Just one single thing.'

MANY THANKS

We hope you've enjoyed reading this story and would consider leaving a review on your favourite review site, or with the retailer you purchased from.

These are not only much appreciated, they also help other readers discover new authors.

For more about other titles in this series, please read on.

ALSO BY TINA CLOUGH

THE GIRL WHO LIVED TWICE

What would you do if you woke up one morning and found that time had rewound exactly a year? Would you revisit your past mistakes and try to do better? Would you try to get revenge on those who had wronged you? Or would you use what you knew to get rich? When Mia finds herself in her own past, she must decide how best to use her pre-knowledge of one year's worth of events and personal issues.

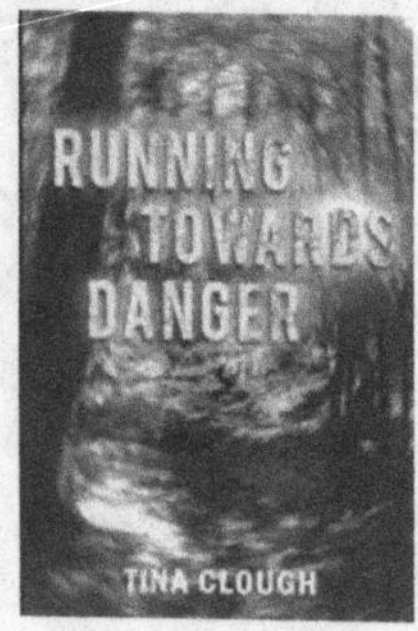

When Karen's flat-mate Nick is gunned down in front of her in the street her life is turned upside-down. Everything she thought she knew about him turns out to be a lie. She becomes a suspect in the police investigation and drug bosses think she knows where Nick has hidden a large sum of money. When her life is threatened, she decides to leave town and disappear.

Karen becomes Cara and creates an anonymous existence, severs all links to her past and adopts a cash-based way of life that leaves no electronic traces. But despite her careful planning danger still stalks her and she is forced to make dramatic choices in the face of threats and brutal violence.

Can she trust the man she is attracted to, or has he been sent by the killers to gain her confidence and find the money they believe she has?

Book 1 - Hunter Grant Series

Army veteran Hunter Grant thought he had left war behind in Afghanistan – a conflict that left him with physical and psychological scars.

But finding an unconscious girl in the Northland bush and gradually untangling her story involves him in warfare of a different kind in his own country.

Hunter sets out to find and punish the man Dao calls Master, but he soon finds there is more to this story than enslavement. Before long he himself is being hunted by the overlord of a drug empire whose sole objective is to kill Dao because she knows too much.

Protecting her and waging war while trying to keep the police from stifling his enterprise takes all Hunter's ingenuity and determination and puts him in deadly jeopardy.

Book 2 - Hunter Grant Series

Journalist Hope Barber disappears two weeks after returning to New Zealand from an assignment in Pakistan, leaving her front door open and her bag and phone inside. The police are tight-lipped about their reluctance to act, and Hunter Grant and Dao agree to help Hope's brother Noah find her. Details about Hope's time in Pakistan gradually emerge but only raise more questions.

Was Hope under surveillance?

Was she linked to terrorists?

And who is the man Hope called 'my stalker'?

FOLDED

Book 3 - Hunter Grant Series

First notes asking for help and folded into tiny origami shapes are found outside a city apartment building, then a physics textbook with tiny writing between the lines and then the woman who found them abruptly resigns and disappears. Are the notes asking for help real or is it a game?

Hunter Grant, ex-army and with a pragmatic view of justice, reluctantly agrees to help find the missing woman.

Things get complicated when a high-powered lawyer arrives form the US, and shortly after his meeting with Hunter and Dao, a "cease and desist" letter arrives from the Cayman Islands. Inspector Bakker - a woman, who in Hunter's words "looks as if she would be useful in a brawl, provided she was on your side" - takes instant exception to his involvement and threatens to arrest him for interfering in an investigation.

Dao sets out alone on a dangerous mission, driven by a compulsive need to find out what has happened to the girl who wrote the notes, and Hunter looks death in the face when he decides to risk everything to put an end to the Darknet forces that threaten their lives.

It is 2026 and individual freedoms are severely curtailed, with state surveillance everywhere. State Security has a Watch List, and being on it means that nothing you do or say escapes the authorities, but does the Kill List really exist? And if it does, how would you know if you were on it?

Coded messages on a found burner phone, top-level government corruption and a shadowy mastermind who calls himself The Broker. In this climate of state control, three unlikely friends start quietly looking for connections and set in motion a deadly game of hide and seek that will change their lives forever.

Trying to uncover the truth means risking your life, and nothing is more dangerous than searching for evidence of government corruption.

ABOUT THE AUTHOR

Tina Clough grew up in Sweden and now lives in New Zealand; dividing her time between writing fiction and translating and editing medical research papers.

Between working and writing she looks after an acre of fruit trees, vegetable gardens and roaming hens.

Apart from reading her interests include photography, wine, growing organic vegetables, making jam and kayaking.

https://lightpoolpublishing.com